# THE

# **REAL MONSTERS**

## ARE

## IN

## YOUR

## MIRROR

# PEEL BACK THE SKIN

FROM BRAM STOKER AWARD® NOMINATED EDITORS

ANTHONY RIVERA | SHARON LAWSON

PEEL BACK THE SKIN
ISBN-13: 978-1-940658-66-7
ISBN-10: 1-940658-66-7
*Grey Matter Press First Trade Paperback Edition - June 2016*

GREY MATTER
P R E S S

Grey Matter Press
**greymatterpress.com**

Grey Matter Press on Facebook
**facebook.com/greymatterpress.com**

Anthology Website
**peelbacktheskin.com**

# DEDICATION

To all the many monsters out there—the readers.
If you don't know who you are, take a look in the mirror.

# Table of Contents

# Mystic
Jonathan Maberry - 8

# The Protector
Tim Lebbon - 30

# Moth Frenzy
Lucy Taylor - 46

# Family Bible
Ed Kurtz - 64

# Life, or Whatever Passes for It
Durand Sheng Welsh - 80

# The Shed
Joe McKinney - 102

# The Greatest Gift
Graham Masterton - 116

# The Lady of the Minch
William Meikle - 138

# Beholder
John McCallum Swain - 160

# Orphans of the Air
James Lowder - 184

# Party Monster
Charles Austin Muir - 204

# Gator Lake
Nancy A. Collins - 234

# Superheated
Yvonne Navarro - 252

# Burning Leaves on an Autumn Day
Ray Garton - 268

# The Long Bright Descent
Erik Williams - 282

---

Declarations of Copyright - 309
More from Grey Matter Press - 313

# Mystic

## Jonathan Maberry

see dead people.

Make a joke. Go ahead, people do.

Fuck 'em.

I see dead people.

Not all of them. My life would be too crowded. Just some. The ones who need to be seen.

The ones who need me to see them.

- 2 -

The diner's name is Delta of Venus.

Most people think that's a pun of some kind, or a reference to Mississippi. It's not. The owner's name's not Venus. One of her girlfriend's was. It's like that.

I had my spot. Corner of the counter, close to the coffee. Out of the line of foot traffic to the john. Quiet most of the time. I dig the quiet. Kind of need it. My head is noisy enough.

It was a Thursday night, deep into a slow week. The kind of week Friday won't make better and Saturday won't salvage. Me on my stool, last sip of my fourth or fifth cup of coffee, half a plate of meatloaf going cold. Reading *The Waste Land* and wondering what kind of hell Eliot was in when he wrote it. World War I was over and he wrote poetry like the world was all for shit. Like he'd peeled back the curtain and the great and powerful Oz was a sorry little pedophile and Dorothy was going to have a bad night. Depressing as fuck.

The coffee was good. The day blew.

Eve, the evening waitress, was topping off ketchup bottles and not wasting either of our time on small talk. Not on a Thursday like this. These kinds of days don't bring out the chattiness in anyone who's paying attention. Outside, there was a sad, slow rain and most of the people who came in smelled like wet dogs.

Then *she* came in.

I saw the door open. Saw it in the shiny metal of the big coffee urn. Saw her come in. Watched her stand there for a moment, not sure of what she was doing. Saw her look around. Saw nobody else look back.

Saw her spot me. And *know* me. And chew her lip for a moment before coming my way.

Little thing, no bigger than half a minute. Sixteen, maybe seventeen. Slim as a promise. Pretty as a daffodil.

Lost and scared.

Looking for me.

People like her find me. I never ask how they heard of me. In my line of work, the referral process is complicated. I get most of my standard clients from asshole law firms like Scarebaby and Twitch. Yeah, J. Heron Scarebaby and Iver Twitch. Real names. Some people are that fucking unlucky, and that dim that they won't use a different name for business. Or, maybe it's a matter of rats finding the right sewer. Not sure, don't care. They hire me for scut-work. Skip traces, missing persons. Stuff like that. Pays the light bill, buys me coffee.

They hadn't sent her, though. She found me a whole other way.

I signaled Eve and tapped the rim of my coffee cup with the band of my wedding ring. Still wore the ring after all this time. Married to the memory, I suppose. Eve topped me off.

"Gimme a sec," I said.

She looked around to see what was what. Looked scared when she did it, which is fair enough. People are like that around me. Then she found something intensely interesting to do at the far end of the counter. Didn't look my way again.

There were five other people in the Delta. Two were regulars: a night watchman on the way to his midnight shift, and Lefty Wright, who was always topping off his Diet Coke with liberal shots of Early Times. Neither of them would give a cold, wet shit if a velociraptor walked in and ordered the blue-plate special.

The other three were a gaggle of hipsters who must have gone looking for one of those no-name clubs, or the kind of dance party that's only ever advertised by obscure Internet posts. Probably got bad directions and brought iffy decision making capabilities with them because they lingered here in this part of town long enough to order pancakes at a place like this. That, or they were hipster wannabes who thought the Delta was retro cool. It's not. And pretty soon they were going to let common sense trump their peer pressure and then they'd fade away.

That left me and the girl.

I didn't turn, but I patted the red Naugahyde stool next to me. Maybe it was the color that drew her eye. I'm pretty sure it's the only color people like her can see. That's what one of them told me. Just red, white, black and a lot of shades of gray.

That's fucked up.

The girl hesitated a moment longer, then she seemed to come to a decision and came over. Didn't make a sound.

She stopped and stood there, watching me as I watched her in the steel mirror of the coffeemaker.

"It's your dime, sweetheart," I said.

She didn't say anything.

I picked up the Tabasco sauce and shook it over the meatloaf. Used enough of it to kill the taste. The specials sign over the kitchen window doesn't say what kind of meat is in it, and I'm not brave enough to ask. I'm reasonably sure that whatever it was ran on four legs. Beyond that, I wouldn't give Vegas odds on it being a cow or a pig.

"You want to sit down?" I asked.

Still nothing, so I turned and saw why.

Her face was as pale as milk. She wore too much makeup and clearly didn't know how to put it on. Little girl style — too much of everything, none of the subtlety that comes with experience. Glitter tube top and spandex micro mini. Expensive shoes. Clothes couldn't have been hers. Maybe an older sister, maybe a friend who was more of a party girl. They looked embarrassing on her. Sad.

She had one hoop earring in her right ear. The left earlobe was torn. No earring. No other jewelry that I could see. No purse, no phone, no rings. That one earring damn near broke my heart.

"You know how this works?" I asked.

Nothing. Or, maybe a little bit of a nod.

"It's a one way ticket, so you'd better be sure, kid."

She lifted her hand to touch her throat. Long, pale throat. Like a ballet dancer. She was a pretty kid, but she would have been beautiful as a woman.

Would have been.

Her fingers brushed at a dark line that ran from just under her left ear and went all the way around to her right. She tried to say something. Couldn't. The line opened like a mouth and it said something obscene. Not in words. What flowed from between the lips of that mouth was wet and in the only color she could see.

She wanted to show me. She wanted me to see. She needed me to understand.

I saw. And I understood.

- 3 -

Later, after she faded away and left me to my coffee and mystery meat, I stared at the floor where she stood. There was no mark, no drops of blood. Nothing. Eve came back and gave me my check. I tossed a ten down on a six-dollar tab and shambled out into the night. Behind me I heard Eve call goodbye.

"Night, Monk."

I blew her a kiss like I always do. Eve's a good gal. Nice. Minds her own business. Keeps counsel with her own shit. Two kids at home and she works double shifts most nights. One of those quiet heroes who do their best to not let their kids be like them. I liked her.

It was fifteen minutes past being able to go home and get a quiet night's sleep. The rain had stopped, so I walked for a while, letting the night show me where to go. The girl hadn't been able to tell me, but that doesn't matter. I'd seen her, smelled the blood. Knew the scent.

Walked.

And walked.

Found myself midway up a back street, halfway between I Don't Know and Nobody Cares. Only a few cars by the curbs, but they were stripped hulks. Dead as the girl. Most of the houses were boarded up. Most of the boards had been pried loose by junkies or thieves looking to strip out anything they could. Copper pipes, wires, whatever. Couple of the houses had been torn down, but the rubble hadn't been hauled off.

What the hell had that little girl been doing on a street like this? Fuck me.

I had a pocket flashlight on my key chain and used it to help me find the spot.

It was there. A dark smudge on the sidewalk. Even from ten feet away I knew it was what I was looking for. There were footprints all over the place, pressed into the dirt, overlapping. Car tire tracks, too. The rain had wiped most of it away, smeared a lot of the rest, but it was there to be read. If I looked hard enough I'd probably find the flapping ends of yellow crime scene tape, 'cause they never clean that stuff up. Not completely, and not in a neighborhood like this. Whole fucking area's a crime scene. Still in progress, too, for the most part.

Doesn't matter. That's me bitching.

I knelt by the smudge. That was what mattered.

It was dried. Red turns to brown as the cells thicken and die.

Smell goes away, too. At first, it's the stink of freshly sheared copper, then it's sweet, then it's gone. Mostly gone. I can always find a trace. A whiff.

And it was hers. Same scent. If I was a poet like Eliot maybe I'd call it the perfume of innocence. Something corny like that. I'm not, so I don't. It's just blood. Even the rain couldn't wash it away.

I squatted there for a few minutes, listening to water drip from the old buildings. Letting the smells sink in deep enough so I could pin them to the walls of my head.

Back in the day, before I went off to play soldier, before I ditched that shit and went bumming along the pilgrim road trying to rewire my brain, smells never used to mean much. That changed. First time I didn't die when an IED blew my friends to rags, I began to pay attention. Death smells different than life. Pain has its own smell.

So does murder.

I stopped being able to not pay attention, if you can dig that. I lost the knack for turning away and not seeing.

There was a monk in Nepal who told me I had a gift. A crazy lady down in a shack near a fish camp in bayou country told me I had a curse. They were talking about the same thing. They're both right, I suppose.

A priest in a shitty church in Nicaragua told me I had a calling. I told him that maybe it was more like a mission. He thought about it and told me I was probably right. We were drinking in the chapel. That's all that was left of the church. They don't call them Hellfire missiles for nothing.

The girl had come to me. Couldn't say what she wanted because of what they'd done to her. Didn't matter. She said enough.

I dug my kit out of my jacket pocket, unzipped it. Uncapped a little glass vial, took the cork off the scalpel and spent two minutes scraping as much of the blood as I could get into the vial. Then I removed the bottle of holy water, filled the dropper and added seven drops. Always seven, no more, no less. That's the way it works, and I don't need to fuck with it. Then I put everything away, zipped up

*Jonathan Maberry*

the case and stood. My knees creaked. I'm looking at forty close enough to read the fine print. My knees are older than that.

Spent another forty minutes poking around, but I knew I wasn't going to find anything the cops hadn't. They're pretty good. Lots of experience with crime scenes around here. They even catch the bad guys sometimes.

Not this time, though, or the girl wouldn't have come to me.

It's all about the justice.

The vial was the only thing that didn't go back into the case. That was in my pants pocket. It weighed nothing, but it was fifty fucking pounds heavy. It made me drag my feet all the way to the tattoo parlor.

- 4 -

Patty Cakes has a little skin art place just south of Boundary Street, right between a glam bar called Pornstash and a deli called Open All Night, which, to my knowledge, has never been open. Someone nailed a Bible to the front door, so take that any way you want.

The tattoo joint was open all night. Never during the day, as far as I know. It wasn't that kind of place. I saw Patty in there, stick thin with a purple Mohawk and granny glasses, hunched over the arm of a biker who looked like Jerry Garcia. Yeah, I know, Jerry's been dead for years. This guy looked like Jerry would look now. His name was Elmo something. I didn't care enough to remember the rest.

"Hey, Monk," Patty said when she heard the little bell over the door.

"Hey, Mr. Addison," Elmo said. He was always a polite s.o.b.

"Hey," I said and hooked a stool with my foot, dragged it over so I could watch Patty work. She was half-Filipino Chinese, with interesting scars on her face. Lot of backstory to her. I know most of it, but almost nobody else does. She knows a lot about me, too.

We don't sleep together, but we've stayed up drinking more nights than I can count. She's one of my people, the little circle of folks I actually trust. We met the year I came back, and she spotted something in me from the jump. Bought me my first meal at the Delta.

She was working on green tints for a tat of climbing roses that ran from right thumb to left. Dozens of roses, hundreds of leaves.

"Nice," I said.

Elmo grinned like a kid on Christmas. "She's nearly done."

I nodded. Elmo was an ink junkie. He'd be back. Not just to elaborate on the tattoo, but because it was Patty sinking the ink. People come from all over just for her. I do. Like me, she has her gifts. Or maybe it's that she has her mission, too. But that's her story, and this isn't that.

Patty sat back and studied her work. "Okay, Elmo, that's it for now. Let it set. Go home and take care of it, okay?"

"Okay."

"Give Steve a kiss for me."

"Sure." He got up, stood in front of the floor-length mirror for a minute, grinning at the work. His eyes were a little glazed. He walked out wearing only a beater and jeans, his leather jacket forgotten on a chair. I knew he'd be back for it tomorrow. They always come back to Patty Cakes.

She got up and locked the door, flipped the sign to CLOSED and turned out the front lights. I stripped off my coat and shirt, caught sight of myself in the mirror. An unenamored lady once told me I look like a shaved ape. Fair enough. I'm bigger than most people, wider than most, deeper than most. A lot of me is covered in ink. None of it's really pretty. Not like those roses. It's all faces. Dozens of them. Small, about the size of a half-dollar. Very detailed. Photo real, almost. Men and women. Kids. All ages and races. Faces.

"Let me have it," she said, holding out a hand. I hadn't even told her why I was there. She knew me, though. Knew my moods. So I dug the vial out of my pocket and handed it to her. She took it, held it up to the light, sighed, nodded. "Gimme a sec. Have a beer."

I found two bottles of Fat Pauly's, a craft lager from Iligan City in the Philippines, cracked them open, set one down on her work table, lowered myself into her chair and sipped the other. Good beer. Ice cold. I watched her work.

She removed the rubber stopper from the vial and used a sterile syringe to suck up every last drop, then she injected the mixture into a jar of ink. It didn't matter that the ink was black. All of my tats are black. The white is my skin. Any color that shows up is from scars that still had some pink in them, but that would fade away after a while.

I drank my beer as Patty worked. Her eyes were open, but I knew that she wasn't seeing anything in that room. Her pupils were pinpoints and there was sweat on her forehead and upper lip. She began chanting something in Tagalog that I couldn't follow. Not one of my languages. When she was done mixing, she stopped chanting and cut me a look.

"You want the strap?"

"No," I said.

She held out a thick piece of leather. "Take the strap."

"No."

"Why do we go through this every time?"

"I don't need it," I told her.

"*I* do. Goddamn it, Monk, I can't work with you screaming in my ear. Take the fucking strap."

I sighed. "Okay. Give me the fucking strap."

She slapped it into my palm, and I put it between my teeth. She got out a clean needle and set the bottle of ink close at hand. She didn't ask me what I wanted her to draw. She knew.

I didn't start screaming right away. Not until she began putting the features on the little girl's face.

We were both glad I had the fucking strap.

- 5 -

It took her an hour to get it right, and I could feel when it was right. We both could.

I spat the strap onto my lap and sat there, gasping, out of breath, fucked up. I could see the pity in Patty's eyes. She was crying a little, like she always does. The light in the room had changed. Become brighter, and the edges of everything were so sharp I could cut myself on their reality. All the colors bled away. Except for red, white, black and all those shades of gray. That's what I saw. It's all I'd see until I was done with what I had to do.

Sometimes it was like that for days. Other times it was fast. Depends on how good a look the girl got and what I'd be able to tell from that look.

Patty helped me up, grunting with the effort. I was two-fifty and change. None of it blubber. A lot of it was scar tissue. The room did an Irish céilí dance around me, and my brain kept trying to flip the circuit breakers off.

"If you're going to throw up, use the bathroom."

"Not this time," I managed to wheeze, then I grabbed my stuff, clumsied my way into my shirt and jacket and stumbled out into the night, mumbling something to her that was supposed to be thanks but might have been fuck you.

Patty wouldn't take offense. She understood.

Like I said, one of *my* people.

The night was hung wrong. The buildings leaned like drunks and the moon hid a guilty smile behind torn streamers of cloud. It took me half an hour to find my way back to where the girl was killed. My eyes weren't seeing where my feet were walking and sometimes I crashed into things, tripped over lines in the pavement, tried to walk down an alley that wasn't there. It's like that for a bit, but it settles down.

Once I was on that street, it settled down a lot.

I stood by the step where I'd found her blood.

This is where it gets difficult for me. Victims don't usually know enough to really help, not even when I can see what they saw when they died. Like I was doing now. Half the time they didn't see it coming. A drive-by, or a hazy image of a tire iron. The feel of hands grabbing them from behind.

It was kind of like that with the girl.

Olivia.

I realized I knew her name now.

Olivia Searcy.

Fifteen. Even younger than I thought, but I was right about the clothes. They were her sister's. Shoes and push-up bra, too. She wanted to look older. No, she wanted to *be* older. But that was as old as she'd ever get.

I knew why she was there, and it was a bad episode of a teen romance flick. She was a sophomore in high school, he was a senior. Good looking, smart, from a family with some bucks. Good grades. A real find, and maybe in time he'd grow up and be a good man. But he was eighteen and all he wanted was pussy, and a lot of guys know that young pussy is often dumb pussy, which makes it easy pussy. So they come onto them, making them feel cool, feel special, feel loved. And they get some ass, maybe pop a cherry, and move on the instant the girl gets clingy. Fifteen year olds always get clingy, but there are always more of them. The boy, Drake, hadn't yet plundered Olivia. It was part of the plan for tonight.

They went to a party at some other guy's house a long way from here, in a part of town where stuff like this isn't supposed to happen, which is a stupid thought because stuff like this happens everywhere. The party was fun and it was loud. They got high. Got smashed. He got grabby and she freaked. Maybe a moment of clarity, maybe she saw the satyr's face behind the nice boy mask. Whatever. She bolted and ran.

She didn't know if Drake tried to find her because she tried real hard not to be found.

She *was* found, though.

Just not by Drake.

For a little bit there I thought I was going to have to break some parents' hearts by fucking up their pretty boy son, but that wasn't in tonight's playbook. Drake hadn't done anything worse than be a high school dickhead. He got her drunk, but he hadn't forced her, hadn't slipped her a roofie. And, who knows, maybe if he'd found her in time he'd have become Galahad and fought for her honor. Might have saved her life.

Probably would have died with her.

Or, maybe the killer would have opted out and gone looking for someone else. A lot of serial killers and opportunistic killers are like that. They're not Hannibal Lecter. They're not tough, smart and dangerous. Most of them are cowards. They feel totally disempowered by whatever's happened to them — abusive parents, bad genes, who the fuck cares? They hurt and terrify and mutilate and kill because it makes them feel powerful, but it's a lie. It's no more real than feeling powerful by wearing a Batman costume at Halloween. You may look the part, but you're a long way from saving Gotham City.

All of that flooded through my brain while I stood there and looked at the street through the eyes of a dead girl. Seeing it the way Olivia saw it right as hands grabbed her from behind. Right as someone pulled her back against his body so she could feel his size, his strength, the hard press of his cock against her back. Right as he destroyed her. Right as the cold edge of the knife was pressed into the soft flesh under her left ear.

I felt all of that. Everything. Her nerve endings were mine. Her pain exploded through me. The desperate flutter of her heart changed the rhythm of mine into a panic, like the beating of a hummingbird's wings against a closed window. I felt her break inside as he ruined her. I heard the prayers she prayed, and they echoed in my head like they'd echoed in hers. She hadn't been able to scream them aloud because first there was a hand over her mouth, and then there was the knife against her throat and those threats in her ear.

And when he was done, I felt the burn.

That line, like someone moving an acetylene torch along a bead of lead. Moving from under my left ear to under my right.

I felt her die because I died, too. Olivia drowned in her own blood.

Then there was a strange time, an oddly quiet time, because I was with her when she was dead, too. When he wrapped her in a plastic tarp and put her in the trunk. It was so weird because while he did that he was almost gentle. As if afraid of hurting her.

Fucking psychopath.

While the car drove from where she'd died to where he'd dumped her, Olivia slipped into that special part of the universe where the dead see each other. Certain kinds of dead. The dead who were part of a family. Victims of the same knife.

*His* people.

Olivia discovered that she was not the only one. Not the first, not the tenth.

She wasn't sure how many because he moved around so much. *Had* moved around. Not so much anymore. Not since he moved to this town. The victims she met were the ones who'd died here.

Twenty-six of them.

The youngest was eight.

I met those victims, too, because I was inside the memory. Like I'd actually been there. That's how it worked. I talked to them, and most of them already knew who and what I was. The first time I'd encountered that it shocked the shit out of me. But now I understood. Not to say I'm used to it, because I'd have to be a special kind of fucked up to be used to something like that. No, it was more like I knew how to deal. How to use it.

Some of them had died just like Olivia. An attack from behind. Everything from behind. No chance of an identification. He varied it a little. One of those nearly patternless killers that the FBI have no idea how to profile. A knife across the throat, an icepick between the right ribs, a garrote made from a guitar string, a broken neck.

Most were like that.

Most. Not all.

There was one who fought. She'd had a little judo and some tae kwon do. Not enough, but enough to make him work for it. It was one of the early ones, after he'd moved here. The one that made him want to never bring them home again. She'd gotten out and he'd chased her into the front yard and caught her before she could wake the neighbors. Single homes, lots of yard on all sides. Cul-de-sac. When he caught up to her she spun around and tried to make a fight of it.

I saw every second of it.

The yard. The house.

Him.

I saw him.

I saw him block her punch, and then a big fist floated toward her face and she was gone. He was a big guy and he knew how to hit. The punch broke the girl's neck, which made it easier on her, if easy is a word that even applies.

I stood there and watched all of it play out inside my head. No idea how long I was there. Time doesn't matter much when I'm in that space. I was there for every second of every minute of every attack. Beginning to end. All the way to when he dumped them, or buried them, or dropped them off a bridge.

Stack it all up and it was days.

Days.

Shotgunned into my head.

I wish I'd had the leather strap. Instead, I had to bite down on nothing, clamp my jaws, ball my fists, clench my gut and eat the fucking pain.

It wouldn't save any of those girls. Not one. And maybe it wouldn't matter that I felt it all but didn't have to live it. Or die from it. I know that.

I couldn't help a single one of them. I couldn't help Olivia.

*Jonathan Maberry*

But as my skin screamed from the phantom touches and the blades and everything else, I swore that I'd help the next girl.

Goddamn son of a bitch, I'd help the next girl.

Because, you see, I saw the house.

I saw the number beside the door.

I saw the tags on the car parked in the drive.

And I saw the motherfucker's face.

I went and sat down on the step next to the blood. Waited. I knew she'd be there eventually. It was how it worked.

Still surprised me when I looked up and there she was. Pale, thin, young, her face as bright as a candle. Eyes filled with forever.

"You can still opt out," I told her. "I can turn this over to the cops. Let them handle it."

She said nothing, but she gave me a look. We both knew that this guy was too careful. There would be no evidence of any kind. He'd been doing this for years and he knew his tradecraft. No semen, no hairs, nothing left for them to trace. The knife was gone where no one would ever find it. And he wasn't a souvenir collector. The smarter ones aren't. They could turn his house inside out and the only things they'd find would be jack and shit.

Even if they watched him, he'd turn it off for a while. For long enough. Police can't afford to run surveillance for very long. They lose interest, even if they thought the guy was good for Olivia's murder.

I sighed. Actually, I wanted to cry. What she was asking was big and ugly and it was going to hurt both of us.

She stood there with a necklace of bright red and those bottomless eyes.

She didn't say a word. She didn't have to.

The price was the price. She was willing to pay it because she was a decent kid who would probably have grown up to be someone of note. Someone with power. Someone who cared. Those eyes told me that this wasn't about her.

It was all about the next girl.
And the one after that.
And the one after that.
I buried my face in my hands and wept.

- 6 -

It took me two days to run it all down. The girl misremembered the license number, so that killed half a day.

Then I put the pieces together. Bang, bang, bang.

Once that happens, everything moves quickly.

I ran the guy through the databases we PIs use, and after an hour I knew everything about him. I had his school records and his service record—one tour in Afghanistan, one in Iraq. Made me hate him even more. He was divorced, no kids. Parents dead, his only living relative was a brother in Des Moines. I figured there were bodies buried in Des Moines, too, but I'd never know about them. He owned three Jack in the Box franchise stores and had half-interest in a fourth. Drove a hybrid, recycled and had solar panels on his house. I almost found that funny.

I was in his Netflix and Hulu accounts, his bank account and everything else he had. If there was a pattern there, or a clue as to what he was, it wasn't there. He was very smart and very careful.

No cops were ever going to catch him.

I parked my car on the route he took to work and waited until I saw him drive past on his way home. Gave him an hour while I watched the sun go down. Twilight dragged some clouds across the sky, and the news guy said it was going to rain again. Fine. Rain was good. It was loud and it chased people off the streets.

Lightning forked the sky and thunder was right behind it. Big, booming. The rains started as a deluge. No pussy light drizzle first. One second nothing, then it was raining alley cats and junkyard dogs.

I got out of my car and opened an umbrella. I really don't give a shit about getting wet, but umbrellas block line-of-sight. They make you invisible. I walked through the rain to his yard, went in through the gate, up along the flagstone path and knocked on the door.

Had to knock twice.

He had half a confused smile on his face when he opened the door, the way people do when they aren't expecting anyone. Especially during a storm.

Big guy, an inch taller than me, maybe only ten pounds lighter. His debit card record says that he keeps his gym membership up to date. I knew from my research that he'd boxed in college. Wrestled, too. And he had Army training.

Whatever.

I said, "Mr. Gardner?"

"What do you want?"

I hit him.

Real fucking hard.

A two-knuckle punch to the face, right beside the nose. Cracks the infraorbital foramen. Mashes the sinus. Feels a lot like getting shot in the face, except you don't die.

He went back and down, falling inside his house, and I swarmed in after him, letting the umbrella go. The wind whipped it away and took it somewhere. Maybe Oz for all I know. I never saw it again.

Gardner fell hard, but he fell the right way, like he knew what he was doing. Twisting to take the fall on his palms, letting his arm muscles soak up the shock. His head had to be ringing like Quasimodo's bells, but he wasn't going out easy.

He kicked at me as I came for him. Tricky bastard. A good kick, too, flat of the heel going for the front of my knee. If he'd connected, I'd have gone down with a busted leg, and he'd have had all the time in the world to do whatever he wanted.

If he'd connected.

I was born at night, but it wasn't last night. I bent my knee into the kick and bent over to punch the side of his foot. I knew some tricks, too.

In the movies there's a brawl. A long fight with all sorts of fancy moves, deadly holds, exciting escapes, a real gladiatorial match.

That's the movies.

In the real world, fights are, to paraphrase Hobbs, nasty, brutal and short.

He had that one kick, that one chance. I didn't give him a second one. I gave him nothing.

I took everything.

When I was done I was covered in blood, my chest heaving, staring at what was left of him there in the living room. I'd closed the door. The curtains were closed over drawn shades. The TV was on. Some kind of CSI show with the volume cranked up. Outside the storm was shaking the world.

He wasn't dead.

Mostly, but not entirely.

That would come a little later.

He wasn't going anywhere, though. That would have been structurally impossible.

I went into the kitchen and found a basting brush. Slapped it back and forth over his face to get it wet, then I wrote on the wall. It took a while. I made sure he was watching. I wrote the names of every girl he had killed.

Every one that I'd met there in the darkness of Olivia's hell.

Gardner was whimpering. Crying. Begging.

When I was done I unzipped my pants, pulled out my dick and pissed on him.

He was sobbing now. Maybe he was that broken or that scared. Maybe it was his last play, trying to hold a match to the candle of my compassion.

Maybe.

But he was praying in the wrong church.

While I worked, I kept praying that Olivia wouldn't show up to see this. Most of them do. None of them should. I didn't want her here.

I looked around for her.

She didn't come.

It helped a little, but not a lot. I knew I'd see her again.

Gardner managed to force one word out. It took a lot of effort because I'd ruined him.

"P-please...," he said.

He wanted me to end it. By then, I think that's what he wanted. I smiled.

"Fuck you," I said.

The storm was raging, and I stood there for nearly an hour. Watching Gardner suffer. Watching him die.

Judge me if you want. If so, feel free to go fuck yourself.

When I left I stole one of his umbrellas.

I'd worn gloves and a ski mask. Everything I had on was disposable. It all got burned. I'm smart about that shit, too.

- 7 -

That night I got drunk. Because it's the only reasonable thing to do.

Me and Patty, Lefty Wright, and a couple of the others. Ten of us huddled around a couple of tables in a black-as-pockets corner of Pornstash. Me and my people. No one had to ask what happened. Patty knew, some of the others maybe. Mostly not. But they all knew something had happened. We were those kinds of people, and this was that kind of town.

We drank and told lies, and if the laughter sounded fake at times and forced at others, then so what?

- 8 -

It was nearly dawn when I stumbled up the stairs, showered for the third time that day, and fell into bed.

I said some prayers to a God I knew was there but was pretty sure was insane. Or indifferent. Or both.

My windows are painted black because I sleep during the day. Mostly, anyway. I had a playlist running. John Lee Hooker and Son House. Old blues like that. Some Tom Waits and Leonard Cohen in there, too. Grumpy, cynical stuff. Broken hearts and spent shell casings and bars on the wrong side of the tracks. Like that.

Stuff I can sleep to.

When I can sleep.

Mostly, I can't sleep.

My room's always too crowded.

They are always there. It's usually when I'm alone that I see them. Pale faces standing in silence. Or screaming. Some of them scream.

I wear long sleeve shirts to bed because they scream the loudest when they see their own faces. It's like that. It's how it all works.

When I'm at the edge of sleep, leaning over that big black drop, I can feel the faces on my skin move. I can feel their mouths open to scream, too. Sometimes the sheet gets soaked with tears that aren't mine.

But which are mine now.

Olivia was there for the first time that night.

Standing in the corner, pale as a candle, looking far too young to be out this late. Thank god she wasn't one of the screamers. She was a silent one. She with her red necklace that went from ear to ear.

My name is Gerald Addison. Most people call me Monk.

I drink too much and I hardly ever sleep.

And I do what I do.

*Jonathan Maberry*

# About Jonathan Maberry

A *New York Times* bestselling author, multiple Bram Stoker Award® winner and freelancer for Marvel Comics, Jonathan Maberry knows his horror.

Among Maberry's body of work are the novels *Predator One, The Nightsiders, Ghost Road Blues, Patient Zero, The Wolfman* and many others. Maberry's nonfiction books include *Ultimate Jujutsu: Principles and Practices, The Cryptopedia, Zombie CSU, Wanted Undead or Alive* and others. His award-winning teen novel, *Rot & Ruin*, is now in development for film, and two of his books, *Extinction Machine* and *V-Wars* are in development for TV.

He edits a number of anthologies including a new series of *The X-Files* books, the *V-Wars* shared-world vampire apocalypse series, *Scary Out There*, an anthology of horror for teens, and the dark fantasy series *Out of Tune*. He was a featured expert on The History Channel special *Zombies: A Living History* and is a regular on the series *True Monsters*.

Maberry writes comics for Marvel, Dark Horse and IDW and his work includes *Marvel Zombies Return, Captain America: Hail Hydra, Punisher: Naked Kill, DoomWar, Black Panther, Marvel Universe vs The Avengers, Bad Blood, V-Wars* and *Rot & Ruin*.

Since 1978, Maberry has sold more than 1200 magazine feature articles, 3000 columns, two plays, greeting cards, song lyrics and poetry. Maberry co-founded the Liars Club and founded the Writers Coffeehouse. He is a frequent keynote speaker and guest of honor at writers' conferences and genre conventions including San Diego Comic Con, The Writer's Digest Conference, The World Horror Con, New York Comic Con, Birmingham Comics Festival and many others.

He lives in Del Mar, California, with his wife, Sara Jo, and a fierce little dog named Rosie.

# The Protector

## Tim Lebbon

Even when the words took me away, part of me always remained in the real world. I was desperate to be all the way there, beyond. On the tropical island with pirates and vagabonds, in the dusty West with grizzled cowboys and trackers, stomping through deep Arctic snow with icicled explorers, climbing cliffs above a rainforest, existing in places I had never been or seen but which I could imagine so well. And I tried.

But I was alert to reality and all its terrible sounds, sights and promises.

True escape was a dream, and it was only in dreams that I found any shred of freedom.

\* \* \*

I heard the front door open and close, and immediately I was ready for the first signs of sadness. It was always like this. There were things to listen for, like mumbling under his breath, or doors and cupboards slamming. Closer, there would be something to smell, too; the tang of alcohol or, if he'd been in another fight, the warmth of blood. Merely looking for the possible confrontation, and the grief to come, had become too unreliable because he was good at hiding fury behind a smile.

Mum knew, too. But I think she was too far gone. I had places I could escape to, at least partially. But Mum always remained behind.

I'd once asked her if he'd always been like this. She'd smiled and said she couldn't really remember.

I sat up in bed and glanced at the clock. It was almost midnight.

I hadn't heard Mum come upstairs to bed yet, and I wished she wouldn't wait up for him. It was later than usual, so he'd had longer to keep drinking.

I heard my father's first shout. Through my closed door and the old house's heavy walls and floors, it was an incoherent roar, rising and falling like the swell preceding a tidal wave. Mum's voice came next, high and soft and almost not there at all. He raged, she pleaded. In the five minutes before silence descended again, I did not make out one single word. It was as if they communicated in the language of hate and fear, a dialect still relatively unknown to me.

But that could not last. Fear grew richer as the hate grew heavier.

I tried to continue reading. I was a small, weak boy, short for my age and always the last chosen for team sports at school. I wasn't bullied or hated, and I had a few close friends. But when it came to kicking a ball around a field or proving myself physically, I was ignored. I sometimes wondered whether to be derided might be better. At least then they'd acknowledge that I was there.

It had never crossed my mind to confront him, at least not while I was awake.

I heard the stairs creaking. Behind and beneath them, a few heavy sniffs as my mother went about locking up the house.

My door opened.

"What shit you reading?"

"It's called *Wizard and Glass*."

"Wizards!" He almost spat the word, stumbling into my room and knocking the door wide. He stank of booze, sweat and cigarettes — the stench of mysterious adulthood. There was a small cut above his left eye and a graze on his chin. I'd learned long ago not to ask. He'd only say, *You should see the other guy!*, and his pride in violence made me feel sick. Sometimes I imagined him saying, *You should see your mother!*, and my growing hate for him fed on that image.

"It's good, Dad. Part of a series. You should —"

"I should what? Fucking crap." He sat on the end of my bed, sighing heavily as the springs creaked. He was a big, strong man, gone to fat in his middle age but still so powerful. Probably no more than six feet tall, in my eyes he was a giant. "You should be out with mates. Football. That sort of stuff. Girls."

"I've got friends, Dad."

"Girls. Your age, I was fucking them behind the village disco. Janey Dickson, she gave me a blowjob, all my mates watching. I tell you that? About Janey Dickson?"

"Yeah, Dad."

"This…this…" He reached for the book and I held it protectively against my chest. He glared at me. His nostrils flared. He had never hit me. "Give," he said.

I slowly lowered the book and slipped in the bookmark before closing it.

He grabbed the book and threw it across the room. "Get yourself a life. A life! Not bloody reading. Sitting in bed reading when you should be…" He waved a hand at my door, the window.

A ghost passed by the door, and I looked up to see Mum's nightdress passing out of sight.

"I need to go to sleep," I said. "Got tests in school tomorrow."

"Tests!" he said, scoffing. I was never quite sure what he wanted of me. To be more like him, big and brash, a man with rough hands and rougher thoughts or, more likely, to be nothing like him at all. I'm not even sure he knew himself.

He staggered when he stood up, slammed my door, stomped into the bathroom. I heard him pissing. He always said a real man pisses into the middle of the water. I always peed on the side.

Laughing to himself, he stumbled across the landing to the bedroom he shared with my mother.

I buried my head beneath the pillow and tried to get to sleep before what came next.

* * *

I approach the top of the steep hill at last. It's been a hard climb, made harder still by the weapons I've carried with me—the sword, forged in the deep Northern Caves of Drandor; the spear, once owned by Helgarth the Spite; the heavy spiked club, used to kill the Granmoorian Giant. But I know that they are necessary. Coming up here unarmed would be the same as throwing myself off the mountain.

Strange winged mammals rise and fall on the currents above me. They're as large as my head with heavily veined wings, colourful duck-like beaks and delicate, long-clawed paws. At a few places on the climb I scared them from their burrows, and I passed close enough to one to see the mewling, pink babies nestled inside. I wonder at a parent's instinct that allowed it to leave its young in the face of danger. Perhaps it's a way of seeing how fit they are to survive.

A strong breeze drifts across the steep face of the hillside. The last two hundred feet are a scramble. Not quite a climb, but steep enough to cause me serious injury if I stumble or fall. I am being very careful. It's not only my life at stake.

At last, summiting the hill and standing on the plateau, I see what no one else has ever witnessed and survived.

There is a forest here, but it is not made of trees. Heavy timber spikes driven deep into the ground bear wretched fruit. Some are still recognisable as people, flesh rotting, hair still clinging onto scalps like the desperate might cling to life. Other spikes bear many remains, so old that the decayed victims have merged into a morass of bone, rotten clothing and shredded skin. The stink is awful. My stomach drops, and my heart cries out as I experience the terror and agony felt across this high, vast plain.

The forest of death continues for as far as I can see. And not too far from me is a flash of pale skin.

*Tim Lebbon*

There she is. Tied to a spike and not yet impaled. Still dressed and moving, still alive. The Draze has not finished with her yet.

As if summoned by my thinking its name, the Draze manifests from the endless fields of spikes. It might have been hiding in shadows, or perhaps it was so still that I could not make it out, but once it starts running at me, it becomes my whole world.

I glance once at the woman and she catches my eye. I see no hope there. Only sadness at the prospect of another life lost.

The fight is epic and heroic, and some time, down through the years, I suspect they will write songs about what happened on the top of that terrible hill.

I lose a hand, the Draze loses an eye. It tears Helgarth the Spite's spear from my grip and snaps it in half, casting it aside. I lure it close and bury the Drandorian sword in its thigh. The Draze screams in agony and delight. I cry out in rage. The beast steps back and rips the sword from its bone and flesh, throwing it out across the hill and two thousand feet down into the valley below.

I heft the spiked club. It has tasted giant's blood, but never something as large as the Draze, never a being so dripping with evil. And one so confident of success.

The club strikes its abdomen and drives it up, back and down onto one of its own spike-trees. It cries out in shock and pain as the spike pierces its chest, bursting from its ribcage with a spew of vile blood and a gush of yellow, poisonous fluid. I climb the beast to finish it. It stares into my eyes.

But it sees no mercy there.

The woman is still alive. I go to set her free, wanting to tell her, *They'll write songs about us.* But before I can reach her —

\* \* \*

It was snowing. I was too old to build snowmen and throw snowballs, but Mum and I went outside and did it anyway. The snow was so deep that no cars were coming through the village anymore. We played in the street with neighbours and children. The streetlights were on, casting spheres of light through which the flakes fell fat and heavy.

"Got you!" Mum shouted. The ball had burst against my cheek and was sliding inside my collar, slick and cold against my skin. "Got you a good one then!"

I ducked behind a car and formed a ball. My heart was pummelling and I was sweating inside my jumper and coat, but this was just the best time. The best.

Dad wasn't there, of course. I had vague memories from my childhood of him building a snowman with me, but he'd marched from the house after work that day, having barely been in for fifteen minutes, saying, "I'm going to the pub. Dave's coming over. Don't wait up." Then, looking at me, he'd said, "Why don't you go and play snowmen, fucking pussy?"

I didn't know what I'd done to upset him. I was almost seventeen then, and some of my mates from school were regulars at my father's favourite pub. The idea of being there with him was horrific.

Mum threw another ball, then leaned back against our garden wall. She looked up into the darkening sky and stuck out her tongue, catching snowflakes. I stood beside her and did the same.

*Why don't you leave him?* I asked her almost a year before. *Because he needs me,* she'd replied, and I'd never asked again. When those bad times came, I only thought it.

We went inside and changed, and Mum made some hot chocolate. I crashed out on my bed and started reading. It was a Ranulph Fiennes book. I loved reading about adventures, pushing extremes, lucky escapes. Dad still thought it was a pointless pastime, and sometimes he told me I should be learning a trade, getting an apprenticeship with a local builder or plumber instead of studying fucking A levels in order to move on and get a useless degree. He often sounded bemused at my choices. On occasion, he became angry with me.

He'd never once laid a hand on me. It was Mum who bore the scars of his confusion.

I heard him coming home from way along the street. He was laughing, his friend Dave laughing along with him. They were both drunk, but even though that state always thickened the atmosphere with trepidation, for once I could only hear his good humour. Eight inches of snow had changed the village landscape completely, and perhaps I was hearing the man he could have been, my dad from another existence.

I threw down the book and turned off the light, opening my curtains and staring out at the glowing, otherworldly snowscape. It was beautiful. The sky had cleared and they were forecasting a heavy frost, meaning that the snow would freeze and stay around for some time. The moon was almost full, and I could have sat there and read in its reflected light.

Dad was swaying along the middle of the street. Dave was with him. They were still laughing, their conversation a confusion of unheard words and jokes. Dave headed off down the footpath that led to his small housing estate, and Dad seemed to freeze. Then he bent over, staggered, nearly fell, stood up again and launched a snowball at Dave's head.

He missed. Dave turned and called him a cheeky fucker, and then the two of them were throwing snowballs at each other, ducking behind cars and slipping on ice. They laughed. They laughed so much they snorted.

I found myself smiling, but sadly. I could not for a second imagine him doing the same with me.

Which was perhaps why I scooped snow from my windowsill and rolled a snowball, ready for when he walked in front of the house.

My shot was perfect, a complete bullseye. Something he'd never praise me for.

He started shouting and screaming at me even as he skidded along the driveway, hateful words that made me feel as if I'd swallowed a handful of ice.

From the bathroom I heard my mum, and her small scream was all the more terrible because it wasn't fear. It was resignation.

* * *

The tree is under siege. I can see it in the distance as I cross the inimical landscape, sight enhanced by suit sensors, alerts sounding as dangers close in. Every circuit of my suit urges me to turn away, but every human instinct keeps me on course. I override tech and good sense and face the future.

The tree is on a hilltop, alone and regal against the stormy red skies. Its branches are huge and lush, laden with fruit and dense with leaves. It's difficult to tell from such a distance how tall the tree might be — a dozen times my height or a mile into the sky. But however small or large, it's clear that the assaulting armies care nothing for its uniqueness. They surge at the hill's lower slopes, like a poisonous sea crashing against unknown shores. They fight the tree's defenders, whose cause is useless, and I rush across the landscape as their only beacon of hope.

The attackers are small from this distance, difficult to make out. The defenders are saplings, hauled up from their planting points, tendril roots waving at the air. They are far too young to be entering into such a fight, but circumstance dictates the need.

I leap ravines whose bottoms are way out of sight. My suit sends probing beams deep down, and they bounce back to tell me the rents in the planet are crawling with life, seething, pulsing with violence. I cross an area of open swamp, trusting the suit's sensors to guide me from one solid outcropping to another. The swamp's waters are sheened with an oily skin, beneath which lie isolated instances of quiet, contemplative intelligence.

The closer I get to the fight on the hill, the more warnings my suit issues. At first they are standard protocols, easy to ignore or put aside, but then the suit's Self makes itself known.

*I advise against this course of action.*

"I can't just leave it," I say.

*The nature of the attackers is uncertain. The source of the tree even more hazy.*

"It's beautiful. It's unique. It might be the only one in the universe, and I can't stand by and let it die."

*Very well. But don't say I didn't warn you.*

"Thank you. Please bring all weapons online."

By the time I leap eighty feet across the river at the foot of the hill, I can feel the potential power in my arms, my hands and nestled across my suit's faze circuits and nano vents.

It seems the attackers can feel it, too. They turn as one and come my way.

For an hour I fight. The attackers are slow but many, and their constant, unrelenting onslaught comes close to overcoming my defences.

They are a strange conglomeration of plant and animal, with stocky bone legs, spindly bodies, and limbs tipped with sharp spikes to pierce and wedge, or saw-like appendages that buzz at the air as they rub them together. Their heads hang low and drip sap, teeth grinding and growling, eyes rolling backwards in their heads whenever they attack.

And attack they do, again and again, wave after wave of them trundling forward across the bodies of their cousins. I blast and burn, vaporise and hack, shoot and freeze. The suit enables my victory, but it does not come without cost. One foot is trapped beneath a pile of corpses, and their blood is toxic and acidic, eating through the advanced materials and exostructure to melt away three toes and half of my foot. The suit keeps the pain at bay and seals the damage as best it can.

Beyond, I see the tree gathering its defences. The saplings are delicate, thin things, and where once there were thousands I now see only a dozen remaining. They plant themselves around the tree—the amazing, wondrous tree, as high as the sky and constantly moving, gathering knowledge, seeding it for the future. Its roots fill the world—they *are* the world—and if the attackers had succeeded, then another existence would have blinked away to nothing in this endless universe.

At last the fight is won. I work my way up the hillside, exhausted and in shock from my injuries. The suit is glitching.

*Three blind mice*, it says, constantly starting a lullaby that it can never finish.

*See how they*—

*See how they*—

I reach the tree at last. The saplings let me by because in me they recognise their saviour. But just as I reach out my hand to touch the tree's bark, and open my mouth to tell it how I feel—

\* \* \*

Mum went to buy a takeaway. She loved having me home from university. This was my third time since I'd left, and she said she always liked a takeaway on the first night. Meant she had more time to talk to me without having to be busy in the kitchen.

Dad would have gone, but he'd had a couple of drinks. "He's lost," she'd told me on the way home from the station. "Ever since you left. Just…lost."

"All right, Dad?" I asked. I dropped onto the sofa, fluffing up a couple of cushions and propping them behind my back. The sofa was almost as old as me.

"Suppose," he said. "You?"

"I'm good," I said. I wasn't. I was lost, too. It wasn't something I could tell Mum because everything she'd ever done, everything she'd been through, had been to make things right for me. After all of that, how could I possibly tell her things were wrong?

The first time I'd come home, I'd expected that being there would make things better. It hadn't.

The second time had been a trial, a tense time filled with explosive outbursts from my father and the familiar silence from my mother.

*Tim Lebbon*

This third time was the last. After this, I was leaving for a long time. All I had to do was find a way of telling her.

"What're you watching?"

"Some shit."

I watched TV with him. He was right, it *was* some shit about arguing families, one of those soap operas that people seemed to watch in search of an escape. It seemed painfully familiar. A man screamed. A woman shouted. A knife was brandished, a son slept with a sister, a husband went missing.

A man raised his hand. A woman cowered. I caught the flicker of a smirk on my father's face.

"You fuck," I said. I reached across and snatched the TV remote from him, clicking it off. Silence settled across the room. "You complete fuck."

"What'd you say to me?" He turned and looked at me like I was a child, and it was the same way he'd always looked at me. Looking *through* me, as if I was barely there at all. He'd never recognised that I'd grown up, got older, turned from a snivelling kid into a young man. I wasn't sure what he saw when he looked at me, but I was only glad it wasn't himself.

"I hate you," I said. And I smiled. Those three words seemed to pour from my whole body, lightening it almost to the point that I floated up out of the sofa. They freed possibilities that had, until now, been weighed down with masses I could not identify or dare touch. I'd felt the hate for so long, but actually saying it felt something like growing up.

"You little —"

"I'm *not* little!" I stood, towering over my father where he sat crumpled in his armchair. His arms were tensed, readying to push himself upright.

"Ungrateful shit," he said, standing, sneering, flexing his hands. I could smell the alcohol wafting off him, seeping through his pores and clogging them with hate, the opposite to what I had just experienced.

"I'm very grateful," I said. "To Mum, for everything she's done for me. For everything she's had to put up with, from you. All she's been through with you, you weak, pathetic bully."

He laughed. Once, loud, like a cough. "Great! So you go to university to study some crap that'll get you nowhere. More fucking books to read. More fucking shit to take in and drown yourself with. Where will that get you, eh? Queer. Fucking queer, are you?"

"Why would I tell you? You don't count for anything in my life."

His fists were clenching again. I heard his knuckles cracking, and I knew for sure that if he came at me, he'd beat me, because that's the sort of person he was. I'd never had a fight in my life, not in real life, at least. In my dreams I had saved whole worlds.

He'd beat me down, but I would win by facing up to him. The first time ever. It felt foolish and brave, but there was no going back now.

"If you hurt her again, I'll kill you," I said.

His eyes went wide. Shock punched him. He took one step forward.

The front door opened. "It's bucketing down out there!" Mum called. The scent of Indian food followed her in, and I smiled at her through the living room door. She paused for a second. But seeing me smiling set her smile in place too, and she moved through to the kitchen. "Come and help me dish up?" she called.

I knew she was asking me. He'd never demean himself by helping her in the kitchen. He had too much important stuff to do.

"I mean it," I said, quieter, stepping in so close that he could smell my breath. "In your sleep, when you're drunk, I'll stick a knife in your eye." I stepped away and threw the remote control at him. It struck his cheek and fell into his chair.

As I walked along the hallway, I heard the TV clicking back on. A woman shouted at a man. A man growled back.

"Okay, son?"

"Yes, Mum," I said. I kissed her cheek and fetched plates from the cupboard.

\* \* \*

I walk through the jungle, searching for the beast, but there is no beast to be found.

The trees are tall and stretch up out of sight, heavy mist obscuring their canopies. The heat is immense, the life here abundant and rich. Spiders the size of my hand eat small mammals, birds of prey swoop down and pluck the spiders from branches, flying lizards larger than me drift through the mist and pierce the birds with serrated tongues. Life circles, and I am cautious, but I know the way. I have lived here for a long time, and my body is well adapted to this environment. I belong here.

Every now and then I pause and listen. I hear no bellows of the beast. But that's not all I'm searching for. I seek also the song of the blessed one, the giver of life who had made all this and still exists within it. She's here somewhere, I know. The beast hunts her, but, already, I am starting to wonder.

I have been searching for a long time, but I carry no weapons. That surprises me because it's so unusual. It's almost as if...

Around every corner there are new wonders. Sometimes these wonders are brutal and harsh because that's how life is. Sometimes they are purely beautiful. Weaponless, I cannot recall whether I have cast the weapons aside because they are bloodied and used, or simply because they are no longer required.

Flowing like life through the jungle, time will tell.

# About Tim Lebbon

Tim Lebbon is a *New York Times* bestselling writer from South Wales. He's had over thirty novels published to date, as well as hundreds of novellas and short stories. His latest novel is the thriller *The Hunt,* and other recent releases include *The Silence* and *Alien: Out of the Shadows*. He has won four British Fantasy Awards, a Bram Stoker Award®, and a Scribe Award, and has been a finalist for World Fantasy, International Horror Guild and Shirley Jackson Awards. Future books include *The Rage War* (an Alien/Predator trilogy) and the *Relics* trilogy from Titan.

A movie of his story "Pay the Ghost," starring Nicolas Cage, was released in 2015, and several other projects are in development, including his novel *The Silence* and his scripts My Haunted House and Playtime (with Stephen Volk).

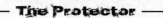

# Moth Frenzy

Lucy Taylor

few weeks after my sister Lina disappeared, I shouldered my backpack and headed out to a ghost town in the desert, looking for a taste of oblivion.

My preferred place to get shit-faced was the crumbled-down ruin of Blileytown, a flyspeck on maps of the 1890s that was once a thriving New Mexican coal mining community. Today, all that remains are the remnants of a chapel and a lonely windmill. I hitched a ride out of Gallup with some affable Indians who shared a joint and warned me of the danger for a woman out here alone. They dropped me off at the crossroads, and I hiked another half mile through the deep maroon dusk along a barely visible, rutted track.

Most of the night that followed is a mishmash of skewed recollection and haywire dreams, a smear of honey and shit on the back of my tongue that I can't seem to scrape off. Near sunset, I arrived at the tumbled-down church of San Felipe, whose tiny, walled graveyard provided some shelter from the clamorous wind. Cactuses clawed at the twilight, and a small tribe of tumbleweeds piled inside the courtyard like a collection of severed heads. I hunkered down with my back to the wall and my feet on a splintery cross. I unpacked my works to the cries of coyotes dismembering a kill, and shot up with skag I'd bought from my dealer, and sometimes fuck buddy, Orlando.

He hadn't lied about it being good shit. Everything mellowed and merged. For a moment, the world seemed surreally pristine, like the scenes on the souvenir beer mugs in the gift shop at the Fire Rock Casino. I flopped onto my back and watched a fat, flirtatious moon perform a splendid fandango behind silken clouds, and I began dreaming the most erotic and terrible dream. I was as high as the Big Dipper and swoony on liquid legs. I twirled out of the graveyard and went traipsing about willy-nilly, meandering among the piñons and creosote bushes in dizzy loops and zigzags, embracing the creaking windmill like we were old chums, calling out to my sister and praying to God that Mami was wrong, that the skinwalker called the Minotaur hadn't gone off with her soul.

Lina didn't answer and neither did God, which didn't surprise me, so I played kickball with the tumbleweed heads and watched a leggy tarantula, resplendent in reddish-brown fur, size me up from its dark hidey-hole. I yahooed to the nude, shameless moon, and the moon leered right back as I whipped off my t-shirt and draped it over the wing of an owl soaring past. The night wind hardened my nipples while stray stars swarmed in my hair, and I swanned around, sighing with bare-breasted glee, aglow in the solace of utter aloneness until I stumbled upon the remains of a dead woman, her bones bare on the moon-dappled sand.

Predators had shredded her clothing and scattered her bones, but cloth clung to some stray ropes of tendon and black hair tufted her bug-ridden scalp. She'd worn a white bra, and a chipped tooth gleamed at the side of her skull.

The bones were helter-skelter, most of them half-buried. In a trance, I picked over them carefully, like a shopper selecting a cutlet for dinner. I decided to pocket a finger bone so that I could later prove to myself the dead woman wasn't just a dream.

While I was bone-picking, the moon tiptoed away behind furrows of cloud. A meteor derailed from its arc and slammed under my ear, and ten shades of scarlet clawed inside my skull. I became legless, an amputee floating in warm, summer air, while tarantulas erupted out of the earth and pattered over my skin, seeking the warm crannies and niches where their kind likes to nest. When I screamed, they crammed themselves into my mouth. I tasted blood and heard a low, throaty bark. A naked man with a bull's head loomed over me, rampant and gleaming with sweat. I dug my nails into the meat of his shoulders and tried to tear off the mask until I realized it grew from his chest. My skin started to ripple with horror and awe and peeled off in long swathes that he draped over his back like a shawl, and we flew through the sky like two sorcerers, my mind all in tatters, my sanity strewn.

I woke up in the graveyard with my pack under my head and my works at my side, as if I'd slept there all night. I felt woozy and sickened, the way the dead woman must have felt as feral teeth stripped off her clothes and rent her flesh. My stomach heaved, and I rolled over as everything in me came up.

Well, not everything. Not the feelings of dread and despair or the pain banging around in my body like a drunk trying to find his way out of a strange house in the dark. My feet throbbed, my tongue bled where I'd bitten it, and even the tiny, deep places where my soul goes to hide felt like my drug-addled romp through the desert had scoured and defiled them.

When I wiped my mouth with the back of my hand, I found I was still clutching the bone that I thought I had dreamed, and I rolled over again and vomited horror and bile into the dirt by the crosses.

Now I can't get the sensations of that lurid dream out of my body, and a craving for poison much worse than drugs has thrust its way into my flesh. I feel reckless and starved; my brain swarms with some awful contagion. Sometimes I think the dream never ended, that it smothered me that night in its musky embrace, and I've been dreaming it ever since.

\* \* \*

Rumors of a skinwalker preying on girls started back in '09, when a trucker making a late run on the 491 between Shiprock and Gallup claimed he encountered a creature who was half-human, half-bull. He said it suddenly appeared by the driver's side window and kept pace even when he accelerated, glaring in at him with obsidian eyes in a bull's shaggy, horned head, but that when he looked down, it had the torso and legs of a man.

A few weeks later, Mami's old boyfriend, the potter Alphonso Nez, was coming back from an art show in Farmington when his pickup broke down. He was aiming a flashlight under the hood when he heard something approach and saw a beast with blood-tipped horns and a man's powerful physique emerge from the brush. Alphonso locked himself in the truck as the creature circled the vehicle for half an hour before it finally disappeared. Over time, his account of the incident became more elaborate. He said the monster resembled the Minotaur of Greek myth, a description that was repeated often enough that later, when two teenage girls from Shiprock vanished, and a woman from Teec Nos Pos disappeared after her car ran out of gas, people said the Minotaur was responsible. More women went missing over the years, but it was usually under dubious circumstances. Girls entangled in bad marriages or in trouble with the law, girls with good reason to run.

Not Lina, though. She had a job at the El Rancho Hotel and was planning to start college in Albuquerque. She was doing fine until the moth frenzy took her.

\* \* \*

"Oh, help me! He has me!" Lina is panting and thrashing when I rush into her room, awakened by the creaking of bedsprings and the thump of her head striking the backboard each time she bounces her hips. Her eyes roll, her tongue flicks back and forth, and she yelps like a dog caught in barbed wire.

"Who is it?" I look around wildly, half-expecting an intruder to leap from the closet or the hallway.

"Oh God, he's here!" She flings back the sheet. Her nightgown is twisted and bunched at her waist, and her knees are bent, exposing slick, maroon folds. I feel heat surge to my cheeks. For a moment, I consider waking up Mami, who snores contentedly in the other room, but I don't want her to see Lina like this.

*Lucy Taylor*

Her good daughter.

I cover her up and fetch my last bottle of Mad Dog, but she shoves it away in disgust. Her eyes blaze and her body shivers, like a doomed moth fluttering near the flames. "Alcohol won't help! Don't you understand? He has me! He's inside me!"

"Don't talk crazy. You're having a nightmare," I say, but I can't stand to stay there and go out into the hall where, unnerved, I chug down the bottle in a few scalding gulps. The alcohol dulls my disgust. I tell myself what Lina says isn't possible, that not even a skin-walker can rape a woman with sorcery.

Still, it takes all my courage to go back into her room.

She's spent now, vacant-eyed and exhausted. In the dim light, I'm shocked by the jut of her cheekbones, which poke up defiantly, no longer obscured by the layers of fat that always softened her face. Her once plump, rounded belly is now a sunken, stretched bowl.

She whimpers, "No, don't," but her hand slides down as her buttocks lift off the bed and she begins a slow, grotesque grinding.

I crack her across the face, grab her shoulders and try to shake her out of the trance. Rage flares in her face. A surge of energy seethes from her skin into mine. Pain scalds my fingers, flenses my forearms and chews into my wrists. My skin blazes an ugly, flayed red, and for a moment the wall I sag against is the only thing holding me up.

"Stop it! You're dreaming," I hiss, but I have no faith in my own words, and I don't try to touch her again.

Unable to watch her contortions, I stare out the window, beyond the portal and the adobe wall, out where the gate to the courtyard blew off in a windstorm last winter and never got fixed. With nothing blocking the view, the desert unfurls like a black throat gobbling down an obscene spill of stars. Alongside the gap where the gate once stood now swarms an unnatural convergence of shadows. In places they are as thick as the beams supporting the portal, in others gauzy as mist. Something massive hunches there in brute stillness. My blood goes a degree or two colder.

The next morning I find Lina sprawled under a clump of piñons a half mile from the house, her nightgown ripped, her feet bloody. Gently I lead her home, bathe her and put her to bed.

"Who's doing this? Tell me!"

She doesn't answer, but her face glows with a terrible radiance, like she's died and been reborn into some glorious hell. "I want him," she whispers, without meeting my eyes.

I know then we've lost her. I know she's bewitched.

* * *

A few nights later, Lina went wandering again, and this time she didn't return. I was in Gallup getting wasted with Orlando. Mami thought Lina was with me and didn't report her missing until the next day. The tribal police got involved, posters went up, and people searched the arroyos and acequias, but then the deaths of four joyriding teenagers in a head-on with a semi out by Church Rock stole everybody's attention. As for me, the only searching I did for my sister was in a heroin haze in the desert after she was long gone.

"So what happened, Drunk Girl? You get arrested again?" Mami snorted when I dragged myself into the kitchen, exhausted after my visit to Blileytown the night before.

I collapsed on the couch, staring up at the whirling ceiling. I tried to find words to explain where I'd been, what I'd seen. Hair and bones poking up out of the sand and something half-human that flew me through an eternal night, impaled and enthralled.

"Well?" Mami demanded when I'd been quiet too long.

She brought her plate into the living room and slammed it down on the table. Crossed her meaty arms. Glowered. "So, Drunk Girl, you know what I do last night when Arthur Yazzie won't let me sleep?"

It took me a second to remember Arthur Yazzie wasn't some hot boyfriend, but how the old people referred to arthritis. She went on, "First I call Leo, because he's wise in the ways of the shaman,

*Lucy Taylor*

and he tells me Lina is probably fine, that she must have ran off to L.A. or Vegas to start a new life. So I say, 'Bullshit, old coot! What do you know?' and hang up. Then I go out in the desert and call to the skinwalker Alfonso Nez saw years ago. I call to the Minotaur to come sit with me."

I had an image of Mami, ponderous on swollen ankles and arthritic joints, armed with her rosary and fetishes, braving the darkness to conjure up monsters.

Any other time I would have laughed, but today I wasn't so sure the skinwalkers weren't real. Still, I tried to dismiss her. "That's a sick fucking joke."

"No joke." She chomped down on frybread folded over a heap of Navajo round steak and gnawed pugnaciously with stump teeth. Bits of bologna spewed from her mouth. I put my arm over my eyes. "I got something to tell him," she said.

"There's no skinwalkers," I mumbled, gummy tongue adhering to furred teeth. "Alfonso Nez was probably doing peyote and ran into a cow."

Mami shook a sausage-thick finger. "You think skinwalkers just a Navajo superstition, but what do you know, Drunk Girl?"

More than I wanted to, I thought, but what I said was, "I know that even if there's some psycho out there hunting women, he's not coming for you. You're too old and too fat."

"Old and fat's better than stupid and squaybe!" She pulled a face like there was a stink to the bologna. "What I want to say to the Minotaur is, 'Listen, asshole, you fucked up when you took my Lina. She had a good life ahead of her. She was a hard worker, a good student. Didn't hang out with trash and slut around and drink herself blind. Didn't bring shame on the family.' She was nothing like you."

"Lina *is* nothing like me!" In my outrage, I lunged up off the sofa too fast. The walls lurched and turquoise paint oozed down the robes of the Virgin in her niche by the kiva. I steadied myself. "Don't talk like she's dead!"

My anger must have frightened Mami—either that or she was scared I was about to projectile vomit again—because she got up and lumbered to the window, squinting out at the shimmering heat waves like she expected Lina to come strolling through them.

"She must've went off to meet somebody she knew, and the Minotaur saw her," Mami said and turned her bitter black gaze onto me. I felt the bone tremble in my pocket like a warning. I knew I should speak, but the words wouldn't come, and I felt a surge of something cold and disloyal.

"You think Lina was so perfect? You should've seen her, humping the mattress and tearing out her own hair!"

Mami stared at me like I was roadkill served up on a platter. When she spoke again, the words unspooled from her tongue like a curse.

"So you know why I called to the Minotaur?"

I felt too broken to ask.

"Cause I want to tell the son of a bitch that I'll make him a trade. I got a girl here who won't get a job or do chores or act decent. Girl who runs wild like a jackrabbit. I tell the Minotaur to come take Drunk Girl away and bring back my good daughter Lina."

\* \* \*

Mami's voice was so full of loathing and scorn that I didn't dare tell her what happened in Blileytown, or show her the bone that I'd found. Worse, I later discovered she'd ransacked my room and thrown out all of my booze so I had nothing to bolster my courage for what I had decided to do. Finally, I grabbed a bottle of Listerine from the medicine cabinet, stuffed it in my back pocket and took the bus to the outskirts of Gallup.

Uncle Leo lived north of the city, in a split-level modular tucked away on a rural road without much else besides cactuses, but his courtyard was tree-shaded and restful, an escape from the punishing heat of midday. Birdhouses hung from the juniper branches and scarlet ristras swung from the portal.

Leo was outside tending his garden of succulents. A sweat-stained t-shirt clung to his back and his grey-streaked black hair was tied back with a bandanna. When I called to him, he smiled and straightened up, wincing with a hand to the small of his back.

We sat in the porch chairs and chatted a while before I asked him if he really believed what he told Mami, that Lina had left town to make a new start.

He spread his big hands, which were calloused and scarred from years of carpentry work. "What do you expect me to say to her, Franki? That I think Lina's in the ground rotting somewhere? That would be too cruel, and besides, we don't know for sure."

I pounced on that. "What if she's alive, but she needs help getting home because a demon's possessed her? You could do an Enemy Way ceremony to protect her from evil."

Leo hefted himself out of the chair and shuffled out into the garden. "Not many young people believe in demons these days. I'm surprised that you do."

So I told him about the fits Lina had suffered, and about the thing lurking out by the gate, but I didn't tell him about my dream of flying through the night with a monster. I was too ashamed to talk about that.

Leo spoke gravely. "That was the moth frenzy that afflicted your sister. She must've caught the eye of a skinwalker and he sent his wild energy into her. He drove her mad."

When he said that, I thought about Blileytown and suddenly remembered finding tarantula hair in my teeth. I clenched my jaw so I wouldn't throw up.

"Do the ceremony for her," I snapped, annoyed with his puttering among the clusters of barrel cactuses and coachwhips with their shiny, spiked leaves.

Leo bent to pluck a dead leaf from a fleshy, blue-green agave. When he straightened again, his knees popped like gunshots. "You know how a skinwalker gets his power? By killing a family member. That's the price for their shape changing, their ability to entice and cast spells. The corpse dust they use, they make that from the bones of the people they kill. You can't fight a skinwalker, Franki. If you'd talked to me earlier, when the moth frenzy first started, maybe I could've done something, but now…"

I'd thought something similar myself. Maybe if I didn't stay drunk and high all the time, I could've done more to help Lina and Mami wouldn't be wishing it was me gone instead. The guilt stung, and I lashed out. "You could still do the Enemy Way ceremony. You loved Lina! Mami always said she was your favorite."

"Your Mami doesn't know everything, Franki."

I didn't know what he meant, so I blurted, "Then I need something else. I need you to get me a gun."

He looked like I'd asked him to help me hold up the Stop N Save. "Forget that. Way you live, too many things can go wrong. Only person ending up dead will probably be you. Now, if you want money to go to that rehab in Tuba City, I might be able to spare a few bucks."

"I'm gonna get sober," I muttered for maybe the five-hundredth time in my life.

Leo sighed and ran his fingers over the leathery leaf of a coachwhip, caressing the plant like you'd touch a pet dog. Although he was standing a good ten feet away, his nostrils twitched and deep furrows ridged his high forehead. "Listerine, Franki? You've sunk to drinking mouthwash these days?"

* * *

I figured Orlando would show me more respect, so I cruised Coal Street until I found him asleep in an oval of shade behind the Fu King Smoke Shop. He came awake growling when I kicked the soles of his boots.

"Shit you want, Franki?" When I told him why I needed a gun, he said I was batshit crazy and besides, guns weren't cheap, but when I flashed the wad of cash I'd conned out of Leo, letting him think I might actually go into rehab, he exclaimed "Howah!" and changed his tune fast.

We went to his Dad's house and I waited while he rummaged through the garage and came back with a .44 Magnum, matte black in a leather holster. It was sexy and lethal-looking and would probably kick me all the way to Las Cruces if I fired it, but I clipped it onto my belt and yanked out my shirttail to cover the bulge. The Listerine buzz was a faint afterburn now, replaced with a shivery nausea. I asked Orlando to get me something to drink. While he was doing that, I spotted a sweet little folding knife inside a table drawer and slipped it in my back pocket.

He came back with a rectangle of black tar, and we shot up and attempted to fuck. When he got sentimental and said going into the desert alone was too dangerous, I told him I'd be okay, and besides, he was going to go with me.

* * *

Near twilight we rode his broke-ass dirt bike out to the cross-roads, banged another quarter mile through the scrub, then ditched the bike in an arroyo and set off for Blileytown. I was the bait, walking up ahead to try and lure out the Minotaur, while he followed behind out of sight.

I'd made this trek so many times I knew it by heart, but tonight the landscape looked surreal and distorted. Even the burnt-orange horizon seemed saturated in gloom. Night didn't just fall here, it dropped like a club to the back of the head. One minute I was squinting into the glare of a fever-red sunset, the next I was stumbling into gullies and slashing my arms on the cholla spines while a paper-thin moon teased hazy light from behind a funnel of clouds. A gritty wind lashed my hair, and coyotes keened a hysterical dirge to whatever poor thing they were rending. When I sensed something coming inhumanly fast at my back, I pulled out the Magnum and almost fired on a rabbit that went bounding past.

Orlando was being a dick, playing some kind of game. He was supposed to keep pace, pausing when I paused, flashing a penlight to let me know he was there. Instead he was either lagging too far behind or following too closely, bumbling into bushes and sending rocks clattering.

Overhead, the sky swarmed with corkscrews of cloud and the stars bled cold, distant light. An owl carved the air with a baleful whoosh and soared past with a mouse struggling in its talons. I hadn't heard Orlando make any noise for some time now. I was starting to think he'd turned back and abandoned me, but I resisted the urge to call out.

I made it another quarter mile, my nerves increasingly fraught, before the jagged silhouette of San Felipe came into view, and I stopped short with shock. Swastikas covered every inch of the decaying walls. It pissed me off that vandals had done this until I realized the black and red geometric designs weren't spray-painted on, but were seething out of cracks in the ancient adobe and scurrying away on nimble, reddish-haired legs. I realized that this was where the tarantulas in my dream came from. Blileytown was their nest. Too numerous to crowd onto the walls, they began scaling the black enamel bowl of the night, scuttling across constellations while comets shot past them like tracers. Sometimes a comet would hit its target and burn one of the spiders to ash, but most missed. The tarantulas, manic and vengeful, laid siege to the sky.

I stared at this lurid sight, mesmerized, until I heard Orlando murmur, "Howah," close by, and that jarred me out of the trance. The word, uttered calmly enough but with a distinct undercurrent of awe, seemed to come from inside the churchyard. I forced myself to climb onto the wall that was now bare of spiders and felt the finger bone shift in my pocket and dig into my hip. It felt alive, like the woman it had belonged to was urging me along. *Go find him. Go kill my killer.*

From my vantage point atop the wall, I searched for Orlando, but the courtyard was black upon blacker. Some celestial joker had unplugged the stars and thumbed out the moon. Jumping down from the wall was an act of pure faith. When my feet hit the ground I thanked a god I had never believed in, then realized my gratitude might be misplaced because what I saw made my blood freeze.

The skycrawlers had scuttled back into their cosmic rabbit holes, but the chollas were ornamented with bizarre and hideous vines, the limbs of dead women draping their branches in pale, fungal-like strands. Caught on the cactus spines, their tattered skin fluttered like the putrid remains of a pageant of crucifixions. Where the flesh had been eaten away gleamed mottled patches of bone.

Orlando had been positioned with a certain crude jest so that his stupefied stare seemed directed between the thighs of a dead woman dangling above him. When I touched his face, an eyelid peeled off like cellophane and fluttered away in the wind, leaving a damp stain on my fingers.

Something veered through the scrub and I whirled, the gun gripped in both hands, firing at a shadow with a gobbet of meat in its mouth. I didn't hit the coyote, but the recoil of the Magnum damn near dislocated my shoulder. I went deaf from the explosion and blind from the flash, and one of my fingers broke when I fought to hold on as the gun was pried from my hand. A suffocating weight mashed me into the dirt, and the Minotaur's huge head, with its matted hair and wide-spaced, bloody horns, lowered itself toward my face.

I found the folding knife in my pocket, but in my desperation to click out the blade I slashed my palm, ring finger to wrist.

The Minotaur opened my legs like a book he was going to rip cover to cover. Beyond his horns I could see the phantom faces of his victims, their eyes bright with a terrible elation that might have been mistaken for lust.

"The dead women," I whispered. "They're here."

Words rumbled from vocal chords not intended for speech. "It's good you can see them. You'll join them soon. They love me so they stay close."

Blood pumped from the gash in my hand, and my fingers were numb, but I felt the curve of the knife hilt and I grabbed it.

The monster's huge nostrils flared. He looked down at the knife. I knew he would take it away from me and probably drive it into my heart, but he instead snatched up the fragment of bone that had fallen out of my pocket.

He held it up, sniffed it. Dog sounds came from his throat. He tilted his massive head back, the better to inhale the scent. "Your sister's. I remember her smell. She was eager. She wanted me all the time."

I stabbed the blade into the base of his neck where the coarse animal hair thinned and a man's blue vein bulged. The shock jolted him upright and his muscles went rigid. He slapped at his throat, a motion which only drove the blade deeper as blood streamed down his chest. I thought he would topple over and crush me, but he lurched to his feet and shambled away, gouts of blood jetting when he yanked the blade out of his neck. I was on my feet, too, and I glanced back as I ran. He had dropped to his knees and was drinking his own blood from his cupped hands, the dead women mournful, coiled around him like ribbons of thin, patchy fog.

\* \* \*

When I finally made it back to the road and was picked up by a passing motorist, I was raving about dead women hung from the chollas and claiming I'd been raped by a skinwalker.

The tribal police found Orlando's gored body stuffed into an abandoned coyote den. His face, apparently, was intact, but the pathologist was baffled by the puncture wounds to his belly, which clearly weren't made by coyotes or by the gun with my fingerprints on it. Around San Felipe, a forensics team dug up the bodies of five women who'd gone missing over the years. None of the remains belonged to my sister, and although I tried to take detectives to the place where I'd found the skeleton, I wasn't able to locate it.

I spent a month at a shelter in Albuquerque for addicted and traumatized women. I felt safe there, even put on some weight, but the day before I went home, someone hung a scarlet ristra on the door to my room. I screamed when I saw it and tore it apart with my hands.

I should have realized this wasn't the end of it.

* * *

My first night at home, I wake up lathered in sweat, my body rippling with energy that arches my spine until I think it will snap and violently jitters my legs. I stuff the sheet in my mouth so I don't scream when my skin starts to crawl off. It slides from my arms like a pair of long gloves, leaving behind only the barest shadows of tattoos and moles, then the rest of it creeps off my body. My face, neck and scalp peel off last with a death-rattle snap, which is when I first see the Minotaur outside by the gap where the gate used to be. Naked and wanton, he snares my skin in his fist and loops it around his groin like a trophy.

After a few nights of this, I stop eating and won't leave the house. Mami thinks that I'm using and starts calling me Drunk Girl again, but how can I think of liquor or smack when I'm wrecked all the time now, my mind reeling, undone, and the phrase 'fuck your brains out' is no longer crass slang, but a dismal, unhinging reality.

One night, in desperation, I drive my head into the wall, but that only makes the assault worse because as my consciousness flickers and dims, his power expands, and I come to convulsing with his violent energy running amok in my veins.

What surprises me isn't that he becomes stronger, but that in some perverse way, I do, too. If I'm corrupted and deadened by his assaults, he too is ensnared. *You can't fight a skinwalker,* he told me, but I have every intention to try.

I enter his yard in the evening via the unlocked front gate, find him sprawled in his garden, sated and snoring, a muscular old man with a bull's bulging shoulders and a pale, lolling cock, a bandanna knotted around his thick neck where an old wound still might seep. Around him, a ring of corpse dust protects him should his enemies, living or dead, come to call.

I hesitate at this boundary, knowing the cost, but when his body reacts to my scent and grows hard, I step inside the circle of crushed and cursed bones. My entry animates the gray powder and causes it to billow in thick, poisonous ropes that sandpaper my nostrils and blister my skin. It kindles a craving for blood in a part of my brain so ancient I thought it went extinct with the trilobites. A cannibalistic hunger to devour and destroy surges through me as I stand over the sleeping old man and aim the gun. The trigger is too unwieldy to squeeze, so after two or three tries, I use my tongue, which is surprisingly pliant and strong. The bullet plows a crater out the back of his head big enough to punch my fist through, which I contemplate doing, except I don't have a fist anymore. The scaled talons aren't practical for using a gun, but work well for scooping out eyeballs.

*You were always my favorite,* he says, but I figure this to be shock. I've never killed anybody before, much less a close relative.

As I leave the courtyard, the corpse dust clings to my misshapen feet and swirls like incense beneath my tough, plated groin. It gifts me with a visual magnitude spanning eons, as well as an unnatural tolerance for the depraved, and it unveils a few extra circles of Hell, a rutting ground for all things bestial stretching back to the Pleistocene. The Minotaur, reborn from the flesh of his former host, looms before me, resplendent in gore.

I belong in this wasteland, and so does he, but first there is carnage to revel in.

The town of Gallup awaits us.

On my four legs, I follow him there.

*Lucy Taylor*

# About Lucy Taylor

Lucy Taylor is the Bram Stoker Award®-winning author of *The Safety of Unknown Cities, Spree, Saving Souls, Nailed* and ten other horror/suspense novels and collections. Her most recent work includes the short story collection *Fatal Journeys* and the novelette "A Respite for the Dead." Recent publications include the short story "In the Cave of the Delicate Singers" and "Wingless Beasts" in Ellen Datlow's The *Best Horror of the Year: Volume 7*, and "Blessed Be the Bound" in *Nightmare* magazine.

Taylor lives in Santa Fe, New Mexico, a land full of mystery, romance and the macabre.

Family
Bible

Ed Kurtz

zra crept around the corner of the Duxom County Drugstore and peeked out at the sparse traffic on Dixon Street. A couple of pick-ups sputtered by, their beds stacked high with feed, and an old crone piloted her Edsel at ten miles per hour, but that was about the extent of it. The boy did not worry about his father catching him in town — the man never came to town on any day apart from Saturday, when he picked up supplies for the coming week — yet there remained the terrifying prospect of some busybody mentioning Ezra's appearance in an off-handed way.

*Saw your boy about this last Thursday, Isaiah. Stalking 'round like a criminal, he was.*

For the sake of meaningless small talk, Ezra would end up on the business end of a powerful whupping.

He scanned Dixon Street again, narrowing his eyes and studying every face, every detail. He thought back to a line from one of the detective stories in the contraband pulp magazine he kept stashed under his mattress: *The coast is clear!* Ezra scrambled around the corner to the sidewalk and rushed into the drugstore.

A tiny silver bell chimed when the glass door swung open. Heads turned. The boy felt like a gigantic spotlight had just been turned on him. Jake Snell stood behind the counter in his crinkled paper hat, wiping out a sundae glass with a rag. He raised an eyebrow at Ezra, a silent question on his face the boy could not decipher. A jukebox at the back wall cranked out a 45 and laid it on the turntable. A second later the drugstore came alive with the sound of a colored man's voice and a pounding rhythm to back it up — a curious juxtaposition with the WHITES ONLY sign posted in the window. Ezra winced. Being in the presence of the Devil's music wasn't helping his anxiety much.

"You need something, boy?" Jake Snell asked. "Looking for somebody?"

A curly mass of golden brown locks spun in the last booth by the window, and Ezra's eyes locked with Annabelle Dell's. The girl smiled, giving a wave with one hand while clutching her milkshake with the other. She sucked on the red-and-white straw, swallowed and said, "Ezra, over here."

Jake Snell smiled and nodded, went back to wiping out the glasses.

Ezra grinned nervously and crossed the tiled floor, overly conscious of the clacking noise his heels made with every step.

Annabelle flashed a toothy smile as Ezra slid into the booth across from her.

"I've never heard music like this before," he squeaked.

"It's the Moonglows," she explained.

Ezra didn't understand, but he didn't let on about it. He just knitted his brow and shook his head like he'd known all along.

"You want a milkshake or something?"

Sweat beaded at his hairline. He was not supposed to have things like that—pops and candy and sweet milk drinks. The suggestion compounded his mounting terror.

"No, thanks," he answered. "I didn't come here for that."

"What else do you come to a drugstore for?" she asked, regarding him quizzically.

"Why, I came for you."

Annabelle blushed. Ezra did, too.

\* \* \*

Duxom was one of Arkansas' largest counties, with one of the smallest populations. Nestled into the state's thickly wooded northwest corner, the county seat—also called Duxom—boasted only four hundred and thirty souls, give or take. Some lived in town, or close to it. Many more resided in old family homes much further out, built on plots claimed by ancestors who came when Arkansas was the Western Frontier. One such property was deeded to Isaiah Durfee, the grandson of the plot's first claimant.

Someday, it would be passed on to Ezra and his brother—the house, the family cemetery, the little tannery out back, everything.

He sat alone on an oak stump and studied the wooden grave markers that sprawled out before him, fifteen in all. The closest belonged to Peter Durfee, Ezra's great-grandfather, the first to come across from Scotland and establish himself in Duxom. The marker was made of cherry wood and shaped like a cross. Behind this resting place the remaining fourteen spread out like an upside-down pyramid. Among those in the very last row was Ezra's mother and infant sister. There was no more room in that row now, not since Mama succumbed to the cancer. The next Durfee to die would have to begin a new one.

Probably Papa. Then either Ezra himself or his brother, Jonah. The Durfees were running a little thin.

It was well past time that Jonah got himself hitched, though there hadn't been any suitable girls around. Papa was getting downright apoplectic about it. In another couple of years, it would be Ezra's turn to face that pressure. He wrinkled his nose, thinking about getting hooked up with some girl and putting a baby in her, another load for another grave in the ground.

He didn't much cotton to the idea.

Behind him, last fall's dry leaves crunched under encroaching footsteps. Ezra pursed his chapped lips and spun around on the stump to see Annabelle emerging from the woods. A yellow picnic basket dangled from her left hand, and she held up a bouquet of wildflowers in her right.

"Purple milkweed," she cooed with enthusiasm. "Never seen them around here before."

"Oh, there's all kinds of flowers 'round here," Ezra said authoritatively. "Papa says it's God's country."

"It sure is pretty," Annabelle agreed. "I was like to get lost in the woods, but I guess I might not have minded so much, pretty as it is."

Ezra stood and shifted his weight from one leg to the other. He eyed the basket, wondering hungrily about its contents.

"Ham sandwiches," she said. "And lemon pops to wash them down."

Ezra frowned, disappointment washing over him.

"You don't like it."

"I don't know if I like it, but I can't eat it," he said. "We don't eat pork. It has split hooves that are completely cloven and it don't bring up its cud."

"Oh."

"That's in the Bible."

Annabelle crooked her mouth up to one side and furrowed her brow. The sunlight came through the tall boughs in luminous shafts that dappled her curls.

Ezra felt his heart punching his ribs from the inside.

"There's victuals in the house, though," he said. "Maybe enough for us both."

He raised his eyebrows and waited while she thought it over. Annabelle shrugged her shoulders, set the picnic basket on the stump and smiled.

"All right. I expect that's okay."

Ezra offered his hand, which Annabelle accepted. Hand in hand they walked down the hill to the old house below.

\* \* \*

The house looked large from the outside, at least larger than most of the outlying homes, but the rooms inside seemed small and cramped. Ezra asked her to take a seat on the worn settee in the front room, which coughed up a cloud of dust when her weight sank into it. He went away to the kitchen, leaving the girl alone with a cramped room full of knickknacks to keep her company.

A clock ticked on the wall, drawing her eyes to the cast iron pickaninny grinning down from the wall beside it. The grotesque, ink-black face leered at her through smiling eyes, and she realized that its gaping, red mouth was a bottle opener. She averted her eyes, vaguely ill at ease with the ugly ornament, and turned her attention to the finished oak bookstand by the fireplace.

Worn and deeply scored in numerous places, the bookstand stood a good three feet or more, a massive book spread open on top. Annabelle glanced around the room and noticed that there were no other books in sight, only the enormous one on such lofty display.

*Likely a Bible*, she thought, recalling Ezra's discomfited regard for the Good Book.

Her people had a family Bible, too—just about everybody did—though theirs rested on the bookshelf in the den between *Spade Cooley's Western Swing Song Folio* and *The Encyclopedia of World History*, rather than the museum-like exhibition Ezra's kinfolks afforded the Holy Writ. And it certainly wasn't half as big as the yellowing behemoth that so fascinated Annabelle at that moment.

She rose from the dusty settee and shuffled over to the bookstand, glancing over her shoulder to see if Ezra was coming back yet. She thought that silly, feeling nervous that she might get caught looking at a Bible. A smile crept across her pink face as she leaned over the crinkly old pages.

It was opened to Ezekiel.

One particular passage was traced over with pencil, darkening and thickening the letters.

*And I will lay sinews upon you, and will bring up flesh upon you, and cover you with skin, and put breath in you, and ye shall live, and you shall know that I am the LORD.*

"Huh," she said, puzzling over the cryptic, ancient words.

"That's Papa's Bible."

Annabelle gasped and pivoted on her heel. Ezra stood in between rooms, a shiny red apple in each hand.

"All I could find," he apologized, passing an apple to her. "Funny, since Papa don't go to town 'til Saturday."

Annabelle said, "Thank you."

"Older n' dirt," Ezra said, his mouth full of chewed fruit. "Older n' the Civil War, even."

"I bet it's valuable," she offered, gently running her fingertips down the page. The paper felt brittle, dry.

"Might could be," he said. "It's worth a lot to Papa. My great-granddaddy made it, you know. Not just the cover, though he made that, too. I mean the whole book; he wrote it down and everything."

"Gee," Annabelle said, gawping at the finely crafted lettering. "He must have been awful religious."

"I'll say. I guess he was sort of like a prophet."

"A prophet?"

"Sure," Ezra said, "like in the Bible days. Smote sinners and all that stuff."

Annabelle mouthed the word: *smote.*

"You remember Elijah," he explained. "Killed all them false priests, the priests of Baal. Well, great-granddaddy Peter found sort of a false church, too, right here in Duxom. Papa says they called themselves Christians, but they was preaching the wrong words, twisting up scripture and all."

Annabelle bit into her apple, her eyes trained on Ezra as he recounted the story. Juice squirted from the fruit's inner flesh, spraying her cheek.

"I guess there was this fellow up in Kansas about the same time, name of John Brown. Story was that John Brown smote sinners with a broadsword on account of they was slavers. Great-granddaddy used a ploughshare."

"They shall beat their swords into ploughshares," Annabelle recited, recalling the prophecy of Ezra's father's namesake.

"That's right," Ezra said, nodding. "Except he done it the other way 'round. He took up his ploughshare and made a sword of it."

"And he...*killed* them?"

"That's what Papa says. Two dozen of them, right in their wicked old church."

Annabelle swallowed hard.

"Goodness," she whispered.

"The way I recollect the story, great-granddaddy'd just about finished writing down his Bible," Ezra said, striding over to the bookstand. He caressed the delicate pages and gingerly closed the book.

The wrinkled amber cover fascinated Annabelle for its starkness—no words scarred the leather, only stitching.

"As for the priest of Baal—that's what Papa always called him—old great-granddaddy cut off his skin and used it to bind this here Bible. We've had it in the family ever since, and that was a hundred years ago."

Annabelle's stomach lurched. Her eyes moved down to the apple in her hand, settling upon a wide brown spot marring the white flesh. Her gorge rose in her throat.

Ezra's lips spread across his face, a mischievous smile.

"You wanna see something?" he asked.

Annabelle regarded him guardedly.

"Come on."

\* \* \*

Above an immaculately made bed in a small, severe-looking bedroom, the ploughshare hung from a hook in the wall. Its wooden handle was cracked and rotting, its dull blade crusted with rust. Annabelle wondered if some of it was old blood, too.

Upon the decayed remnant of the handle, a legend was branded into the wood: ISAIAH 5:25.

"Therefore is the anger of the Lord kindled against his people," Ezra said, noticing Annabelle's focus on the legend. "And he hath stretched forth his hand against them, and hath smitten them: and

*Ed Kurtz* ————————————————————— **71**

the hills did tremble, and their carcasses were torn in the midst of the streets. For all this his anger is not turned away, but his hand is stretched out still."

"Does your Papa make you remember all those passages?"

"I study a lot," he said. "That's how come I don't go to school. They don't teach what's really important. That's what Papa says, anyhow."

Annabelle kept her eyes on the corroded old ploughshare, at its position of prominence in the stark room. Little else embellished the space apart from a framed photograph on the nightstand of a handsome woman, and a simple, unadorned cross that hung on the opposite wall. She presumed the woman to be Ezra's mother. He'd told her she died in the spring. But even she did not receive the distinction given to the old prophet's ploughshare-turned-sword.

She found it gruesome, yet vaguely exciting, like something out of an H. Rider Haggard story. She was somewhat surprised to discover how little the grisly artifact bothered her. In an odd sort of way, it served to further endear her to the reticent boy by her side. He came from a colorful family background and had stories to tell. Annabelle, conversely, came from boring old Duxom stock. Her father was a sharecropper.

"Ezra," she said softly after a while. "My school's putting on a dance in a few weeks. A sock hop—do you know what that is?"

He shook his head.

"Well, it's just a regular dance, except you gotta take off your shoes so as to not ruin the gymnasium floor."

"Oh," he said.

"There'll be lots of nice kids there," she went on, "and punch and cookies, that sort of thing. I already asked my mother if it was all right, and I'd sorta like you to take me."

"Take you?"

"To the dance, silly."

Ezra narrowed his eyes and scrunched up his face. He had met Annabelle only two weeks before, during one of his unsanctioned escapes into town, but he'd already taken a profound liking to her. She was forthright and charming and kind, and her startling prettiness only helped. Other boys promenaded for her attention, but Annabelle said she preferred Ezra's shyness, his gentle demeanor.

*Some boys will paw at a girl,* she'd told him to his marked wonder. *I'm glad you don't think I'm that kind.*

He did not know what kind she meant, but Ezra was glad, too.

"You don't have to, of course," Annabelle squeaked, her eyes a bit shiny.

"No, no," he protested. "I'd like that. I really would."

The girl sighed and smiled sweetly. She reached for Ezra's hand, squeezed it, and touched her soft, pink lips to his cheek.

He felt a mild tremor work its way up his spine.

\* \* \*

Jonah wiped the sweat from his brow with the back of his hand and exhaled noisily. He'd been hauling logs and hefting the axe over them for the better part of an hour, yet Ezra was nowhere to be seen. The boy was shirking his chores.

"He becometh poor that dealeth with a slack hand, Ezra," Jonah grumbled.

He buried the ax blade in a stump and stretched his aching back, mulling over how sulky and silent his brother had been these last few days. It frustrated the older boy to no end, but more than that it worried him. Ezra was not even practicing his penmanship or copying the scriptures as he was expected to do. If he failed to finish his Bible in time, Papa would be cross. Terribly cross.

Jonah snatched up his shirt from a low hanging branch and used it to wipe himself down as he made his way to the house.

In Ezra's bedroom, he found his brother staring dubiously at his Sunday clothes laid out on the bed.

"What are you doing? You're supposed to be helping me chop firewood."

Ezra snapped his head up and gawped at his big brother.

"And what're you doing with them clothes? It's still Saturday, you know."

"I'm just—I'm just getting ready for worship," Ezra stammered. "That's all."

"Baloney. It ain't like you have to make up your mind about it. Never have before."

Ezra frowned, started gathering up the clothes to put back in the closet.

Jonah planted his hands on his bony hips. "What's going on?"

"Nothing's going on," Ezra barked. "Mind your own business."

"That's rich," Jonah said. "You'd better mind yours. There's wood to chop, and Papa'll be back before sundown. If you wanna get whupped, then get whupped. I'm gonna chop wood."

With that the older boy stalked out of the room. By the time he reached the front door, his anger melted, giving way back to the concern he had before. Something was going on, and it bewildered him deeply. If it was at all indicative that Ezra might be straying, Jonah decided he was going to have to keep an eye on his brother.

There was a dwindling legacy to think about, after all.

\* \* \*

As instructed, Annabelle waited in the clearing beyond the Durfee place. She stood atop a mound of brown pine needles, shielding her eyes from the setting sun with the flat of her hand, wishing she had a wristwatch. Even without it, she was fairly sure Ezra was late.

She wore a pink-and-white striped circle skirt dress, with three large Lucite buttons running down the front that had ribbons tied into them. Her mother said she looked *dee-vine*. Annabelle worried that she was sweating too much in it, standing out in the warm late afternoon like she was. She hoped Ezra would show up soon.

Finally, she heard the crunch of feet smashing forest detritus,

*Ed Kurtz*

coming from the general direction of Ezra's house. The girl perked up, checked herself over for anything that might have gotten stuck to her dress on the way into the woods. She wanted desperately to look nice for Ezra. She'd never been to a dance with a boy before.

And he was such a nice boy.

Presently, a figure appeared amongst the trees, silhouetted by the sun at its back. Annabelle managed a nervous smile, clasped her hands together at her breast, and stepped forward.

"You," the figure seethed.

"Ezra?" Annabelle called back. "Is that you?"

"You have the brazen look of a prostitute, and yet you refuse to blush with shame."

"What?" she asked, her skin prickling with anxiety and confusion. "Ezra?"

The shape emerged into the light of the clearing. He looked an awful lot like Ezra—he sported the same brown flattop and his nose was similarly thin and crooked—but this boy was taller, skinnier. At his side, the rusty ploughshare hung from his hand.

"The Lord is filled with fury against you when you do all these things," the boy growled at her, "acting like a brazen whore."

"I don't understand."

She stepped back, her pink shoes rustling the pine needles.

The boy closed the distance. He tightened his grip on the worn handle, obscuring the branded legend with his bloodless hand.

He felt the blood of his great-grandfather throb in his veins.

"I reckon you're no priest of Baal, but a sinner's a sinner, and you'll just have to do."

Annabelle stumbled backward, raising her hands over her sweat-drenched face when her heel snagged a root and her body jerked with a single violent spasm. In an instant she collapsed to the ground in a heap. She twisted her upper body to right herself, tearing the top button from her dress. It disappeared among the dead pine needles. A wet sob bubbled up from her throat.

"No," she rasped.

Jonah raised the ploughshare high above his head. The receding evening sun glinted rust-red off the metal of the blade. He then brought it down hard and squeezed his eyes shut before the blade crunched through shoulder and neck.

Blood sprayed across the front of the cupcake dress.

\* \* \*

As the afternoon wore on, Ezra eventually gave up on the bedroom door. Usually it was Papa who locked him in, but this time it was Jonah, exercising his authority as the eldest son. There was no getting it open, not even by slamming his shoulder against it. He regretted giving in so easily, telling Jonah what he'd planned to do. But by then it was much too late to do anything about it, so he relented and spent the time copying the venerable words in to his Bible. He'd made it through Second Kings at last, and he now worked on First Chronicles. His wrist and knuckles ached, but he had to be careful to keep the letters looking nice and even. He had gotten sloppy halfway through Deuteronomy back in the spring, around the time Mama passed on, and Papa was like to make him eat the pages he'd ruined. Now the youngest son was considerably more vigilant in his work.

As the sky outside his bedroom window went from purple to black, Ezra felt his heart sink. It was foolish to have agreed to take Annabelle to the dance in the first place, but he hated himself for standing her up. He wondered how long she would wait in the clearing before realizing he was never going to come. He wondered how much she hated him and if she was going to feel that way forever.

A warm tear dropped from the edge of his eyelid and splashed the page, leaving a dark spot in which the ink smeared. He grimaced and crumpled the page into a ball.

He was never going to finish. Everything felt so hopeless.

A key crunched into the lock and the bedroom door creaked

*Ed Kurtz*

open. Ezra bolted up from the floor where he was working to see Jonah emerge from the shadows. He was wearing his undershirt and blue jeans, both spattered with blood.

He was breathing hard and his face dripped with sweat.

"You'd better tell Papa you done it," he wheezed.

"Done what, Jonah?"

"He'll be back any minute. I better get cleaned up for supper."

"Done what?"

Ezra heaved himself up to his feet and stared, open-mouthed.

"And I'm not doing none of the peeling or the stitching for you, neither."

A lump formed in Ezra's throat as he watched his brother vanish around the corner. He just stood there, gaping at the darkness beyond the room, knowing what Jonah meant but still trying to make sense of it.

Ezra reckoned he would be the youngest Durfee to ever finish his family Bible. Papa was bound to be prouder than an old peacock.

But it didn't help the heartache much.

# About Ed Kurtz

Ed Kurtz is the author of *Nausea, A Wind of Knives, The Forty-Two* and *Angel of the Abyss*, among other novels and novellas. His short fiction has appeared in numerous magazines and anthologies including *Thuglit, Needle: A Magazine of Noir, Shotgun Honey*, and *Psychos: Serial Killers, Depraved Madmen, and the Criminally Insane*. He work has appeared in *The Best American Mystery Stories 2014*.

# Life, or Whatever Passes for It

Durand Sheng Welsh

During the early '70s, just before the two spans of the old Sunshine Skyway Bridge shook hands two hundred and fifty feet above Tampa Bay, the unopened southern approach became an informal layover point for the rough characters migrating down to Miami and the Keys. Myself, I'd gone AWOL from the Air Force — a conscientious objector, if the girl asking was pretty enough — and had journeyed there via those interconnected fingers of land near St. Pete: Treasure Island, Madeiras Beach, Pass-A-Grille. Names to make a restless man think of toucan birds, jaunty pirates and the freebooter's lifestyle.

Of course, no toucans greeted me on the Skyway's southern approach. The freshly concreted two-lane had all the charm of a bail jumpers' convention: rusted out camper vans, vagrants dossed down in sleeping bags and the smells of beer and marijuana mixed in with the aromas of raw bait and the salt breeze. No one blinked an eyelid at my ruin of a '56 Chevy and my bullet-holed Airstream.

That first night I had a fugitive's wanderlust, so I scrounged a bottle of watered-down Jack Daniels off an enterprising fisherman, and then had the crazy idea of checking out the view from the bare bones of the south span. I wasn't the first man to blame Vietnam for his loss of faith in God and country, but, nonetheless, I felt a coward for running, and there are few cures for cowardice as good as booze and an act of grand stupidity.

By the time I reached the spot where the jumbled girders thinned out to a lone tight-walker's strut, the bottle's contents were in my gullet and the bottle itself had taken a long dive into the bay below. I walked out onto the steel ribbon, each foot going toe-to-heel like a Russian gymnast.

That was where I met Sharkbait Sutter.

He was perched on the end of the beam, solemn and still, at peace with the night, the long drop beneath his heels and the slow rumble of the ocean. An unlit cigar twitched between his teeth, and he leaned forward. I thought he meant to jump, probably because suicide and death were never far from my thoughts in those days, but then I caught the silhouette of a rifle.

He was sighting down an old bolt-action military piece.

Having discarded my best manners, along with my sobriety, I sidled closer and asked him what he was shooting at.

"Not communists," he said, which made me think about the fading tan lines under my shirt where my dog tags had been.

"What are you shooting at?" I repeated, a meaner edge in my voice.

"Thin air," he said without turning around.

"Try not to miss."

Sutter laid his head closer to the rifle's scope and fired off a round so thunderous that I lost my balance. I teetered on the beam's edge, glimpsed the dark and cracked shell of the ocean far, far below. My stomach butterflied into my throat, and I did a passable impression of a doomed cartoon character teetering on a cliff. Sutter grabbed my shirtfront and yanked me straight again. I doubled over laughing after I'd caught my breath.

Sutter adjusted the scope and hefted the stock back onto his shoulder. He was wearing a snow parka, a bulky nylon get-up that had to be ridiculously hot. If I'd been less drunk I'd probably have thought harder about his choice of clothing, but right then I was fixated on the fact the lunatic was taking pot-shots at empty water. The rifle stock seemed a hunk of worn and dark-grained obsidian, the barrel a spear of starlit bronze. I followed the barrel's line out across the ocean, tracking the curve of the earth and the tide that swept out into the Gulf. To my surprise, an orange light swooped and bobbed out there, its afterimage uncoiling like a Chinese dragon dancing with the wind.

The Gulf of Mexico has always had a reputation for the unexplained. In further testament to my drunkenness, I took a tipple from the local reservoir of superstition and wondered if I were indeed witness to a glowing visitor. Then the sharp crack of Sutter's rifle broke the mystic moment, and a split-second later the light winked out.

"What the hell did you do?" I asked belligerently, as if Sutter had just tossed a puppy onto a campfire.

"Hopefully caught me a shark," Sutter said. Then he turned around, teeth clenched hard on his cigar, and the look he gave me was sobering. I took the hint and left him to his fishing.

\* \* \*

Next morning, dried out and nursing the hangover to prove it, I ran into Sutter on the Skyway's approach. He was sitting astride a chunk of broken concrete, a protruding length of rebar sticking up between his thighs like a satyr's glory. Between his hands he held a car inner tube, one end tied to a length of small-gauge chain. The chain trailed four feet to a hook that looked about the right size to hang a pig carcass.

He wore a heavy wool sweater, shapeless and baggy. It reminded me of his fashion choice the previous night, and it made me wonder if some mental health issue wasn't behind his overdressing. I didn't mention him saving my life, figured I wouldn't have lost my balance if he hadn't spooked me with that rifle shot in the first place. Still, I found myself shuffling up to where he was working. I guess when a man saves your life, even if you don't want to thank him, some sort of acknowledgment should occur. Maybe a person's life feels more worthwhile, less pointless, if the saving of it isn't just disregarded.

Off to one side were a couple of deflated sacks. "What are those?" I asked, ice-breaking and small talk not being great strengths of mine.

"Weather balloons," Sutter said.

I looked at the blue sky. Looked back at Sutter. Looked up again. He ignored me. I asked him why he had a weather balloon.

"Hitch the balloon to the hook and let the tide carry her out into the deep waters. When you shoot out the balloon, the hook and bait will fall, fall, fall." He angled his fingers downwards and wriggled them to make his point.

"Couldn't you take the shot from down here?" I asked.

Sutter scratched his chin, silver with stubble. "Probably could." He went back to checking the tension of the inner tube, his big hands torturing the squealing rubber, stretching it out and out.

"What's with the tube?" I asked.

"Why you so keen to know?"

"Just making conversation is all."

"Can't you go do that by yourself somewhere?"

I used a hand to shade my eyes from the sun's glare. "Probably could," I said, echoing his earlier response.

Sutter's jaw tightened and his skin took on a curious grey tinge, but then the door of his trailer opened, interrupting the usual chain of consequences that comes from two recalcitrant men getting edgy with their words. A fox-faced girl stepped out. She wore an expression that indicated she found the sunlight bouncing off the bay even less therapeutic than I did. Either that or she'd taken offense to the pervasive stink of fish guts. Given her alabaster skin, and the stains on the oversize singlet that was pulling double-duty as a miniskirt, it wasn't hard to figure out which was the more likely option.

"Darlene, the kid wants to know what the tires are for. He can't figure it out," Sutter said.

"Stop teasing him," she said, throwing a dismissive look my way. "They're shock absorbers. For when he hooks the big fish. He wants you to ask, you know. So he can hold court and be the keeper of the knowledge."

Sutter's expression darkened for a moment, but then he chuckled and threw back a private insult of some kind. The two of them traded them casually, to and fro, while I stood on the sidelines. I mused on how the sultry Tampa breeze was playing havoc with the singlet's hemline. The tenor of Darlene's banter with Sutter made me sincerely hope that the two of them weren't father and daughter.

"Baby, now you've finally gotten your sweet tail out of bed," he said, "why don't you fetch me some soup off the stove."

Darlene gave him a hard look that made me wonder if maybe she'd once turned tricks—or still did—before skulking off to the camper with one last flick of her behind that answered any remaining questions about whether she was wearing underwear.

"She's a peach, ain't she?" Sutter asked, watching me with eyes that glittered like wet stones.

"You'd know better than me," I replied.

"Ain't that the truth of it," he said in a weary voice as he tightened the chain around the inner tube. "You think this'll hold?" He held up the tube; it looked like a conger eel that he'd strangled to death.

"Sure," I replied, still thinking of Darlene's ass.

Sutter laid the tube down across his lap, freeing his hands. He reached down to a bucket next to him. His fist came out gripping a wicked filleting knife. The bucket was filled with bloodied water, but when the water sloshed back and forth, I heard hard objects bumping the tin sides.

"Turn around," Sutter said.

"I heard that one before," I said, eyeing the knife.

"C'mon now, aren't you forgetting you owe me your life after last night? It's a bit early for me to go collecting that debt. I got to fillet some bait for the hook, is all. Bait bucket's just behind you. You going to help me out and throw me a chunk of chum or are you just going to give me bullshit all day?"

My pride finally overcame my fear—not exactly shattering news to anyone who'd known me back then—and I spun about, saw a halved grouper in a bucket, and spun back about with the fish dangling from my fist.

"Suspicious critter, ain't you," he said, eyeing me carefully. "So, which branch of the military you cut and run from?" He gestured for the fish I held.

"I never said I was in the military."

"No, you never did." Sutter feigned puzzlement. "Here now, I thought you wanted to make conversation."

I leaned over, inches away from the filleting knife, making my point, and dropped all twenty pounds of wet fish onto his lap. "Air Force," I said. "Not telling you which wing, though. That's my business."

"See much action?"

"If you're asking that, then you weren't over there. But yeah."

"Kill many gooks?"

There was a pause, a lull during which the Tampa Bay itself seemed to tighten itself around the pylons like its surface was a skin of heated shrink-wrap. I got whammied with a second of vertigo, and I could smell the blood of the halved fish mixing with the remembered stench of burning flesh. The black inner tube sat in Sutter's lap under the bleeding fish, looking for all the world like the scorched dead husk of a baby.

"So?" Sutter said.

Darlene broke the silence by pushing out the camper door with a pot of steaming soup balanced in one hand and a cigarette dangling from the other. She paused to blow equal parts smoke and cool breath over the top of the soup and then set it down next to Sutter.

"He give you a sermon about the mermaids?" Darlene asked, staring out across the bay.

"Nope," I said.

"He's crazy for mermaids."

"They aren't mermaids," Sutter said, and he seemed on the verge of getting up and belting her. She met his gaze, as if daring him to, and I got the sense that there was some secret message, some shared history, that passed between them in that exchange of looks. Sutter smiled grimly and dropped his gaze to the bowl of soup.

"Why don't you explain it yourself," she said. "And don't give him no crap about fishing for sharks. That story almost makes you sound sane." She gave me a wink that didn't change any of the hard-luck expression south of her smeared mascara, and then she left.

"Mermaids?" I asked.

Sutter blinked as if coming out of a fugue. "Ah, hell," he said and shook his head. "She's not talking about those mariner's fairy tales, mind you. The real ones look more like sharks."

"So, they got all the usual womanly charms from the waist up?" I asked, playing it straight.

"Yeah, plus a shark's dorsal fin. And teeth sharp as razors. Before you go and have a proper laugh, you ever hear about the Fountain of Youth?"

I admitted that I had no knowledge of that scholarly topic.

Sutter wasn't a big speech sort of guy, so it was very much the abbreviated story of the Spanish conquistador Ponce de Leon and his quest for the mythical fountain in what is now Florida.

"It's out there," Sutter said, nodding with severity toward the mouth of Tampa Bay. "Sandwiched between the thermals and the sandbars and the tidal currents is a rill of hard-core junk that Ponce de Leon would have given his left nut for."

*His left nut. Poetic.*

"You got any proof of that?" I asked.

"Just the mermaids."

"And where are they?"

Sutter nodded his head at his ride, a Ford 150 with a taut blue tarp pulled over the rear tray. Figuring this might be funny, I walked over to it. As I got closer I saw blood, old and new, scabbing the metal sides of the tray, and I heard the buzzing of flies trapped under the tarp. I loosened the tie-down cords from their eyelets and lifted one corner. The sun shone through the tarp with a murky blue light. Between the hazy light and the stench it took me a moment to focus on what I was seeing: shark tails. At least six, the smallest a two-footer with tiger-stripe markings.

"I slice the fins off, where the fountain's elixir concentrates, and throw the torso back. Let the tide and the crabs have them. There's places around here that'll pay for the tails. They'll grind 'em up and sell it as scallop. Keeps Darlene in the lifestyle to which she is accustomed."

I stared hard at the severed shark tails and wondered how bat-shit crazy Sutter was. Just as I was set to release the tarp, I saw a hank of pale red hair lying on the grooved tray bed. Looking closer, I saw it was blonde and had been dyed by the blood collecting in the grooves. I let the tarp flap shut.

"The passage from youth to age is a journey of metamorphosis," Sutter said with grim assurance. "So the fountain must both renew and transform." He started cutting the grouper to fit the hook. "Those fancy words, I stole them out of a book. Smarter men than me, or you for that matter, have failed where I've succeeded. I've found that rich vein out there in the Gulf of Mexico. Damned if I haven't. And only three people in the world know about it."

*Me, him and Darlene.*

Sutter looked like the kind of guy who kept his loose ends tied off. I thought about the Colt Python .357 I had stashed under my pillow in the Airstream.

"Why are you telling me?" I asked.

"Because you remind me of myself when I was twenty-one or so." I worked hard at not taking that as an insult. "And I want to ask you whether you think I'm crazy."

I would have preferred the conversation take place without him holding a knife, but my preferences never had held much sway with the world. "Insane crazy?" I asked.

He nodded, biting his lip, the boisterous version of him gone. "Some days…none of this seems quite real, you know? It's like I'm waking up after a weeklong bender and the world still has that blurry, slick feel to it."

Casting an eye at his shitty camper, I wondered why Sutter would want to live forever. That alone ought to have tipped him off that his head wasn't right, but I wasn't going to be the one to break the news. "No more crazy than a whole lot of people I've met," I said, which was close enough to the truth.

He narrowed his eyes at me, weighed my answer and grinned. "What was I talking about? Oh yeah. I don't care about living forever. That's a fool's game, believe me. I plan on getting rich. How much you reckon some of the wealthy chumps on Snell Isle would pay to be able to enjoy their views for all eternity?"

It wasn't really a question. I wondered if Sutter knew which camper was mine and made a mental note to make sure he never did know. Even visions of Darlene's sweet behind weren't enough to tie me down to the vicinity of this lunatic. Might be I wouldn't wait for the Skyway's grand opening, would make south for Manatee County the long way around, and sooner rather than later.

"The trick is distilling the elixir, bottling it." Sutter lay the hooked grouper down and picked up the soup. He ladled a steaming serve into his mouth. "But I reckon I've got that figured out." Something grey bobbed up and down in the soup.

"Shark fin soup," Sutter said. He held the bowl out. "Try some." I declined.

"Your loss. It's a powerful aphrodisiac." He winked and laughed. While his jaws snapped open and shut, I saw a strand of blonde hair hanging out the gap between his front teeth.

"What would you pay to live forever?" Sutter asked when he'd reined in his good humor.

"Doesn't interest me."

"Yeah, because you're still young. You already think you'll live forever."

No. Pretty early on in my deployment I'd learned the hard facts about mortality and death. I knew I wasn't living forever, and maybe it was just me being a gloomy putz, but I sort of liked the idea that one day I'd have to account for my sins.

Changing tacks, Sutter asked, "Don't you wish you had the time to make right the things you screwed up?" For some reason he wanted my agreement, as if by agreeing with him I'd somehow validate his crazy pursuit. "Don't you have a regret that you could put right if you had the time?"

"Doesn't everyone?" I didn't tell him that all I'd put right would be to put a bullet through the head of a man named Lieutenant Chalvers Monroe, and that the time for that had come and gone. The conversation had well and truly soured for me by then, and so I took my leave and walked a long, circuitous and secretive route back to my camper.

* * *

Three days later my Airstream was still chocked on the fresh-laid concrete of the southern approach, and given that thieves had stolen the wheels off my Chevy, those chocks weren't coming out anytime soon. I'd found a bar and grill a short way off the approach that sold moonshine under the counter, and I spent most nights sloshed midway to comatose, staring out at the Gulf or up at the dark steel fingers of the two Skyway spans as they strained to touch. Occasionally I heard the report of Sutter's rifle and saw a flash of light, knew that somewhere, out in the Gulf, about six pounds of raw meat and a wicked hook was falling into the lightless abyss.

Hunting for mermaids. Christ almighty. It was just like they said: every sort of transient weirdo got down to Florida in the end.

I caught Darlene, now and then, in the shadow of Sutter's camper, huddled around a joint and so doused in perfume that if she ever dropped that lit roll-up into her lap she'd explode like a Roman candle. She gave me a wave one time—if you can call a flick of the fingers a wave—and then went back to brooding on the miserably bright sun. I waved too because I was twenty-one and horny and because I'd just come back from Vietnam and didn't know how to be scared of jealous boyfriends. It used to be that

*Durand Sheng Welsh*

I'd known and I'd accepted the boundaries of the civilized world. Thou shalt not kill — that whole laundry list of tawdry sins a decent man avoided. But since coming back, the civilized world seemed off its axis. I couldn't find my feet in it, couldn't get my balance.

I walked over to Darlene.

"Can't spare any weed," she said. "I can hook you up with the guy I buy off, though."

I told her I wasn't interested. She asked me what I was interested in.

"Nice tattoo," I said, pointing at the angel tattooed down her right thigh. It wasn't nice, but girls expect you to lie about those things. The ink had faded to the watery blue you'd expect to find on a grizzled ex-con's forearms. She must have gotten it when she was twelve.

The name Michael was scripted above the angel's wings.

"My son's name," she said.

"You got a kid?"

"Had a kid."

I took a moment to process that. I expected her expression to harden up, but it did the opposite, grew soft and thoughtful. I had a brief vision of her as a different person, smiling, laughing. It made me feel sad.

"He was one of a kind. He used to love trains. He used to be terrified of ferns and spiky plants and masks. He used to lean over the edge of the bath with his pudgy feet swinging off the ground and try to turn the hot water tap on. I used to get so mad at him. One day there's so much life there, and then there's nothing. Just an empty crib and a quiet house and the lingering baby smell of him. I hope you never know what that's like. A piece of me died with him, I think." She sucked on the joint and closed her eyes.

I thought of green jungle, smoke and ashes, a charred baby, a woman crying while cradling that smoked ruin of an infant in her burned arms. *Put them out of their misery for Chrissakes,* Lieutenant Monroe had said.

"It's a terrible thing," I said to Darlene. "It truly is."

She looked at me and part of me fled from her gaze.

"I think you know it is," she said. "So many people have no idea."

I nodded.

"What's the point of living if the people you love are dead? What's the point?"

I had no answers.

"You take what you can get. Whatever passes for love, whatever substitute is on offer. That's what you do." She scratched at her neck, and for the first time I noticed the pale skin at her throat was scarred. The scars could have been ligature marks, or they might have been made with a blade. *Self-inflicted?* Hard to tell. Whatever had caused them, she knew all about death. From the looks of it, she'd come close enough herself. "It was a long time ago. A long time ago. Say, what'd you want again?" she asked, brow furrowed.

I couldn't for the life of me remember why I'd approached her in the first place. As I walked away, I glimpsed Sutter staring at me through the camper's window. He grinned at me and tipped the bill of his baseball cap.

\* \* \*

That night, at 2:00 a.m., I got a knock on the side of my camper. I rolled out of my cot to find Sutter standing in my open doorway. I froze, the late night consumption of a bottle of hospital-grade alcohol still fogging my thoughts.

*The Colt, idiot,* said the part of my brain that had gotten me home from Vietnam in one piece. I fumbled for it, but Sutter was already inside my cramped quarters. He stunk of cigarettes and butchered fish.

"I know you think I was lying the other day," he said.

"What?" I asked, reaching under the pillow for the Colt and feeling nothing but filler herniating out a rip in the pillow's underside.

"You thought I was spouting shit."

"I never said that," I said, still groping. "Never thought it neither."

"Oh, hell. Unclench your sphincter. I'm not here to have it out with you. I just want to show you that I'm an honest man." He hiked his baseball cap up high on his forehead, all the better to give me a meaningful look of measure, as if to say, *are you man enough, boy?*

"Truth is, I need help with gaffing my catch."

"Catch?"

"You were the one asking about mermaids the other day. You lost interest in seeing one, now, have you? Darlene's coked out of her brain tonight. If I have to, I'll take her rather than yourself, but I know she'll fuck up, then she'll blame me, then it'll all get ugly." He clenched his fist and I could guess what kind of ugly he meant.

I didn't want Darlene to get a beating just because I was too lazy to humor her lunatic boyfriend, and in any event, I figured I owed the world at least one good deed. "Give me a sec to get some pants on," I muttered.

Sutter backed out the door and stood in the rectangle of bluish gloom, smoking a cigarette while I dredged up my pants from the darkened floor. I had no intention of ruining my night vision by lighting up the oil lantern near my bed, and getting dressed in the dark was one good talent that had come out of my time in the service.

I never did find the Colt Python that night. Turned out I must have been drunk enough to shove the gun under the mattress rather than the pillow. I don't believe in fate, but maybe fate had plans for me that night that didn't involve plugging Sutter with a heavy grain slug.

We walked along the flat approach to the hump of the bridge proper, where there were scaffolds and the squat shapes of lifters and loaders and mixers. Sutter gestured to a big-game rod he had wedged against the seaside railing and fixed in place with what looked like enough rope and chain to hog-tie a rhino. "My catch knocked her head on the pylon as I reeled her in. I think she's still dreaming, buddy boy. You want to go first?" He snatched up a big gaffing hook as he spoke to me.

Keeping Sutter in the corner of my eye, I peered over the railing, followed the silver thread of the line as it plunged down under the approach's roadway. On this section of the approach, shy of the stratospheric bridge itself, the drop panned out to a mere ten feet, give or take. Still, whatever was snagged at the line's other end was too far underneath the roadway for me to see it.

*It's goddamn dark down there,* I thought.

"She's caught under the pylons. Water's shallow, though. Sand-bar stretches out from here and curves back toward the Pasadena side of the bay. These pylons are sitting high in the water. Knee-deep is the worst it'll get." Sutter handed me the gaffing hook, straddled the railing, leaned over to look down into the dark water, and then dropped over the side.

He had a hurricane lamp next to the fishing rod, but although the metal shell felt warm, I couldn't see anything to light it with. The warm Gulf breeze whistled between the railings and sent a low chop spuming up the pylon legs. Sutter took his leisurely time dragging his catch out from under the bridge's overhang.

There was a little light shining across the water from a porta-ble admin shack the construction workers used, and it was just enough to cut Sutter's silhouette out from the black sheet of the sea. He was bent over a shape propped against the pylon, and he was buck-naked. I pulled one hand down my face as if I could tug the sight away. Spray burst up and over him. He looked amphibious, inhuman. Shirtless, his back had an odd kink about halfway up the vertebral column. *A knot, a ridge? A vestigial fin?*

Take or leave his physical problems, I decided that man's mar-bles had long ago been traded in for gumballs. I was gripping the gaffing hook so tight that it seemed to be humming like one of those bridge cables getting strung up further north. I should have

*Durand Sheng Welsh*

dropped it and walked away, but Vietnam aside, at that age I never had known when to walk away. It's a lesson many a young man has to learn the hard way, his older self looking back with equal parts envy and dismay.

Sutter's catch squirmed. Beneath the water, its lower body began thrashing. The upper body was a woman's. I could make out just enough in the bad light to see that. I couldn't have described her face to a police sketch artist, or even said whether I'd met her before, but I knew I wasn't seeing a manatee or dolphin.

Sutter bent over her. He had an object clamped between his teeth—a knife. Her lower body flopped up and down, a rippling kick, like a worm under a boot heel, or like the throes of one of those shark-tailed mermaids Sutter craved.

Sutter slid the knife into her neck, then turned up to face me and shouted, "Gaff her, kid." His mouth yawned open too far. It looked as if it were crammed with serrated teeth.

I was so damn terrified I pissed in my jeans. Even the Viet Cong couldn't lay claim to that modest feat. I dropped the gaffing hook. The Tampa Bay chose that moment to drag the woman from her seat against the pylon. She keeled sideways, and then she was gone, vanished into the glassy black.

I expected him to rail and shout, but Sutter only laughed. He threw the knife in after his mermaid. Then he turned around to face me, his nakedness both absurd and frightening. At first I thought the shadows were playing tricks with me, but the longer I stared at him, the more clearly resolved his freakish—how shall I put it—masculine equipment became. Hell with it. In plain speak, Sutter had two pricks. Both of them were as thick and long as a barracuda's belly.

"I'm twice the man you are, boy," he said. "Sharks get all of nature's perks, don't they? Go on, take a good long gander, hombre. You should have tried the soup I offered. Freshly stewed out of primo mermaid cuts. A marvel, a tonic that is both a longevity elixir and a ferocious aphrodisiac."

"Did you have to kill her?"

"You'd eat her alive, would you? I damn well hope not."

"Jesus, eat her?"

Ocean spray exploded around him. "It's like those heavy metals, working their way up the food chain. They...accumulate... that's the word. They accumulate."

"What accumulates?"

"The fruit of the fountain, the rich vein of the eternal that bleeds into the Gulf. It accumulates in those mermaids, and now that I've had my fill of them, it has accumulated in me."

With that he closed his eyes and his face took on a tortured expression. I thought that perhaps he was having a seizure or 'episode,' as I heard the doctors call the post-traumatic stress reactions of returned soldiers, but too late I understood that what I saw was bliss.

His pricks twitched, and his ejaculate spurted the full ten feet up onto the roadway. Great dollops of it landed near my boots, but more of it sloshed into a tin bucket by the fishing rod. It was his bait bucket, the same one he'd taken his knife from that first day I'd met him by the camper. A hollow scrabbling came from inside the bucket.

I backed away, stopping only to snatch up the gaffing hook. The bucket was shaking and jumping now. Water foamed over the sides. It toppled and three fish heads came out, mouths gasping. Behind them they dragged their flensed spines, white ribs scratching against the concrete. Half a crab followed, cut cleanly along its center, one stalked eye bobbing and weaving as it dragged itself sideways towards the road center.

I smashed them all apart with the gaffing hook. When I was done, Sutter was still down there, waiting. "You believe me now? Or do you think I just offed some whore down here, her legs knotted tight at the ankles and her mouth shut with electrical tape? Say, like that bitch Darlene."

I said I hadn't much considered that.

He told me I should, and he laughed some more. I figured I'd leave him there and go have a harder look for that Colt of mine when something he said stopped me cold.

"Don't you want to live forever?"

There he was, hunched over and streaming with saltwater, motioning to the twin bulbs of his pricks as they yearned upwards toward the empty space in the sky where in a few months the two jagged halves of the old Skyway Bridge were destined to intertwine their cable, concrete and steel. "Don't you want to fucking live forever, boy?"

"You're talking to the wrong guy."

"Am I? Even if you think your own future isn't worth pissing on, you telling me you've never wanted to bring someone back from the dead? You telling me you've never had that wish? You've never watched someone die and wished, really wished, that you could bring them back?"

Near my boot one of the fish heads was still alive, its mouth opening and closing, gill slits clenching and unclenching. I kicked it off the edge of the roadway and into the sea.

* * *

A place can sneak up on you. One day it's not a pit-stop any longer, it's a home. One day you realize you've got a job, a mailing address, and keep your whiskey in a glass cabinet rather than on the bedside table.

Yeah, things sneak up on you, time most of all.

In 1980, I was living in a shack on Sunset Beach when the freighter *Summit Venture* plowed into the old Skyway Bridge during a storm, sending six cars, a truck and a Greyhound bus plummeting into Tampa Bay.

In '86, I moved into a rental out the back of a Crabby Bill's in St. Pete. That year I stood on the new Skyway Bridge and watched *Challenger* climb heavenward on rocket fuel and the cheers of us proud Floridians. And I stood there on the bridge as those cheers turned to tears and the traffic stalled and people climbed from their cars to watch our champions return to earth as ash.

In 1993, I called in sick at my job and drove twenty minutes to watch the old Skyway be demolished. Explosive charges pulverized the concrete pylons into dust so fine I could taste it through my open car window. I remember it being a beautiful, sunny day.

At times I stare out at the Gulf and think about Sutter. For all his bluster he didn't live past that night, let alone forever. I left him hard up—to pen a crude pun—in the humid Florida night. Come morning two beachcombers found his corpse washed to shore near Fort De Soto. No one's sure how he died. His body was torn up pretty bad. There are a lot of hungry critters in Tampa Bay and the inter-coastal waterways.

As for Darlene, sweet Darlene, what of her? You ask me, Darlene's still out there. See, lately someone's been following me. I don't know for certain who it is, but I have a reasonable suspicion, as the lawyers say.

So, I've taken to watching my street from the living room easy chair, the Colt Python laid in my lap. That's what a scared man does. Sits and waits and watches. Supposedly, those talents also come naturally to an old man, probably because being old and being scared are generously thought of as being a sad fucker's two-for-one deal. Supposedly. At least my hands don't shake much for an old codger's. I'm a keener shot than I was at twenty-one—just ask many a floating beer can in the swamplands—and I've learned better than to stash my gun under a pillow.

My residence backs onto a marshy culvert thick with cattails, and I've got an eye cocked out that way too. At night you can hear the cattails whispering and the water burbling over the mortared joints of the culvert. In Tampa Bay it never gets cold enough that you need to shut your windows to the breeze and the salt air.

Straying too far from water makes my back ache and my skin crack, so Tampa's hooked me good for now. Toss a coin in my hat and bleed me some sympathy, sure, sure.

Point is, I'm never far from the blue Floridian ocean. Darlene, the lovely lass, she won't have to travel far to find me. Sharks, gators—anything with teeth, a tail and a hunger for meat finds its way to Florida in the end.

I can guess at, too, what's finally drawn her to me. No one wants to suffer, but it is even truer to say that no one wants to suffer alone. *You take what you can get. Whatever passes for love, whatever substitute is on offer.* That's what Darlene had said, the young girl with the old, old eyes.

I dare say, though, that it won't be that skinny girl—won't be a girl at all—who comes a-knocking on my window pane in the dead of night. Thirty years of Sutter's gift percolating through her will have put paid to that. Nothing in this life comes without a price.

Strange to say, but what I'm most scared of is that she'll want to talk. She knows how Sutter died, I reckon. She knows what he offered me, too, I reckon.

Maybe she thinks her and I are bound by some unholy pact, by a commingling of circumstance and blood. Whatever she accuses me of, though, I intend on denying. There'll be no dark confessions in my living room tonight, or any other night. Nothing to be done now but wait, and I'm better than most men at that.

# About Durand Sheng Welsh

Durand Sheng Welsh has worked as a police officer in Sydney, Australia, for the past 14 years. He is currently based at the Coroner's Court, just above the morgue. Down the hall from his office is a long flight of stairs that bottoms out at a doorway that reads: CAUTION NECROPSY AREA. One day he's going to open it.

Welsh is a graduate of Clarion 2008 San Diego, and the winner of the Apex 2007 Halloween competition. He has published stories in several venues, including *Phantom Drift 4*, *Crossed Genres* and the anthology *Midian Unmade: Tales of Clive Barker's Nightbreed*. He is currently working on a grimdark SciFi/Crime novel.

# The Shed

## Joe McKinney

hom Campbell stood at the kitchen window with a cup of coffee in his hand, watching his twelve-year-old daughter, Megan, slip into the shed in the backyard.

From the backward glance she gave over her shoulder, it almost looked like she was trying to get away with something.

Or, maybe, she'd just heard a noise.

Christ, who knew anymore?

He sure didn't.

For the last two years, the girl had been a complete mystery to him. Some days he was so fed up he was ready to give up. Let her live in the house until she was eighteen, then they'd toss her ass out and forget about her. Other days, when he hated himself for thinking some of the mean things he thought about his oldest child, he just wanted to crawl into a bottle and pickle himself.

It had gotten that bad.

But most days he was able to tough it out. Yeah, she was a mess, but she was his mess, and he would love her, and he would deal with her shit because he loved her. No matter what, he loved her.

Still, loving the girl was hard.

It was a Saturday morning in early April and he was doing the taxes. Thom worked as a paramedic for the Austin Fire Department, twenty-four hours on, forty-eight hours off. He'd worked the day before, and after what his Fitbit claimed was a meager three hours and forty-two minutes of sleep, he'd dragged himself to the dining room table, fired up the computer and started plugging away at the old Turbo Tax, grumbling at paying taxes for a government that he felt was increasingly full of shit.

He'd been at it for an hour.

Sometime during that hour Megan had come downstairs, surprisingly dressed in something other than her pajamas, and asked him what he'd done with her phone.

"It's your phone," he'd said. He and his wife Sarah were always walking on eggshells around Megan, bracing themselves for the next screaming fit, but some days his patience was too thin for that and he'd let the passive-aggressive part of his personality take over. "Why would I know where your phone is?"

"I'm just asking. You don't have to be so mean."

"Baby, I'm not being mean. It's your phone. That means it's your responsibility. I don't know what you did with it."

"You hid it, didn't you?"

"What? No."

"You did! Why are you so mean to me?"

"Mean? How am I mean? Baby, I'm just sitting here trying to do the taxes."

"Great. Nice. You don't care."

"About your phone? No, I don't care. It's your phone. It's wherever you left it last. Now come on, I'm trying to do the taxes."

"You don't care!"

"Please, baby. I'm really —"

"Stop!"

"Stop what?"

"Stop it! Just stop it. You don't care."

Just like that. Zero to fucking freak-out in no time flat.

"You don't care!" Megan said. She clapped her hands over her ears and ran to the living room couch where she crawled up into a ball and screamed, over and over again, "You don't care! You don't care!"

If he tried to say something, he'd be met with shrieking. "Stop it! Stop!"

It was like that almost every day now.

The freak-outs.

Sarah was no better at it than he was. She and Megan would

spend hours yelling at each other, Sarah pleading with her to make sense. He couldn't even count the times he'd watched Sarah, sitting on the floor, leaning against Megan's door, begging her to say something. *Just talk to me, baby.*

Sarah tried. She really did.

When Thom would get into it with Megan, Sarah would intervene. She'd scream at Thom, actually bark herself hoarse. "What are you doing? You can't yell at her like that."

"She's fucking insane, Sarah. What do you want me to do?"

"She's just twelve, Thom. Can't you see that? She's our little girl."

But the long and short of it was that Megan was out of control.

He and Sarah were both at the end of their rope, and they knew it. Neither one of them had any idea how to move forward. He felt helpless and angry and hopeless and bitter beyond belief. The whole family was hurting. They were in real danger of tearing themselves apart, and there was no relief in sight.

They'd been to therapy. They'd been to shrinks. They'd had her tested again and again. The first doctor, the only one they'd even thought might be credible, told them it was Oppositional Defiance Disorder coupled with severe depression.

She wouldn't prescribe medication though, and she didn't take their insurance.

So they found someone closer and in network.

No help there. ADHD this time. New medication, but all it did was make Megan so constipated she'd taken to spending hours in the bathroom behind a locked door, crying her eyes out.

And it had been that way through eight different shrinks. A different opinion every time but no answers. The latest jackass wanted her tested for freaking autism, for God's sake.

Thom put his coffee cup down on the table. A little harder than he'd meant to.

He wanted to punch something.

He wanted to grab the back of a chair and twist until it broke apart in his hands.

Instead, he took a couple of deep breaths and refocused on the shed in the backyard. Megan had left the door open, just a little. *What in the hell was she doing out there?*

The shed was one of his projects, something he'd been meaning to work on since they bought the house three years earlier. The thing was starting to look a little ratty, but it was still in okay shape. They kept the Halloween and Christmas decorations out there in large plastic tubs. He had plans, though, to turn it into a woodworking shop. He had plans to fix the back patio awning too, and he thought the shed would be the perfect place to put a band saw and a hobbyhorse.

Then Megan came out of the shed and closed the door behind her.

Her tears were gone.

She wasn't screaming, for once.

She was actually smiling.

She crossed the yard and came in through the back door. She saw him standing there in his jeans and t-shirt and gave a little wave. "Hey, Dad," she said. She didn't stop to talk, though. "Love you," she said and walked up the stairs to her room.

All Thom could do was watch her go.

\* \* \*

She'd looked so pleased with herself.

These days, he'd come to distrust anything she did or said that wasn't done while screaming, and so he waited for her to close her bedroom door and then went out to the shed to take a look.

Nothing too terribly out of place.

She'd taken the Halloween decorations and pushed them into neat stacks on the right side of the shed. On the left she'd arranged the Christmas decorations. Her bedroom always looked like a trailer park after a tornado, but the rest of the things in Megan's life always had to have a home. Everything had to be in its place, so it didn't surprise him that she'd come out here and put some order to the mess.

It didn't even surprise him that she'd taken some pains to wipe down and clean up the workbench he'd made.

She'd actually done a really good job.

She couldn't pick up laundry to save her life, but if it was something she set her mind to, she made damn sure it got done.

And done well.

Laser focus, Sarah called it.

Like the workbench.

Spotless.

So too were the insides of the cabinets above the bench. He closed the cabinet door and frowned.

*What was she up to?*

\* \* \*

As the distance between he and Megan had grown over the last two years, Thom had become more and more attached to their Jack Russell terrier, Bartleby. He never thought he'd like a little dog this much, but Bartleby stayed by his side constantly. He couldn't turn around without nearly tripping over the thing. He couldn't nap on the couch without the dog climbing up beside him to snuggle, whining whenever he stopped with the belly rubs.

He'd fallen in love with Bartleby.

In the back of his mind he knew what he was doing.

It had been like this with Megan, back when she was little. She'd snuggle with him, laugh with him, fill the house with giggles.

But as her attitude had turned poisonous, he had transferred some of that affection for Megan to the dog. It was pathetic and wrong and horrible on all kinds of levels, and he knew that.

He couldn't help it, though.

\* \* \*

That Monday, while Megan was at school and their youngest, Jacob, was inside watching cartoons—he was four—Thom took Bartleby out back to throw a tennis ball around. One wild throw ended up with the ball under the shed. Bartleby tried to get it, but too many treats had made him fat and he couldn't get all the way under. Thom pushed the dog out of the way and glanced beneath the shed.

"What the hell is that?" he said aloud.

It looked like...bed sheets.

Megan's bed sheets.

He pulled them out. They were cream colored, with princesses all over them.

Definitely Megan's.

And they were wet.

He sniffed the sheets. It was pee.

*What the hell?* She'd wet her bed. She'd done that a lot when she was little, but she was twelve now.

*And why in the hell would she bury them under the shed?*

\* \* \*

That afternoon after Sarah got home from work, the two of them confronted Megan with his discovery.

They sort of pussyfooted around the accusation, but once it was out, he could feel Sarah stiffen beside him.

They waited for the screaming.

To his surprise, she just shrugged. "Bartleby peed on my sheets," she said.

"What?" Thom asked.

"I don't know. I went to shower, and when I came back there was dog pee on my bed."

"But he was in his crate when I went downstairs," Thom said.

"I don't know. Maybe Jacob let him out."

"And then put him back in?"

"I guess."

Thom and Sarah both heard the pitch of Megan's voice change.

They'd been trained, after two years of this, to know when to back off.

"It's okay, baby," Sarah said. "Do you want me to wash your sheets for you?"

"No way. They've got dog pee on them. Just throw them away."

"Sheets are expensive," Thom said. "That's money we don't need to be throwing away."

"It's not my problem," Megan said. She made a move to push her way past them. Thom, for a moment, thought of holding her back, but they'd been down that road before. Megan was too big now to control physically without a fight. The last time he'd tried it had gotten so ugly a neighbor had called the cops. The cops had taken one look at Megan's ranting and raving and they'd responded by simply giving Thom a pat on the back and wishing him luck.

But the point was made: he could no longer physically control his daughter without putting himself in serious legal trouble.

And he had no intention of doing that.

So he let her pass.

She went into the bathroom and he heard the toilet lid come up and he knew they wouldn't see her for at least an hour.

"Well, at least she didn't scream at us," Sarah said.

"Sarah," he said, "she was lying to us. You saw that, right?"

"But isn't what she said possible? Bartleby has peed on the carpet before."

"But not in her bed. He's scared to death of her."

"He's not scared to death of our daughter."

"Are you kidding? He won't go near her, even with me in the room."

"That's not her fault."

"But peeing in the bed is. Please tell me you see that? Our daughter just lied to us."

* * *

A month later, with summer coming on, Thom was spending a lot more of his time in the backyard. He'd taken the little cash they had left over each month and planted a garden on the back patio. It was a pretty good one, too. Lots of herbs, tomatoes, zucchini – stuff they could eat.

The patio was looking good.

One Saturday morning he rose from another night of restless sleep and went down to the kitchen for a cup of coffee.

Sarah was at the store, buying their weekly groceries.

Jacob was, as always, on the couch watching cartoons.

He couldn't find Megan, though.

He walked around the house, calling her name, assuming she probably had those damn headphones on again—she couldn't hear a train wreck with those things on—until he got to the kitchen.

Nobody had bothered to feed Bartleby, so he did.

That done, he put his coffee cup on the counter and turned his attention to the patio garden.

But he was immediately drawn to the shed.

There was smoke coming out of the roof.

He was a paramedic by training but a firefighter by nature, so he grabbed the fire extinguisher they kept in the pantry and ran for the backyard.

He threw open the door and saw Megan inside. She had a pile of Jacob's G.I. Joe dolls laid out on one of Sarah's cookie sheets, and they were burning.

She was smiling, happy as a lark, the lighter still in her hand.

"What in the hell are you doing?" he asked.

"Stop it!" Megan said.

"No, what in the hell are you doing?"

"Stop it! Stop!"

Megan clapped her hands over her ears and ran from the shed.

"No, goddammit," he yelled after her. "What are you doing?"

"Leave me alone!" Megan yelled, and ran inside.

Through the windows at the back of the house, Thom could see her work her way up the stairs and then to her bedroom, where she promptly slammed the door.

Done for the rest of the day.

The firefighter in him turned his attention back to the fire she'd started. Seven different dolls, burning pretty good.

He doused them with the extinguisher and left the heap of burnt plastic sitting on his workbench.

And when Sarah got home, they had words.

* * *

Thom hadn't trusted Megan for a while, maybe a year.

The kid lied all the time.

Lied about stuff there was no reason to lie about, like wetting her bed and stuffing the blankets under the shed.

It made no sense.

But the bit with burning Jacob's G.I. Joe dolls was the last straw.

"We are not leaving her alone with Jacob," he told Sarah. "There's no way. In fact, I don't think we should leave her by herself at all."

Sarah, her arms wrapped around her ribcage and her eyes full of tears, could only manage a nod.

That was their life for the next two weeks.

It was Hell.

Megan wouldn't talk to them. Wouldn't even scream at them. But every time she passed them in the hall or caught their eye from across the room, she glared at them, at Thom especially, like she hated him.

Hell, she totally did. She thought he was a pile of what Bartleby had left on the lawn.

That Saturday he got up a little after eight, went to the kitchen and poured himself some coffee. Sarah liked to do her weekly shopping early in the morning, to beat the crowds, and she'd taken Jacob with her. Megan was somewhere. He had no idea where.

And, of course, nobody had bothered to feed Bartleby, so he scooped out some food for him.

"Bartleby," he said. "Come here, boy."

Nothing.

Ordinarily, the dog came running just at the sound of the food getting scooped out.

"Bartleby!"

He checked the backyard, to see if maybe Megan had let him out to poop, but rather than see the dog, he saw Megan slip into the shed.

*What the hell?*

He opened the back door and called out to the girl. "Megan, have you seen Bartleby?"

No answer.

"Goddammit," he muttered. He didn't want to face the screaming, not another day of it. Then he kicked himself for being scared to talk to his own daughter. It shouldn't be this way.

He went to the shed and pulled the door open.

Megan was standing at his workbench, her back to him.

She was dressed in old jeans and a dark t-shirt, and even as his mind was processing the strangeness of Megan dressed in something other than pajamas before noon, before breakfast even, he saw the blood on the workbench.

"Megan...?"

He took a step to one side and saw Bartleby's headless body on the bench.

"Oh Jesus," he said. "Oh, oh, oh."

His stomach lurched and he felt the bile rise up in his throat. Rage didn't even enter his mind. All he felt was shock. His legs were like water.

"What did you do?" he asked. "Bartleby...?"

Megan was standing next to the bench, her face utterly expressionless. No emotion. Stone cold.

And then, in an awful moment of clarity, he understood.

He understood his daughter.

He understood what she was. And what she could become.

He'd thrown words like psychopath around, but he'd never really believed them. Not *really*.

But it was worse than that, wasn't it?

The high intelligence but poor performance in school. The excessive antisocial behavior. No guilt, no remorse. All the lies.

And now the bed wetting. The arson. And animal mutilation.

What did the cops call it? The MacDonald Triad.

He was raising the Devil.

"Baby, what did you do?"

Her expression never changed. Not even a flicker of humanity. Not even when she lashed out with the knife and caught him across the throat.

He gasped without sound.

A second later she was all over him, plunging the knife into him again and again.

The last thing he saw was his blood spattered on his daughter's face.

\* \* \*

Megan went to the garage and got the gas can.

It was heavy, and she had to lug it back to the shed with it balanced on her hip. She screwed off the cap and pulled out the nozzle thingy and poured the gas all over everything, the benches and the Christmas decorations and the dead dog and right on her Daddy's face.

She was careful, though, to save just enough to splash the walls of the shed, inside and out, and then lit the whole thing ablaze.

It went up so fast.

Fire always made her happy.

*Joe McKinney*

# About Joe McKinney

Joe McKinney has his feet in several different worlds. In his day job, he has worked as a patrol officer for the San Antonio Police Department, a DWI Enforcement officer, a disaster mitigation specialist, a homicide detective, the director of the City of San Antonio's 911 Call Center, and a patrol supervisor. He played college baseball for Trinity University, where he graduated with a Bachelor's Degree in American History, and went on to earn a Master's Degree in English Literature from the University of Texas at San Antonio. He was the manager of a Barnes & Noble for a while, where he indulged a lifelong obsession with books.

McKinney published his first novel, *Dead City*, in 2006, a book that has since been recognized as a seminal work in the horror genre, and one of the cornerstones of zombie literature. Since then, he has gone on to win two Bram Stoker Awards® and expanded his oeuvre to cover everything from true crime and writings on police procedure to science fiction to cooking and Texas history. The author of more than twenty books, he is a frequent guest at horror and mystery conventions.

McKinney and his wife Tina have two lovely daughters and make their home in a little town just outside of San Antonio, where he indulges his passion for cooking and makes what some consider to be the finest batch of chili in Texas.

# The Greatest Gift

## Graham Masterton

*"Oh would some power the gift give us,*
*To see ourselves as others see us!"*
Robert Burns.

"You're mad, do you know that?" laughed Cathy as the speedometer needle touched 80. "You're totally, utterly, irredeemably crazy!"

"What do you mean, crazy? I'm not crazy, I'm just *practical!*" Robin shouted back over the buffeting of the slipstream. "Life is too damn short to go slow!"

They were driving north on Bedford Road toward Katonah. It was a bright day in early October, unseasonably warm, so Robin had put down the roof of his silver Mustang so that the wind would ruffle their hair. As they sped along, overtaking every other car on the highway, they left behind them a whirling cyclone of crimson and yellow leaves.

Robin was always frightening Cathy, which was one of the reasons she loved him so much. He was tall and sculpted and handsome, with brushed-up black hair, a strong jawline and sapphire-blue eyes that always looked as if he was finding life amusing. If they were eating outside on a restaurant balcony, he would jump up when the check was put in front of him and throw himself over the railings, regardless of how far down he might fall. If they were swimming in the Housatonic, he would climb up to the bridge and dive headfirst into the water, even though the river was dangerously shallow. He would challenge anybody who annoyed him—parking attendants, shop assistants, cops, other drivers.

Cathy had never met anybody so fearless. He always seemed to be daring the world to stand up to him.

"We can stop at Willy Nick's before we go to your sister's," Robin shouted. "I'm jonesing for some of their crab cakes!"

"Okay, but careful!" Cathy shouted back as Robin had to swerve to avoid an oncoming bus.

"Careful? What does that mean?" he asked.

Those were the last words he spoke as they neared the intersection with Parkway where a huge maroon truck pulled out across the road in front of them. He stood on the brakes, but they were driving twenty miles an hour too fast. The Mustang was nose-heavy and slid sideways with its tires screaming in a shrill operatic chorus.

Cathy clung to the door handle, and all she could see was trees and road signs rotating around her and then the huge white letters MOVING MAN INC. The Mustang slammed broadside into the truck with a deafening crash, although Cathy didn't hear anything at all. Her door was flung open and she was thrown out onto the road, almost as if somebody had taken hold of her arm and forcibly yanked her out of the passenger seat. She tumbled over and over, grazing her shoulder and knocking her head hard against the concrete.

She lay on her back for a moment, shocked and concussed, staring up at the sky. She could hear a high singing noise in her ears. Then she heard a stentorian roaring sound, and a wave of heat rolled over her. She managed to turn over onto her side and prop herself up on one elbow. It was then that she saw the Mustang was burning fiercely, orange flames leaping up the side of the truck.

The driver and his mate were climbing down from their cab, two black men wearing maroon overalls. They tried to approach the Mustang, but the heat was too intense. They had to raise their arms to shield their faces and back away,

At first, Cathy couldn't see Robin, and she thought that he must have managed to escape. Surely he had managed to jump out, in the same way that he jumped off balconies and bridges, but she didn't see him anywhere. At that moment, though, the wind fanned the flames to one side, and she saw him still sitting in the driving seat, a scorched black figure with his brushed-up hair alight, frantically wrestling to free himself from the wreckage. His eyes were still white but circled with red. He looked more like a Halloween demon than a man who was being burned alive.

"Robin!" she screamed, or thought she screamed. She climbed to her feet and made her way unsteadily towards the blazing car, but as soon as she came within twenty feet of it she found that the heat was unbearable, hotter than an open oven, and like the men she couldn't venture any closer.

Meanwhile, the truck's driver had run to his cab and was now hurrying back swinging a large yellow fire extinguisher. While his mate was calling 911 on his cell phone, he unfastened the nozzle and started to spray the burning Mustang with foam. He sprayed Robin first, turning him instantly from a black demon into a struggling parody of a snowman. Flecks of white foam were whirled upwards by the heat and blown into the trees by the wind, where they clung like blossoms.

A station wagon stopped not far away, and a stocky man in a tan suede jacket ran up, carrying a smaller fire extinguisher. He and the truck driver gradually managed to subdue the flames, and at last they guttered out, although the tires were still smoldering, and so much acrid grey smoke was billowing from the upholstery that the Mustang was intermittently lost from sight.

Cathy cupped her hand over her nose and mouth and made her way into the smoke, as close to the car as she could, even though it was still far too hot for her to try and open the driver's door.

Through streaming eyes she saw Robin sitting behind the steering wheel with his head bent forward, still clutching his seat belt buckle. His hair looked like a yard-broom that had been burned right down to the last few spiky bristles, and the skin on his hands and forearms had blackened and split so that scarlet flesh showed through.

The truck driver came up through the smoke behind her and laid one hand on her shoulder. "Ain't nothing you can do for him, lady. I'm sorry. We've called for the paramedics and the police. You'd best take care of yourself, make sure you ain't got no bones broken, nor done yourself any other kind of mischief. I saw you come flying out of that car and it was almost like the angel of the Lord reached down and hauled you out of there his self."

Cathy nodded, too shocked to be able to say anything. She found it almost impossible to believe that this grotesque figure sitting in the car was actually Robin—the same Robin who had made love to her this morning, just as it was growing light. The same Robin with whom she had been laughing and joking only minutes ago. They were supposed to be going to Willy Nick's and then to visit her sister Jeanette. How could this have happened? How could this incinerated effigy be him?

"Come on, lady, come away," said the truck driver. "Like I say, there ain't nothing you can do to help him now. Nothing that nobody can do for him, no how."

Cathy was about to turn away when Robin lifted his head. His face was a ghastly mask, with rags of burned skin hanging from it, but he opened his red-rimmed eyes and stared at her.

"Cathy?" he croaked between cracked and bleeding lips. "Cathy, save me."

\* \* \*

It was early on a Friday morning in the second week of January when Cathy's iPhone warbled. She was standing in the kitchen filling the kettle to make tea. It was still dark outside, and a light but steady snow was falling.

"Cathy? This is Megan."

Megan was Nurse Megan Wing from the Burn Center at Bridgeport Hospital, where Robin had been taken after the crash, and where he had been undergoing specialized treatment ever since.

*Graham Masterton*

She sounded emotional, and Cathy's heart sank.

"What is it?" she asked. She could see her face reflected in the kitchen window, and she thought she looked like a ghost standing in the snowy yard outside, staring in at her herself. "What's happened?"

"It's good news, Cathy. Robin has come out of his coma. He opened his eyes for the first time about an hour ago, and he's actually managed to say a few words. He asked where he was and he also asked where you were."

"Oh my God, really?" Her eyes were instantly crowded with tears. "Is he still conscious now?"

"He's under heavy sedation, of course, but he's been drifting in and out. I'm sure that when you come over today, he'll be able to speak to you. "

"I'll come right now. It's snowing some, but it doesn't look too bad."

"Just take it easy on the turnpike. I saw on the news that there was a pile-up at the Route 1 intersection."

"Oh, you can bet I will. I've had enough car wrecks for one lifetime. Thank you, Megan. I'll see you later."

\* \* \*

Cathy hurriedly dressed in her pink roll-neck sweater and jeans, then shrugged on her dark-brown duffel coat. She was sitting on the stairs, pulling on her UGG boots, when her cousin Holly came out of her bedroom door, yawning.

"You're not going out already? It's only ten after six. And look out there—it's snowing!"

"The nurse at the Burns Center just called. Robin's woken up. He opened his eyes and he actually spoke."

"He's awake?" Holly asked. "That's amazing." She made no effort to sound enthusiastic. They had argued about this over and over again. Even if Robin survived, Holly had insisted he would never again be the handsome, athletic daredevil that Cathy had fallen in love with. He had suffered over 70 percent burns, especially to his head and arms and upper body, which should have been more than enough to kill him. It would take years of intensive therapy for him to be able to perform the most rudimentary functions, such as feeding himself and bathing, and apart from that, he would be hideously scarred. Even Nurse Wing had warned Cathy that underneath the pressure mask that was protecting his face, he no longer had a nose or lips, and his ears had been burned off. Even the most skillful of reconstructive surgeons would not be able to give him his good looks back.

But Cathy had said, "I don't care how much he's changed. He's still Robin underneath. Can't you understand that? His soul is still Robin. Nurse Wing said the first thing he asked was, 'Where am I?' and the second thing was, 'Where is Cathy?'"

As she went to the front door and opened it, Holly followed her. "You know how much I care about you, Cathy. You really need to think about what you could be getting yourself into. You're only twenty-two, for Christ's sake. You're clever, you're pretty. You have so much to look forward to. Don't saddle yourself with a cripple for the rest of your life."

"Holly! How can you use a word like that? I love him!"

"You love the memory of him, sweetheart. The way he used to be. But he'll never be like that again. And being all burned up like that, it will have changed his personality, too. There's no way he's ever going to be the same. How could he be? Would *you* be, if you hadn't gotten out of that car and had burned up with him?"

Cathy sat in the driveway in her car, with the engine running, and the windshield defroster switched on to full blast to melt the thin layer of pearly frost that had formed overnight. She knew how much of a challenge it would be to take care of Robin. But he was still alive, and now he was awake, and he had asked about her. That was all she could possibly ask for.

*Graham Masterton*

\* \* \*

Nurse Wing was waiting for her in the smart, open-plan reception area of the hospital. She was tall and Swedish-looking, with blonde hair scraped back into a short pony-tail and pale blue eyes. As soon as Cathy came through the doors, she walked across and took hold of both of her hands.

"Oh! You're so cold! But I hope this news will warm you up a little. Doctor Fremont says that he cannot believe that Robin is making such a strong recovery. He is still very sick, of course, but we have taken him off the danger list."

"Is he awake?"

Nurse Wing smiled and nodded and led her by the arm along the corridor. "I told him that you were coming and he said that he couldn't wait to see you. When I told him how long he had been unconscious, and yet you had come every single day to sit by his bedside, he couldn't believe it. I think if he still had any tear-ducts, he would have cried."

They reached the end of the corridor and Nurse Wing opened the door labelled STAFF ONLY. Inside, there was a small changing room, and just as she had done every day when she visited Robin, Cathy took off her coat and put on a green surgical gown and cap, and a mask. She took off her boots, too, and replaced them with pale-green theatre clogs.

When they were ready, they crossed the corridor to a room labelled MR ROBIN STARLING. STERILE AREA. NO UNAUTHORIZED ADMITTANCE.

The room was dimly lit, and the venetian blinds were drawn, although Cathy could still see snow clustering on the windowsill outside. Robin's bed was in the center of the far wall, two drip stands and a monitor softly beeping beside him. Robin was propped up by two large pillows. His face was covered with a transparent TFO mask, which allowed his doctors to see how the healing of his face was progressing. Cathy had already been told that even after re-constructive surgery, he would have to wear the mask for twenty hours a day for at least the next two years.

Both of his arms and his chest were still wrapped in white, mummy-like dressings.

Cathy approached the side of his bed, and he turned his head towards her. All she could see underneath the plastic was a knot-ted mass of reddened welts, but his eyes were open and glistening, and she could see that through the holes in the mask he was staring at her.

"You shouldn't have come," he whispered. His voice hadn't changed.

She pulled up a blue plastic chair and sat down close to him. "How can you say that? I love you. I've been coming every single day."

"Megan told me. I don't know why you bothered. Look at me. And the same could have happened to you."

"Robin, it's going to take time. I know that. Years, even. But I've talked to your doctors, and they'll be able to give you a whole new face."

Robin's eyes rolled uncontrollably. "They've told me that, too. But what kind of a face? I don't have a nose anymore. My ears are gone. I've seen people whose faces have been burned as badly as mine. It doesn't matter how good the surgeons are, they all look the same. Like monsters."

Cathy laid her hand on his bandaged arm, and he grunted in bitter amusement. "You won't even be able to hold my hand, do you know that? I've lost all of my fingers. Oh, I think my left thumb managed to survive. I won't be much use to you in bed, either. Not unless you like your wieners extra well-done."

Cathy shook her head, and she couldn't stop her eyes from fill-ing with tears. "I don't care, Robin. I love you. I'm not going to walk away from you, ever."

Robin started to cough, harsh and phlegmy, and Nurse Wing

*Graham Masterton*

came forward with a plastic bottle of water so that he could sip some through a straw. "Thanks, Megan," he said when he could speak again. He turned his gleaming, masked face back towards Cathy and added, "Megan...she's been sent directly from heaven. She treats me like I look normal."

"You *do* look normal, Robin, for a burn victim," said Megan. "And from now on, you can only begin to look better."

"Hunh," said Robin, and then lapsed into silence.

Cathy didn't really know what to say to him. Should she tell him about everything she had been doing since the accident? How she had moved from her parents' house in New Milford to stay with Holly in Fairfield so that she could be closer to Bridgeport? Somehow it seemed rather petty and self-congratulatory to tell him about that. *I'm such a martyr. You look hideous, but I haven't abandoned you.*

After a long silence, Robin lifted up both of his bandaged arms like a frustrated teddy bear and then let them drop back onto the bedcover. "Cathy, the first thing I thought about when I woke up was you. To tell you the truth, sweetheart, I haven't been able to think about anything else."

Cathy smiled and said, "I don't care how long it takes, Robin. I'll always be here for you."

"That's what I've been thinking about," Robin said, and coughing again, but when Nurse Wing came forward with the water bottle, he waved her away. "You're such a pretty girl, Cathy. I can't expect you to devote the rest of your life to a man who looks like me. I'm going to be a freak, no matter how good they try to patch me up. What do you think people are going to say when you walk into a room with me? They're going to pity you, that's what. They're going to whisper about you behind your back, and they're going to feel sorry for you. You don't deserve that."

"Robin, my feelings for you, they haven't changed at all. If anything, they've grown stronger."

"Well I'm afraid that's just too bad, Cathy, because I'm not going to let you waste yourself on me, not the way I am now. God made you beautiful, and you need a handsome prince in your life, not a burned-up mess like me."

"Robin—" Cathy began, but he started coughing again, and his coughing was so hard and so harsh that it sounded as if he were ripping his esophagus into shreds.

Nurse Wing touched Cathy's shoulder. "I'm afraid I think you should leave him for now, Cathy. He's very distressed," she said.

Robin went on coughing and coughing, gasping for breath at the end of each spasm, and so Cathy pushed back her chair and stood up.

"Please," Nurse Wing said, and so she left the room, feeling both guilty and abandoned.

*Does Robin really not want me anymore, or is he just saying that to spare my feelings? How can he possibly understand how I feel? I don't understand it myself. I should walk out of this hospital now and drive home to New Milford and forget I ever knew this man. But for some reason I can't. He touched the very core of me, not just because he was so good-looking, but because he was always prepared to challenge everything that was ordinary and boring and conventional. He set me free, and I can't just turn my back on him, no matter what he looks like now.*

She sat down in the reception area and, after a few minutes, Nurse Wing came out to join her.

"Robin's reaction is only to be expected," she said, taking hold of Cathy's hands. "Most of our patients with severe facial disfigurement feel the same way. We call it disturbed body image. They have a preoccupation with the change in their appearance and the loss of their normal looks. They also develop a strong fear of other people's reactions and of being socially rejected."

"Is there anything I can do to help him cope with it?" Cathy asked.

Nurse Wing shrugged. "You can continue to tell him that you still love him. But that's only if he allows you to go on visiting him. He just told me that he doesn't want to see you again. I'm sorry,

I really am, but he feels so strongly that you're a beautiful young woman, and that you should find somebody else."

"I'll come back tomorrow anyway. Maybe he will have changed his mind," Cathy said.

"Why don't you give it three or four days? Even a week. Doctor Fremont and Doctor Mazdani will be talking to him tomorrow about facial reconstruction, which may give him more hope of returning to a normal life. Besides, if you leave him for a while, he may start to realize that he misses you."

\* \* \*

When she turned into the driveway of Holly's house, Cathy saw that Holly's car was missing, leaving crisscross tire tracks in the snow. When she went inside, she found that Holly had left her a note on the kitchen table.

> Cathy,
> Mom not well. Gone to Darien for the weekend.
> Probably back Tues or Weds.
> XX

She went to the kitchen window and looked out. Although the backyard was still blanketed in snow, and the sky was still slate-grey, the snow had stopped falling and the wind had dropped. The world was silent and very cold, as colorless and motionless as a black-and-white photograph.

*So what do I do now? Do I forget Robin? Or is there a way to make him think differently about me? His one reason for telling me that our relationship is over is my looks. I know I'm pretty, but supposing I wasn't? Then he wouldn't have any reason to end our relationship. Suppose I was just as monstrous as him.*

She opened the cutlery drawer. Inside was a clutter of corkscrews, slotted spoons, potato peelers and spatulas. There were also several kitchen knives, including a very sharp knife with a six-inch blade which Holly used for cutting up chickens and trimming steaks.

*If I can still recognize Robin underneath his disfigurement, then he'll be able to recognize me, no matter what I look like. That morning before the accident, he said he loved me. He told me that he had never felt the same way about any other girl.*

She took out the six-inch knife and cautiously ran her fingertip along the edge. It cut into her skin, although not deeply enough to draw blood. It was so sharp that she didn't even feel it.

She took the knife into the bathroom and stood in front of the sink, staring at herself in the mirror. There would be blood. There would probably be a lot of blood, so she pulled one of the bath towels off the heated rail and folded it over the rim of the bath, well within reach. Then she took off her pink sweater and removed her bra so that she was bare-breasted.

Her face in the mirror was pretty, but it was totally expression-less. There was no appeal in her eyes for her to change her mind, to forget Robin and find somebody else. She took hold of her left ear and pulled it outwards, and then she positioned the edge of the knife in between the top of her ear and the side of her head.

The knife hadn't hurt her when she had cut her finger and it didn't hurt her now. She drew it downwards and forwards at a slight angle, and in one stroke she sliced her ear off completely. Blood immediately flooded down the side of her neck, and she dropped the ear into the sink so that she could reach for the bath towel and press it against the side of her head. She felt hardly any pain at all, more of a chill, although the blood was warm as it ran over her collarbone and dripped off her breast.

Surprisingly, the flow of blood stopped quickly. Cautiously, she lifted away the sodden bath towel and turned her head to one side so that she could examine what she had done. Her ear was noth-ing more now than a bloody hole, but it still looked neater than the shrivelled-up bacon rind of Robin's ears. She looked down at her severed ear lying in the sink. It could have been some kind of mollusk, and she found it hard to believe that a few moments ago it had actually been part of her.

She placed the sticky-handled knife in her other hand and grabbed her right ear. She was quicker and more decisive this time because she knew that it wasn't going to hurt very much, and she sliced it off without any hesitation. Again, she let it drop into the sink, and again she pressed the blood-soaked towel to the side of her head. She looked at herself defiantly in the mirror, with runnels of blood all down her chest, and she thought, *yes, I can do this, I can change myself so much that Robin will love me for what I am.*

Her hands were trembling, and she realized that her system was beginning to show signs of shock, but she was determined to continue. Now she leaned forward closer to the mirror, and lifted up the tip of her nose between finger and thumb. *Look at you, little piglet,* she thought. Then she placed the knife underneath her nostrils like a shining steel mustache.

She cut upward into the septum, but this was much harder and much more painful than cutting off her ears. She couldn't stop herself from letting out a strangled moan as she was forced to cut upward again and again, until at last she reached the bone. Blood poured over her upper lip into her mouth and dripped off her chin.

Gagging and shaking, she sliced the knife across the bridge of her nose so that she could twist the nub of flesh away from her face. She staggered backwards, dropping the knife with a clatter onto the tiled floor, and when she reached out to stop herself from falling over, her hand left a crescent-shaped smear of blood across the wall.

Cathy stood in the middle of the bathroom, giddy with shock. It took her almost a minute before she was able to approach the sink again and look into the mirror. Where her nose had been there was now a gory cavern, and she could see right into the dark recesses of her sinuses. As she breathed, she made a thick bubbling sound, and she could feel the blood pouring down the back of her throat, which made her retch.

She had begun her self-mutilation, but she knew that what she had done was not enough. Robin was disfigured much worse than she was — well beyond any chance of ever having his original good looks restored. He was suffering third-degree burns over most of the upper half of his body, and as he had told her, he wouldn't be of much use to her in bed, so his genitals must have been shrivelled up, too.

Cathy bent down, blood still spraying out of her sinuses with every breath, and she picked up the knife. She felt numb and detached, as if she were having an out-of-body experience, or watching some other young woman in a horror movie. Her hair was sticking up in a tangled fright wig, and her chest was varnished red with gradually-drying blood.

She took hold of her left nipple and stretched it outwards in the same way that she had stretched her ear. She hesitated for a moment while she swallowed a mixture of blood and vomit, and then she sliced upwards and cut her nipple clean off. She dropped it into the sink along with her ears and the lumpy remains of her nose.

Next, she cut off her right nipple, and she stood there with both breasts bleeding, as if she were ready to wet-nurse an infant vampire.

She let the knife fall into the bath and then she shuffled back into the kitchen, leaving a trail of bloody footprints behind her. Robin had suffered burns to turn him into a monster, so she had to suffer burns too. She went to the cupboard where Holly kept her blender and her weighing scales, along with the chef's blowtorch that she used for melting the sugar on top of crème brûlée.

Cathy took the blowtorch down from the shelf and slowly made her way out of the kitchen and along the corridor to her bedroom. She sat down on the bed, and as she did so, she could see that it was snowing again. She was finding it very difficult to breathe now, and she kept making a terrible snorting sound.

It seemed to take her hours to wrench down her jeans and push

*Graham Masterton*

them off her feet. Her head was throbbing and her breasts hurt so much that she couldn't stop the tears from running down her cheeks. Robin would have to love her after she had suffered so much. When he saw what she had done to keep him, he would have no choice.

She dragged down her thong, left it dangling around one ankle. Then she picked up the blowtorch, thumbed off the safety-catch, and pressed the button to light it. She sat there for a long time, staring at the pointed blue flame while the snow continued to fall outside. She wondered if she secretly wanted the blowtorch's butane gas to run out so that she wouldn't have to do what she intended to do next.

*This will ruin me forever,* she thought. *But then I'm ruined already. I'm a monster and there's no going back.*

She leaned forward and played the flame of the blowtorch up the inside of her left calf. The skin reddened and blistered instantly, and she gave a honking scream of agony through her noseless face. But somehow, the sheer intensity of the pain made her even more determined to do it again, and now she directed the flame at her knee and then her inner thigh. As she burned away the outer layers of skin, and then her nerve endings, she felt as if she understood completely what Robin must have experienced when he was burning in the driver's seat of his Mustang—unbearable pain, but then a strange absence of any sensation at all. She continued to direct the flame at her inner thigh and felt nothing.

Cathy lay back on her pillows where her Raggedy Ann doll was lying with its ginger hair and its fixed, silly smile. She opened her legs wide and turned the blowtorch onto her vulva, so that it looked for a moment as if she were being penetrated by a penis made of blue fire. She smelled burning hair and burning flesh and her lips curled up like living worms thrown onto a hotplate.

There was no name for a pain like this, but Cathy lay back and continued to hold the blowtorch between her legs until her brain shut itself down. The blowtorch dropped to the floor. The snow fell. Cathy twitched and shuddered, her eyes half-open, only the whites showing. She dreamed that she was dead, and in a way she was because her brain refused to allow her to wake up.

\* \* \*

It was the second day of June when Nurse Wing came into Robin's room at the Bridgeport Hospital. He had undergone his third operation to remove the keloids on his face and to rebuild his nose, but he was still wearing his transparent facial orthosis. The sun was shining and white cumulus clouds were hurrying northeastward, as if they were panicking.

"Robin, I have a visitor for you," said Nurse Wing.

Robin was sitting in a chair by the window, wearing a thick maroon robe. His bandaged wrists peeked out of his sleeves. The time to fit him with prosthetic hands would come later, when his burns had completely healed.

"Really? I'm not expecting anybody, am I?" Robin had caught something in the tone of Nurse Wing's voice. Usually, when his sister or one of his friends came to visit him, she sounded cheerful and upbeat. Not now, though. She sounded almost as if she were trying to give him a warning.

Before Nurse Wing could say any more, the door behind her opened wider and a young woman walked in. He didn't recognise her at first because her face was completely covered by a flesh-colored mask, made out of the same material as pressure bandages. She could have been a giant doll. She was wearing a flowery summer frock in red and blue and yellow, but her legs were also covered by flesh-colored pressure bandages, and she was pushing a walker.

Nurse Wing attempted a smile and said, "I'll leave you two together then. Call me, Robin, if you need me."

She left the room and closed the door behind her. The doll-like young woman stood unmoving for a few seconds, and then she pushed her walker up to Robin. Before she could say anything, he realized who she was. It was the perfume she was wearing, the same perfume that he had given Cathy the week before the accident.

"Cathy? You *are* Cathy, aren't you?"

The doll-like woman nodded.

"Holy Christ, Cathy, what's happened to you? Did you get involved in another wreck?"

Cathy sat down in the chair next to him. "No," she said in a strangely hollow voice, as if she were speaking through a megaphone. "Nothing like that."

"Then what? What's happened to your face?"

"I did it myself, Robin. I did it for you. Well, that's not really true. I did it for *us*."

"I don't understand, Cathy, You did *what* for us?"

"You said you didn't want to see me again because you were going to turn out to be a monster, and I was pretty."

"I know," Robin said. "I know I did. But I only wanted to be fair to you. You shouldn't have to spend the rest of your life with a gargoyle like me when you could snap your fingers and have any man who takes your fancy."

"That's why I did it. I love you, Robin. You and me, we're soul mates. Now we're more than that. Now we look like each other, too."

With that, she reached behind her pressure-mask and unfastened it. She bent her head forward, carefully eased it away from her face and then looked up at Robin, her brown eyes bright, her lips smiling.

Robin couldn't speak. He simply stared at her in revulsion. Her brown eyes may have been bright, and her lips might have been smiling, but there was nothing but two triangular caverns where her nose had been, and she had no ears. She looked like a ghastly parody of Lon Chaney playing *The Phantom of the Opera*.

"That's not all," she said, and she eased herself up so that she could lift her dress and show him the purple braided scars between her legs. "No other man is going to want me now, Robin, so you don't have to worry about me. We can be together forever."

Robin said, "Cathy, pull your dress back down. And, please, put your mask back on."

"Aren't you happy? Aren't you pleased I did this? I still have a whole lot of surgery to go through. But they're treating me here at Bridgeport, too. I come here two or three times a week, so we can see each other all the time."

"What in God's name have you done to yourself?"

"I did it for you, Robin. I thought you'd be pleased. You *are* pleased, aren't you?"

"Cathy, just because I look like this doesn't mean that I want a partner who looks like this. I might be a freak myself, but that doesn't mean that I'm going to be attracted to another freak."

Cathy's eyes filled with tears. "What are you saying? You're not saying that I shouldn't have done this? Robin, I did it for you!"

Robin closed his eyes for a moment. While he did so, Cathy replaced her pressure-mask and fastened it. When he opened his eyes he said, "I'm going to have to be truthful with you, Cathy. What you've done to yourself, I think you must be psychotic. You look inhuman, and that's the kindest thing I can say. Don't blame me for it."

He reached across and pressed the bell beside his bed. After a few moments, Nurse Wing came in.

"I think visiting time's over," Robin said. "I don't know what to say to you, Cathy. I'm totally shocked."

Nurse Wing walked over and helped Cathy to stand up. Cathy's shoulders were quaking with grief, although she wasn't audibly sobbing.

"I don't know what's going to happen to you now, Cathy," Robin said. "All I can do is wish you the best of luck, and say that I'm very, very sorry for you."

"So there's no chance at all?" Cathy asked in a choked voice.

Robin shook his head and lifted one of his bandaged stumps towards Nurse Wing. "Me and Megan, we've become really close. She's been taking care of burn patients all of her life, and they don't put her off. And I have to say that she's beautiful, like you used to be."

\* \* \*

Holly was waiting for Cathy in the reception area. She didn't say a word as they walked out into the windy afternoon and across the parking lot to Holly's car. She could guess what had happened, and she didn't want to say, "I told you so."

They were speeding back to Fairfield on the turnpike when Cathy said, "Well. It seems like I have only two choices now. I could join a circus. Step right up! Come and see the noseless, ear-less, unfuckable woman."

"Oh, Cathy. What's the other choice?"

Cathy sat quite still for a while with her hands in her lap. Then she unbuckled her seat belt, opened the car door and threw her-self sideways out of the car and onto the road. She bounced, and bounced again, her arms and legs flying, and then she was hit by a huge Mack truck and disappeared from sight.

Later, when the police and the ambulance had arrived, Holly went over to the truck driver, who was sitting on the steel divider in the middle of the road, still badly shaken.

"It wasn't your fault," Holly told him.

The truck driver shook his head. "Never seen nothing like it. Your car door come flying open, and do you know? It was like the angel of the Lord plucked her out of there, in person."

# About Graham Masterton

Graham Masterton is a British horror author. Originally an editor of Mayfair and the British edition of *Penthouse*, his first novel, *The Manitou*, was released in 1976 and was adapted into a film of the same name. Further works garnered critical acclaim, including a Special Edgar Award by the Mystery Writers of America for *Charnel House* and a Silver Medal by the West Coast Review of Books for *Mirror*. He is also the only non-French winner of the prestigious Prix Julia Verlanger for his novel *Family Portrait*, an imaginative reworking of the Oscar Wilde novel *The Picture of Dorian Gray*. Masterton was also the editor of *Scare Care*, a horror anthology published for the benefit of abused children in Europe and the USA. *Buried*, the latest book in his Katie Maguire crime series, was released in December 2015.

Masterton's novels often contain visceral sex and horror. In addition to his novels, he has written a number of sex instruction books, including *How To Drive Your Man Wild In Bed* and *Wild Sex for New Lovers*.

Masterton currently lives in Surrey, England.

# The Lady
## of the Minch

### William Meikle

├┼┼┼┼┼┼┼┼┼┼┼┼┼┼┤

The red door behind him rattled.

It didn't bother John Ratchett. In fact, he welcomed it. It reminded him of better days. He sat at the kitchen table reading his paper. The radio was tuned to BBC 4, and the long-loved voices and laughter of the studio audience soothed him.

"Tonight, we promise you a nail-biting contest, which will be followed by a nose-picking contest."

*Old friends.*

He finished the sports section and had moved on to the crossword when he remembered to look up at the clock.

*The last crossing is late again. Mr. Phillips will have words to say.*

He'd gone as far as laying down his pencil and pushing his chair back from the table when he remembered. He sat back with a heavy sigh.

At ten thirty he finally gave up on the crossword, folded the paper neatly and made two cups of hot chocolate. He left one on the kitchen table as he headed for the stairs and bed.

*There you go darling. Careful with it, it's hot.*

From the bottom of the stairs he could still hear the rattle of the old door, but by the time he got to the bedroom, all was silent.

*Too quiet.*

He sat on the edge of the bed and sipped at the hot chocolate. It tasted bitter tonight. He placed it on the bedside table and lay back against the too-soft pillow. He knew Bettie would be annoyed with him for not removing his clothes first, but he was tired all the way through to his bones.

*I'm getting too old for this.*

He lay there for a long time, staring at the shadows that waltzed across the ceiling, listening for the ferry whistle.

* * *

In the morning, the red door rattled again as he went to the fridge for milk. A flake of paint fell off to join a small pile of others at the foot of the door. He'd thought, several times over the years, that he should give it a fresh coat.

*But Bettie wouldn't like it.*

Bettie liked things to stay the same from one day to the next, an even keel and a steady ship.

*Everything in its place and everything to the timetable.*

John tried hard not to disappoint her, even long after she'd passed on.

*There, now you've done it you old fool. You've remembered again.*

He closed the fridge door quietly and went through to the front of the house. The living room — *the parlor*, as Bettie called it — was to his left, but he hadn't been in there for years. That was Bettie's domain, and woe betide anyone who trespassed.

His daily paper lay on the floor inside the main door, but he didn't feel up to bending down for it just yet. Not before his constitutional.

He left the paper on the floor, fetched his coat and went outside. Not for the first time he considered getting a dog, a companion that he could share his walks with.

*But Bettie wouldn't like that. Dogs have hairs, and hairs mean mess. Bettie wouldn't like mess.*

It was a warm, sunny day. He took his time, enjoying the morning as only a man who realizes he may not have many left can. His mind wandered in long-past days, but his legs knew the way, taking him along paths ingrained by many years of repetition. The morning check had become almost a religious ritual. More than that, it had become a necessity, ever since the Jones boy and his gang had discovered the pier office block.

He walked through the town slowly. No one spoke to him, but that wasn't unusual. Most of the people he'd ever known were long since gone, and the young don't talk much to the old outside their immediate family. It reminds them too much of their own mortality.

*Some of us don't need reminding.*

The old ferry point on the pier was near as dead as his friends were. The passage of time wasn't treating it kindly. Ivy ran rampant along what was left of the walls. The windows were boarded shut, and the old doors were covered in the vilest graffiti. He'd long since given up trying to maintain the exterior — that was the domain of the local youth.

*I'm glad Bettie isn't here to see what things have come to.*

The interiors, where his memories were stored, that was another matter.

He went along to the night watchman's office first. Weeds flowered where cargo trolleys had once ran, and the old rails were rusted and crumbling atop timbers that had become rotten and ravaged by the weather. John kept the office in working order, just in case. There was always a slim chance of a reversal. He just hoped he'd live long enough to see it.

The door to the office lay partly open.

John's heart sank.

*Not again.*

Something scuffed inside then went quiet.

"The little buggers," John muttered, then clamped a hand over his mouth. Bettie never stood for any swearing.

Something scuffed again, and a child giggled.

"No more warnings," he said loudly. "You're in trouble now."

He climbed the short steps into the office. He wondered what it would be this time. Over the past year he'd found empty bottles of beer, magazines that he'd never be able to talk to Bettie about and, on one occasion, a perfect spiral of human shit right in the middle of the floor. He'd reported it to the authorities of course, but nothing was ever done, and he'd often hear the Jones gang laughing at him behind the walls as he did the rounds. Sometimes they threw things at him—eggs, tomatoes and even stones.

He bore it. Bettie would never allow him to take his anger out on children.

*You would have made a great mother Bettie.*

They'd never had any children of their own. It hadn't been for want of trying. The old bed in the room above the ticket office had seen plenty of action in those years. But when the bridge was built, and the ferry was closed down, all they had to take with them when they left were their memories and the old red door from the ticket office, as a memento.

Bettie's father hadn't let them put it in the front of his house, but when John installed it at the back of the kitchen, Bettie thanked him and pecked him on the cheek.

"It's perfect," she said. "We'll see it every day to remind us of the way we were."

When the old man died, John had broached the subject of the door again, but Bettie proved true to form.

"Father was right. The front of the house is what everyone sees, but the important things go on round the back. It's in its rightful place," she said, and would hear no more.

\* \* \*

He came out of his reverie standing in his kitchen in front of the red door with no idea how he'd got back from the dockside. By the angle of light from the back window, he knew it was already mid-afternoon.

*I'm getting too old for this.*

More and more he'd become lost in the past, reliving happier times.

*I miss you Bettie.*

He made a pot of tea, letting it steep for a while, just the way she liked it. When it was ready he sat at the table reading his paper, the radio once again tuned to the BBC. The long-loved voices and laughter of the studio audience washed over him.

The paper was full of the usual bad news. The world was going to hell.

*You wouldn't like it Bettie.*

The crossword was more difficult than usual and he welcomed the diversion it supplied. He lost track of time for a while. He only looked up once, not really expecting the last ferry but unable to break the old habit.

The red door rattled behind him.

*Maybe I'll just fix the hinges. Bettie wouldn't mind me doing that.*

Then it did something new. It squeaked.

A cold chill hit the back of John's neck and ruffled the paper in front of him on the table. He turned, half-expecting to see a figure standing in the doorway. Sometimes visitors came straight to the rear door, knowing that he spent most of his time in the kitchen.

But there was no one there. He pushed himself up out of the chair, fighting against new stiffness in his back. The door lay open by a good six inches. A faint light—orange and flickering slightly—showed from beyond.

*That's not right.*

The handle was cold in his hot palm as he pulled the door further open and stepped out onto a foggy pier.

*That's not right at all.*

He looked left and right. The pier was empty, a slight fog hanging down at sea level.

A tannoy rang out, tinny and echoing, but he recognized Mr. Phillips's voice, even after all these years.

"The ferry approaching is the nine-thirty from Kyle."

The long remembered *peep-peep* of a steam whistle sounded in the distance. A few yards along the pier, the handle of the waiting room door squealed and started to turn.

He almost threw himself back into the kitchen, slamming the door shut behind him. He stood there for a long time, just listening to his heart thump in his ears, struggling with each breath, terrified that, at any moment, he'd hear a ferry pull in to a platform just outside — outside in the back garden. But once his heart slowed, he noticed that all was quiet and still.

As he stepped away from the door, it rattled again, just once.

He went to the cupboard and took down the whisky. Years ago, he'd convinced Bettie to buy some "for medicinal reasons." The last time it had been opened was the night of her funeral, and he had to wipe a thick layer of oily dust from around the cap before untwisting it. He poured a large measure into his teacup and swallowed it without tasting. The fire, as it hit his belly, reminded him that he was still alive.

He stood there, looking at the door.

On the radio they were playing "Mornington Crescent" and cackling loudly. Suddenly the voices sounded just a bit too forced, too mechanical, like a tannoy on an impossible pier on an equally impossible shore this far up the hill out of town. He played with the tuning until he found a wash of innocuous music. It was only then that he could start to settle and begin to try to make sense of what had happened.

*You're getting too old for this, John.*

He'd been having the blackouts for months now, ever longer periods of fugue. He didn't mind so much. They passed the time between sleeps. But this was different. This had been a visual and auditory hallucination, more real than any dream.

*Maybe Bettie was right. Maybe the old house is haunted after all.*

But John didn't believe in haunts. If things like that existed, Bettie would have come back to him years ago. The night she'd gone, even as she lay on her deathbed, she'd promised to be with him, forever.

*I'll send you a sign. Just so you'll know it's me.*

And like an old fool, John had waited. Years and years he waited. But she didn't come. Even when he talked to her, all through the day, she never talked back. That's when he knew there was nothing beyond. His Bettie would never have been able to stop herself from talking back.

After years of no response, John had given up waiting and had settled into a life of sleep, checking the ferry offices and reading the newspaper. It was a daily routine that had suited him perfectly.

*Until now.*

As he made up two cups of hot chocolate, he was remembering the first night they'd spent in this house.

\* \* \*

The ferry had stopped forever that very same morning, and Bettie was teary all day, weeping at the slightest provocation. Just the sight of the red door being taken down in the ticket office, replaced by a cheap plywood board, sent her into a crying fit that lasted two hours. Even after they got into bed, she pressed against him, sobbing quietly for a long time.

At some point she fell quiet, and he had thought she'd finally gone to sleep. He was proved wrong when the cupboard door across the room opened with a loud creak, and she sat straight up in bed as if given an electric shock.

"Hayden Brooks!" she shouted. "Go away. You're not welcome here."

He tried to hold her, but she was taut with tension, trembling all over, refusing to take her gaze from the shadows that crept around the open cupboard door. It took him another twenty minutes to calm her, and that involved turning on the lights, shutting the cupboard door and holding it closed with the back of a chair, checking under the bed and making sure the windows were locked.

Even then she was reluctant to say any more. When she finally relaxed she was embarrassed by her outburst, berating herself for behaving like a slip of a girl. But after some coaxing, she told him a story of a cuckolded ship's captain, a descent into alcohol and a trio of missing children who were never found.

"Hayden Brooks was his name. And he was the most evil man ever to live in the town. He went to the gallows for his crimes but he never repented. His house used to stand on this plot. They had it burned to the ground and the ashes scattered. My family put this house up some years later."

"When did this happen?"

"In the old days," was all she'd said, suddenly sounding like the little girl John knew she kept hidden deep inside. "But Brooks is still here. He can't leave."

All that night she'd clung to him.

"Mother said he couldn't harm us, that he was just a haunt, with no power over God-fearing folks. And during the day, I know she was right. But some nights, it's hard to remember that."

The next morning he put up the red door in the kitchen.

\* \* \*

John realized he was standing over two cups of cold hot chocolate. The clock struck twelve.

*Sorry Bettie. I'm getting too old.*

He poured the drinks down the sink and made a new batch. He left Bettie's mug on the table, as he'd done every night since she passed, and dragged himself up the stairs. Before he settled, he checked under the bed and put the back of a chair against the cupboard door.

\* \* \*

He almost felt normal again the next morning. The red door didn't rattle at all while he had his cereal and toast, and the jolly lads on the radio kept up a constant stream of witticisms that even had him smiling as he went out into the sunshine.

The first inkling he had that something was wrong came as he turned out of his drive and headed down towards the main street.

*William Meikle*

Two policeman stood outside the post office, talking gently to a young woman who was near hysteria. John kept his head down and walked past quickly.

Bettie never liked getting involved in other's business. Where other local women would gather for gossip and spend hours over their shopping trips, Bettie was in and out in minutes. John always followed her example. The people of the town had long since learned not to try to engage him in chatter, and John liked that just fine.

There were more people out and about on the street than usual, gathered in small clumps, chattering animatedly, but none of them paid John any heed as he made his way to the pier.

The building was never going to win any style awards, not even in its heyday. It was little more than a two-story box with a roof. Some of the top floor had caved in now, the portion that would have been Mr. Phillips's room. John hoped he'd be long dead before the room where he and Bettie had lived fell into such ruin. Several of the upstairs windows still had glass in them, but most of them had been broken by a combination of the elements and stone-throwing youths. Up in the eaves, two empty hanging baskets swayed gently in the wind. In the pier's pomp Bettie would have them full of a starburst of color that brought gasps of delight from the travelling passengers.

As he got closer, the vision of the night before started to prey on his mind, but all apprehension was forgotten when he saw that the main door lay wide open.

*Someone got inside.*

He broke into a shuffling run. By the time he got to the door and into the offices proper, he was panting like a dog. He cried out when he saw what had been done.

Day-Glo pink letters, over a foot high, ran along the wall opposite the ticket office, *his* ticket office.

OLD MAN RATCHETT EATS SHITE.

A neat spiral of all-too-human feces provided a full stop on the floor at the end of the script.

John shook with rage, hot tears running down his cheeks.

*You're better off out of it, Bettie.*

He knew this was going to take all day to clear up, and that he'd have to get started sooner rather than later, but the ritual needed to be observed first.

He did the rest of his rounds. He went to the night watchman's office first. The door was closed. Nothing seemed to have been touched. He couldn't remember checking here yesterday, but, then again, that was nothing new. He rattled the doorknob and it didn't budge.

*Maybe I'm not as old as all that.*

He walked along the pier back to the office buildings. A vivid memory came to him, of standing on this very spot, waving his father off to a war from which he wouldn't return. He'd realized years before that his attraction to the old pier was more than just sentiment. In a very real sense it held what little history there was that defined him as a person, from that day waving to his father, to meeting Bettie one day on his way home from the mainland, to all those days and nights handing out tickets. He was the one who ensured everyone got to where they wanted to go; the static hub in the town's wheel.

He shook his head.

*Wool gathering again, John. This won't do. There's work to be done.*

He continued past the ticket office. He didn't look in at the graffiti—he'd be seeing it up close soon enough.

The door to the waiting room was closed, and for that he was thankful.

*Bettie wouldn't want any of their kind in her room.*

He eyed the door handle warily. It didn't move. Even so, he gave it a wide berth as he passed it on the way to the storage shed, and again on the way back.

Two hours later, he had made progress on removing the graffiti. He could still see a faint outline on the wall, and he'd always know it had been there, but at least no one else would ever have to suffer the sight.

He scraped the feces from the floor and into a bucket. The water supply had long since been cut off to the pier, so he dropped the mess down the nearest drain and washed it away with bleach.

Satisfied he'd done what he could with *that*, he turned his attention to the door. Luckily, fixing it was simple. All it needed was a few new screws around the lock and it was solid again, probably even better than before.

When he closed it behind him to head home, he felt an air of satisfaction.

*Job well done.*

It lasted just as long as it took for the first ripe tomato to fly through the air and *squelch* on the door behind him. He had to duck to avoid another.

*Little buggers!*

The rage came back, twice as strong. He ran, screaming, straight for the low wall from which he guessed the bombardment had come.

\* \* \*

Later, as he stood once more in his kitchen, staring at the red door, he was ashamed at how he'd lost control so quickly. And he hadn't even caught the youths. One second he was running for the wall, the next he was lying on his back on the gravel track, staring at the sky and wondering how he'd got there.

All he'd achieved was getting muck and grime all over his clothes.

*Bettie would be disgusted with me.*

He showered and changed. By the time he got back to the kitchen another day was almost gone. They were playing silly word games on the radio.

*Axiomatic. A machine for chopping wood.*

There was a lot of laughter, but John didn't join in. The exertions of the day were catching up to him.

*Haven't had as much excitement for many a year.*

He made tea and some dry ham sandwiches, then settled down at the table with the day's paper. He couldn't concentrate. Even the football results made little sense, and it would be useless to attempt the crossword with his brain so addled by fatigue. He laid his head in his hands and was asleep in seconds.

He was woken by a cold chill at the back of his neck. A faint light—orange and flickering slightly—showed from outside.

*That's not right.*

Somewhere, deep down, he knew that he should just get up and close the door. Maybe even take a dive into the whisky bottle. Even though he wasn't a drinker and it would surely make him as sick as a dog in the morning, at that moment it seemed preferable to any alternative.

But the urge to see was stronger still.

He moved slowly to the door.

Once more the handle was cold in his hot palm as he pulled the door further open, and once again he stepped out onto an empty pier.

He knew what was coming next.

The tannoy rang out, tinny and echoing. Mr. Phillips's voice came loud and clear.

"The ferry approaching is the nine-thirty from Kyle."

The *thwup* of the paddles sounded in the distance, and a mournful whistle announcing the *Lady*'s arrival. A few yards along the pier, the handle of the waiting room door squealed and turned. John's breath steamed in front of his face.

He felt strangely calm, as if all potential for fear and excitement had been leeched out of him during the day.

The waiting room door swung open, a yellow light spilling a long rectangular outline on the pier.

*The ferry will be here soon.*

John stepped forward so that he was standing in the light from the waiting room.

Inside, something shuffled.

His heartbeat started to go up a bit. It was a struggle to take another step.

The *thwup* of the paddles in the water got closer.

"Please stand well clear of the edge." Phillips's voice said loudly.

John could see half of the waiting room from where he stood. The yellow light came from an old light fitting. He recognized it straight away. In fact, he knew it intimately. Over the years he'd changed the bulb many times and cleaned out the shade even more often. No one had cleaned this one for a while. The half-dome of glass looked grimy with dust, and black flecks showed where a small army of flies had crawled in and been cooked in the heat.

Something shuffled again. There was a scrape.

*Someone just stood up from the bench.*

Three figures moved forward, faces deep in shadow, bodies little more than silhouettes. The larger person in the center led the other two by the hand.

Suddenly, John couldn't breathe.

The paddle noise grew so loud he could hardly hear. The pier trembled at his feet. He stepped aside as the three figures came out of the waiting room. The pier filled with steam and fog as the paddle ferry pulled in to the dock.

He couldn't take it anymore. More by instinct than judgement his hand found the handle of the red door and he threw himself into the kitchen, slamming the door hard behind him. He lifted the whisky bottle and poured half of it down his throat without a pause, then stood, head spinning and guts on fire, until reality started to fill in around him.

It was only later as he dropped, exhausted, into bed that he realized.

For the first time, he hadn't left Bettie her hot chocolate.

* * *

John approached the pier with a degree of caution the next morning, as if somehow the events beyond the red door would have imprinted themselves on the physical building. But the only echoes of the past that came to him in the clear light of day were the ones created by his own memory.

The ticket office stank of bleach and carbolic soap, so he left the front door open wide while he did the rest of his rounds. He had to take a few minutes to clear up the rotting tomatoes from around the entrance, and he eyed the wall warily as he cleaned. But there was no giggling from behind it and no bombardment.

*Maybe I did accomplish something yesterday after all.*

After cleaning up he sat at the stool behind the ticket window, reliving old times. He'd done this for many years now, at least three times a week, playing pretend games like a child's tea party, welcoming invisible customers and passing out imaginary tickets for a ferry that had long since stopped running.

Previously he had always gone home feeling slightly sad, but somehow closer to the old days, closer to Bettie. Today, all he felt was cold, damp and tired.

His day didn't improve when he arrived home to find two young policemen on his doorstep.

They wouldn't tell him what it was all about, but they asked a lot of questions about the Jones gang, and John was only too happy to tell his tales of woe all over again. They came in and shared a pot of tea, and he noticed that they had a good look around, one even going so far as to go upstairs. He said he was going to the bathroom, but John knew his house. He knew the steps above them meant the man was in his bedroom.

But he had nothing to hide, and the law is the law. He let them poke around and ask their questions. By the time they left, they were a lot more relaxed than they'd been on his doorstep.

*Policemen in the house. Bettie would be mortified.*

That thought made him guilty for forgetting the hot chocolate the previous night. In penance, he washed all his dirty clothes.

*William Meikle*

Once done, he poured the whisky down the sink and put the bottle in the bin.

*Never again. That's a promise Bettie.*

He made a pot of tea, just the way Bettie liked it, put the radio on, and sat at the table with the paper.

*That's much better.*

The BBC lads were making jokes about politicians. He'd heard most of the material many times over the years, but the sheer nostalgia of it all settled him, and he started to feel more like his old self.

He got lost in the crossword so didn't notice the time. It was only the cold draft on his neck that told him the door behind him had opened once more.

The orange light flickered from beyond, but this time he had no trouble ignoring it. He stood and went to the door but didn't go out.

"The ferry approaching is the nine-thirty from Kyle."

He heard it pull into the pier and smelled salt air and smoke.

He closed the door gently.

The room fell quiet, save for the studio laughter from the radio. He went back to the crossword. At ten-thirty he made two mugs of hot chocolate and left one on the table for Bettie.

That night he slept soundly for the first time in weeks.

There were no dreams.

\* \* \*

It was raining when he got up, one of those steady drizzles that looked to be settling in for the day. But a little rain wasn't going to stop him. He put on his overcoat and headed for the pier.

The young policemen were back at the green. This time they were surrounded by a group of women. The women's voices were high and shrill, but the rain deadened the specifics and John wasn't interested enough to attempt to make out what was being said. Two of them pointed in John's direction, and one made to cross the road towards him but was held back by the policemen.

John put his head down and kept going.

*It's none of my concern.*

He was pleased to note that nothing had changed at the pier. There was no new vandalism, and all the doors and windows were secure. He felt so good that he walked along the dock and stood beside the waiting room door.

As he put his key in the lock and turned the handle, he half expected the tannoy to start up above him, but all he heard was a rustling in the room beyond, the telltale *whump-whump* of a pigeon taking to the air.

He pushed the door open, slowly. There was only darkness inside, and a musty dry smell that stung at his nostrils and in his throat. He fumbled for the light switch and turned it on. Nothing happened. Overhead, a pigeon cooed softly then went quiet.

His eyes started to adjust to the darkness. The room was just as he remembered it, although it had been several years since he'd last opened the door. Long benches ran round the walls of a square room. Years ago there would have been a heater in one corner and sometimes a newspaper or two left behind by the passengers. Now there was just the benches.

He walked to the center of the room and looked up. The light fitting above him was intact, just as it had been in his vision. The black specks where the dead flies lay even looked to be in the same pattern.

He backed out of the room, no longer feeling quite so relaxed.

"Eat *this*," a voice said behind him.

He turned just in time to see the Jones boy swing a baseball bat towards his head.

\* \* \*

When he came back to himself, he was in the kitchen, staring at the red door. He had blood on his hands and a gash above his right eye. He'd been dripping on the floor and there was a spreading crimson puddle at his feet.

*Sorry Bettie.*

He felt light-headed and groggy. He remembered nothing but the sight of the boy's grin and the *swoosh* of the bat as it came towards him.

*I need to tell those policemen.*

But before that he had to clean up, first the floor, then himself.

It took a while, and when he finished he was surprised to see that the sun was going down. He made tea, put on the radio and sat at the table. He tried to read, but his eyes refused to focus on the text, showing him only black specks and daubs on a sheet of white.

He switched his attention to the radio, but the usual laughter was absent. The announcer was deadly serious.

"Tonight, police have launched a search for three young boys—"

He rose and switched the radio off.

*Don't want Bettie getting upset.*

The red door started to swing open as he turned back to his chair. The orange light flickered outside.

He was about to move towards it when there was a pounding at his front door.

"Police, Mr. Ratchett. Open up please. We need to talk to you."

*Oh no. Bettie wouldn't like that. She wouldn't like that at all.*

He stepped out onto the pier.

The tannoy rang out, tinny and echoing. Mr. Phillips's voice came loud and clear.

"The ferry approaching is the nine-thirty from Kyle."

He heard the *thwup* of the approaching paddles and the mournful whistle announcing the ferry's arrival. A few yards along the pier, the handle of the waiting room door squealed and turned. John's breath steamed in front of his face. The waiting room door swung open, a yellow light spilling a long rectangular outline on the platform.

*The ferry will be here soon.*

John stepped forward so that he was standing in the light from the waiting room.

Inside, something shuffled.

The *thwup* of the paddle-steamer got closer.

"Please stand well clear of the edge," Phillips's voice said loudly.

Something shuffled again. There was a scrape.

Four figures moved forward, faces deep in shadow, bodies little more than silhouettes. The larger person in the center came forward first, the three smaller figures following meekly behind.

Suddenly, John couldn't breathe.

The paddle noise grew so loud he could hardly hear. The pier trembled at his feet. He stepped aside as the figures came out of the waiting room. The pier filled with steam and fog as the ferry pulled in to the dock, so much so that the figures became even more vague and indistinct.

He heard a shout in the distance from the front door of his house.

"Mr. Ratchett, if you don't open this door we'll have to break it down."

*Bettie wouldn't like that at all.*

He turned towards the red door. He was stopped by a voice whispering his name.

*John.*

That was all she said. That was all she had to say.

*Bettie?*

He turned.

She was there, smiling, holding out a hand towards him. Behind her, three children hugged at her coattails. The largest peered around her and smiled. He'd seen that grin before somewhere but couldn't quite remember where.

*She makes a great mother.*

Back in the house the front door crashed open and wood splintered.

"Mr. Ratchett. Where are the boys?"

Even from the pier, John heard the thudding of feet on the stairs. He knew he should be concerned, but his mind was focused on the figure in front of him.

"Bettie? Is it really you?"

Her voice came as a whisper from far away, as thin as the smoke that surrounded her.

*Come on John. We're taking a little boat trip. The whole family.*

The noise from back in the house was getting louder. There were crashes as furniture was thrown aside and shouts of frustration.

But Bettie didn't seem to mind.

*And if Bettie doesn't mind, then neither do I.*

A figure stood at the far end of the pier. He was wreathed in smoke, but John recognized the tall hat and long coat. He waved, and the harbormaster raised a hand and waved back. Suddenly he didn't look quite like the man that John remembered. But who else could it be?

*All aboard!*

Mr. Phillips wasn't one to wait for stragglers. Bettie shooed the children aboard up the short gangway and waited until John took her arm. Together they stepped up onto the gently swaying deck of the ferry. John immediately felt at home. Bettie put her arm around him and stood, cuddled close beside him, with the three children standing straight-backed and quiet to one side.

*A family outing. That sounds nice.*

The ferry pulled out of the dock and John caught a last glimpse into the kitchen.

The young policemen ran into the room.

The red door swung gently closed.

# About William Meikle

William Meikle is a Scottish writer, now living in Canada. Around 1991, and after being given a push by his new wife, he began submitting stories to a number of UK small press magazines. Meikle now has twenty novels published in the genre press and over 300 short story credits in thirteen countries. His work has appeared in a number of professional anthologies and magazines. His novel, *The Hole*, rose to the Top 20 of the Amazon Horror chart.

Meikle chooses to write mainly at the pulpy end of the market, populating his stories with monsters, myths, men who like a drink and smoke, and more monsters.

He lives in Newfoundland with whales, bald eagles and icebergs for company. When he's not writing he plays guitar, drinks beer and dreams of fortune and glory. He writes to escape. He hasn't managed it yet, but he's working on it.

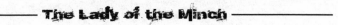

# Beholder

## John McCallum Swain

had not seen Aubrey Debrunner since I was a kid, and for me, being a kid was a long time ago. When I finally saw him again after four decades, I couldn't help being repulsed by the memory of his missing eyes — those empty sockets and flaccid lids — and my abhorrence when I saw what he had placed inside those gaping holes, or my terror when he whispered *"Now I can see you,"* as he had done once before so long ago.

## 2

Aubrey and I grew up in Kitchissippi, a town in Canada's Ottawa Valley. While we lived on the same street, it's not like I really wanted him around. As a kid, he was tolerated, much like the ass-end of winter in February, or clouds of black flies in June.

Some of us were military brats whose fathers worked at Canadian Forces Base Petawawa and some of us were "civvies," but we all lived together in the same small town and attended the same public school.

Kitchissippi no longer exists. A lot of bad shit went down there in the seventies, and by 1981 it was a ghost town. I'm sure there's a good story in the bitter decline of what I will always think of as my boyhood home, but that's not my story to tell.

I want to tell you about Aubrey.

## 3

Aubrey was the kid we all ragged on. Make no mistake, my

friends and I were losers. We were kids who were singled out for minor differences in a typically homogeneous Canadian town that remained, right up to the end, almost exclusively the domain of white Protestants and Catholics. There was the fat kid, the kid who had seizures and the kid whose parents were raging, street-fighting drunks. There was the kid whose divorced mom dated too many different guys, the kid whose motorcycle-riding dad was turned into a red smear on Highway 7 and the kid whose little sister died in a fire. And then there was me, the one with red hair, nerdy glasses and a wild imagination that made him blurt out weird shit at the most inappropriate times.

We were all about the same age and attended all the same classes for years. We called ourselves the Group of Seven. We had stolen the name for our gang from a bunch of Canadian artists who painted landscapes so bleak you wanted to cry or kill yourself for just looking at them. Aubrey wasn't one of the Seven.

He may have had certain advantages, but he was a coddled only child who couldn't do anything risky. He couldn't swim in the Petawawa River, or slide down the steep sandy hill near Boyd's Pond on sheets of cardboard, or skate on a frozen creek in winter, or even help the rest of us build tree forts in summer, the latter being arguably the grandest of traditions among Kitchissippi children. He was susceptible to colds and infections that either kept him out of school or required that he fire down handfuls of antibiotics like the rest of us gobbled up Maltesers. Among the other kids, the Group of Seven were near the bottom of the social ladder, and Aubrey was a rung below us.

And then there was that damned name his parents had burdened him with. *Aubrey.* Holy whistling Jesus, could it get any worse than that?

Aubrey's family had a really nice house on the west side of Kitchissippi, nicer than anything the rest of us knew living in rented apartments or PMQs, and I recall him saying both his father *and* mother were artists who worked all over the Ottawa Valley, including at the National Gallery and the Museum of Man. That got a lot of weird looks from the other eleven- and twelve-year-old kids who heard this, kids whose dads were mechanics or worked on loading docks, whose mothers were housewives.

His parents were a different breed, and they treated Aubrey differently. That made him seem different to the rest of us. Hell, they might as well have painted a target on his back.

Aubrey was pale and slim and ripe for being shit on, yet he kept hanging around, no matter how much grief we gave him. I guess you had to give him points for that.

I remember Aubrey showing up to school one day with big sunglasses. He had a note allowing him to wear them in class. That was in September of 1976, and we were all starting the sixth grade. Aubrey looked like an albino Roy Orbison in those shades. After a few weeks of creeping along the halls with his eyes hidden behind tinted plastic lenses, Aubrey began leaving school early. It was said that he was getting headaches all the time, bad headaches.

The few times Aubrey showed up at school in October were unsettling. He was horribly pale; his veins showed through his skin as if someone had drawn on him with a blue marker. It was just before Halloween when we realized Aubrey was losing his hair, and he looked so wretched that our Group of Seven felt bad making him the target of our teasing or the butt of our jokes.

Somebody, it may have been Mark, asked Aubrey what was going on with him and Aubrey said he was getting chemotherapy and radiation, which instantly filled us with dread since we knew — thanks to the movies — that radiation either melted you like a death ray or mutated you into a giant monster.

Horrific stories started making the rounds, stories about Aubrey losing his eyes. It was said he had cancer, that he had tumors on both of his optic nerves and that the doctors would soon have to surgically remove them, along with his perfectly healthy eyes.

That remains one of the most disturbing things I've ever heard. When I was young, kids weren't as sophisticated as they are

PEEL BACK THE SKIN

today. Our knowledge base and playing fields were narrower. We didn't have cable TV or the Internet, smart phones or Xboxes. We didn't have the entire world at our fingertips. What we had was reruns, the public library and endless woods; the truths and the lies our parents told us to enlighten and protect us; the utter bullshit our older siblings fed us just to screw with our heads; and the grapevine of communal childhood information that was part mythology and part hearsay, all of it distorted by the lenses of wonder, inexperience, fantasy and fear.

We weren't exposed to everything the world had to offer back then. We had no idea how apocalyptically messed up some people were, and for that I have always been grateful. There's a lot of good in the world and a lot of ugliness. I was spared most of the ugliness, and I spent my childhood simply being a kid.

And that's why I thought the stories about Aubrey had to be true.

I've always enjoyed writing, and I had a knack for making stuff up even at that age. Long before I ever put pen to paper, I began telling poorly crafted stories that were completely uninhibited flights of fancy, but cancerous tumors of the optic nerves? No kid I knew could have imagined something like that back then. It was too ghastly to be anything but real.

When you were a military brat you got used to kids disappearing. Fathers got transferred and sometimes families had to pull up stakes on short notice. You got used to packing and moving, saying goodbye to old friends and making new ones. I have friends now that have spent their entire lives in the same town, and to me that seems strange.

A week before my family left Kitchissippi, Aubrey disappeared. And I welcomed both events.

It was in the spring of 1977, and my dad had been posted to Chilliwack, out in BC. The upside was I was leaving Kitchissippi. The downside was that I had to say goodbye to my friends. But that was just as well as my friends were disappearing in the worst

**164** ———————————— *John McCallum Swain*

way imaginable. They were being murdered. And I think it was Aubrey who was killing them.

After Keith and Lorne died, Aubrey's parents left town. One day they were there and the next they were gone, but not before they had their own son committed to an asylum, the Leander Meade Convalescent Home and Sanatorium, Renfrew County's notorious mental hospital north of Kitchissippi.

That aging facility, constructed at the same time as Canada's Parliament buildings, using the same Ottawa Valley sandstone, was troubled from the start. Once a wellspring of terrifying stories whispered among the children of Kitchissippi, Miramichi and Petawawa, the vacant hospital is now a shuttered Gothic curiosity, its sculpted towers and arched windows slowly being swallowed by the dark outgrowth of Algonquin Provincial Park.

After one too many scandals involving inexplicable operational expenditures, rumors of sexual abuse and purported accidental deaths — not to mention acquisition of the notorious and unflattering sobriquet *La Maison Sombre* — the institution was shuttered a few years after Aubrey's arrival.

Where Aubrey went once the asylum was shut down, or what he had endured while he was there, no one knew. During the turmoil of the hospital's dénouement in the winter of 1979, a brief, bleak note on his release was inscribed in a register of patients. It read simply that he was "turned out."

- 4 -

Like many people my age, I recently began using Facebook to recall and share memories of the past, reconnect with old friends from high school and college through pages set up to commemorate a specific time and place, or to host groups for military brats. When I received an invitation to join a group called Remembering Kitchissippi, I was surprised that anyone wanted to recall that town, and amazed that anyone found me.

I had been living in northern Alberta the last few years, in Fort McMurray. I never stayed in one place very long. From British Columbia to Newfoundland there are thousands of men who share my name, John MacDonald. It's a name than comes with a certain amount of anonymity. And while I do make a very public living writing, I publish everything under a pseudonym. Yet someone had connected this John MacDonald, me, with a place two thousand miles away and forty years gone, knowing that the full-bearded, ponytailed man living now was the fresh-faced boy who lived then.

The creator of the Facebook group used an alias: Perseus Jones.

I had read a lot of Greek mythology as a kid, and for a moment the ancient tales of Perseus seemed to have some significance, but it eluded me and I let the thought go.

Access to the page was granted quickly, and I soon saw some familiar names. Kent was out in BC. Eddie was in Halifax. Mark was in Montreal. Darren was in Toronto. All that remained of the Group of Seven. We chatted on Facebook for months and played with schedules until we realized we could all meet during the first week of August. We choose Miramichi as ground zero; it was the closest town to the now empty houses, deserted businesses and overgrown lots of Kitchissippi.

- 5 -

When we finally got together in the restaurant of the Best Western, it was surreal. I could see the boys in the faces of the men around the table, people I had not seen in forty years. We all had greying or thinning hair, too many wrinkles, and for some of us, too many extra pounds.

We shot the shit for a while, tossing each other the highlights of our lives, getting to know who was married, who had kids, who had a nice house or a job worth bragging about. We had all been close as kids, but too much time had passed. We had moved too far apart. I didn't care much about the full lives being shared with me, but I did care about what I thought of as the real reason we were here.

"Time to fess up," I said. "Which one of you is Perseus Jones?"

Blank stares all around.

"It's not me, so it had to be one of you."

"It isn't me," Darren said. He had been chubby as a kid and still carried a lot of extra weight. His round, ruddy face was the most youthful at the table. He had five little girls and a wife who was still slim and gorgeous. Go figure the odds on that one.

"Me either," Eddie said as he sipped a Canada Dry club soda and muffled a belch with a fist. His parents were drunks who had trashed their own home a dozen times over in fantastic brawls, and now he was a high school counselor. Seeing the club soda in his hand, I wondered if he had inherited the family genes.

"Sure as fuck wasn't me," Mark said. He had been a small kid with a sweet face, and rumor had it that his mom had been an easy lay—a lush, a tramp, a harlot. All the old epithets came back to me as I looked at Mark. Now he was all sinew and callous, one of those wiry guys that can be so dangerous in a fight. He taught advanced self-defense classes. When we had met he smiled and shook my hand, squeezing hard, and I had noticed a raw hostility in his eyes that saddened me. He'd been a nice kid. Now he looked like a bastard.

Kent just shrugged. His once glossy black hair was now grey, but he had the same big jug-handle ears and friendly grin. He restored old cars. If that sounds like he was a grease monkey messing around in his garage on Saturday afternoons, let me clarify things: he sold his cars to collectors like Jay Leno.

I was biting back the urge to say it was me, just for the hell of it, when our waitress came to the table. She was probably all of twenty years old, and for a moment as I looked at her, I felt my age like a great weight on my bones.

She set a folded card on the table, gestured to a faux-antique clock on one wall and said, "I was told to give this to you at 10:00 p.m."

I opened the card.

Inside, there were two small photos that looked as if they had been cut from an old grade-school yearbook and glued in place. The photos showed the smiling faces of the two members of our Group of Seven who were no longer with us, Keith and Lorne. Written on the card in a childish scrawl was a message:

*Meet me at the Playhouse, at midnight.*

The Maitland Playhouse had been Kitchissippi's only movie theater. It had been boarded up in 1979 after being overrun by rats that had proved damned near invincible.

The message was signed *Perseus Jones.*

I passed the card to Kent. He read it and passed it on. No one said a thing as the card circled the table.

When it came back to me, Kent pointed at the card. "Anyone notice the word midnight?"

"Somebody scratched out the letter *i*," Eddie said. "Both of them."

"You gotta be fucking kidding me," Mark said.

"Aubrey," Darren whispered.

I sat back from the table, remembering what happened the last time we had all been together.

People in Kitchissippi said the trouble with Aubrey started when he killed a cat. I believe it started a few weeks before that, when Aubrey lost his eyes.

- 6 -

Aubrey had left school for good at the end of November in 1976. He underwent surgery at a hospital down in Ottawa two weeks later, and had his recovery over the winter break.

I believe Kent and I are the only two people Aubrey reached out to after his surgery. It was Aubrey's mother who had invited us to drop by on the day after New Year's Day. I can only imagine how excruciating the lead-up to those phone calls could have been for Aubrey, with Mrs. Debrunner asking her son if he would like to invite any friends over, and Aubrey trying to come up with the names of one or two kids who might actually show up, not blow him off and use the request as fuel for more cruel taunts, all the while lost in a darkness that was newfound and forevermore.

In the end, Kent and I agreed to visit Aubrey, but not because of pressure from our parents. My mom and dad didn't know the Debrunner family, but they were sympathetic to their grim situation as the parents whose poor little boy had "lost his eyes," as if they had fallen out of a hole in his pocket. No, we ultimately decided to see him out of morbid curiosity because we were kids.

At the urging of the others, Kent and I went to Aubrey's house on Sunday, the day after the Group of Seven attended a New Year's Day matinée at the Maitland. It was a typical double bill of older flicks, which in this case were *The Devil's Rain* and *Race with the Devil*. I don't think Pete Maitland ever showed a first-run feature in his theater. He was too cheap for that. The stupid bastard turned down a chance to screen *Star Wars* and make a mint at his concession stand.

It was between a chapter of a pretty decent Republic serial called *The Purple Monster Strikes* and the first feature when I mentioned that Aubrey's mom had called to ask if I would could come over and visit him. Instead of ragging on Aubrey as a loser, we sat silently watching the spastic antics of a cartoon bag of popcorn that exhorted us with disturbing desperation to visit the snack bar, until Kent spoke up and said his mother had received the same call.

Eddie, Mark, Darren, Keith and Lorne insisted we had to go. We had to find out exactly what had happened to Aubrey and then report back.

So we went.

- 7 -

"Do you think this is a good idea, Johnny?"

I tried to focus on Kent's question and not let irritation distract me. I hadn't been called Johnny since I left Kitchissippi, and I wasn't too keen on hearing the name again.

"Sure, why not?" That was bullshit. I was scared, but I was also compelled to go back to my old hometown and find out exactly who was screwing with us.

We were heading down Highway 13 in the minivan Darren had driven up from Toronto. Eddie was driving now; he was the only one of us who hadn't had any drinks with dinner.

It was a warm night and the windows were rolled down, the air heavy with the humidity that was the scourge of Ottawa Valley summer. Darren's satellite radio was tuned to an oldies station, the volume turned low. Bachman Turner Overdrive whispered to me from the past, telling me that I ain't seen nothing yet. As we turned off the old highway onto Laplante Road I heard the unmistakable call of a loon out on the flat black expanse of Lake Kewasowock. Miramichi was behind us. The ruins of Kitchissippi lay ahead.

"Sounds like some practical joke," Mark said. He was half-cut on Canadian Club whiskey and looked meaner than ever.

A moth hit the windshield with a soft thud and left a palm-sized greenish smear on the glass. Darren jumped. He looked scared, and I wondered why he had come along.

"Jesus fuck," Eddie whispered, turning on the wipers. "I forgot how big the bugs were out here."

We drove on without speaking. The minivan turned onto Laurier Street, and then we were in the dark and haunted belly of Kitchissippi.

"We're back in the Kitch'," Mark said. "And ain't it a bitch."

Eddie took a left, and another left and then we pulled up in front of the Maitland Playhouse.

As kids we'd all had some grand times in that old movie house. The movies had been my only escape from this town until my family moved away. Seeing that it had become a boarded-up, graffiti-tagged ruin broke my heart.

"What a mess," Darren said.

"What a drag," I said.

Kent nodded. "I know, eh?"

There were sheets of plywood across the entrance. The glass was broken out of the ticket booth, and more plywood sealed the booth off from the rest of the building. Someone had used chalk to draw a crude pair of eyeglasses on one sheet, head-high. Centered in each of the chalk lenses was a knothole. Written over the knotholes, in an oddly-canted hand, was a challenge:

*Are you brave enough to look inside?*

*Or will you run away and hide?*

Still drunk, Mark nearly fell out of the minivan, read the words on the wall and said, "Fuck that shit." He unzipped his fly and began pissing on the side of the ticket booth.

Eddie stepped past him and stood close to the plywood wall. He peered through the knotholes and then screamed in pain as someone rammed the long steel tines of a two-pronged hay fork through his eyes and out the back of his skull.

- 8 -

I rang the Debrunner's doorbell on that chilly day in January. Kent was taller than I so he reached up and used the brass door knocker.

"Before we got here, I was hoping this would be kind of weird," he said. "Now I hope it's not."

Aubrey's mom opened the front door, and for a moment I thought she was getting ready for a role in a play as her face was powdered almost white, her lipstick was such a dark red it was almost black and her eyelashes looked like the legs of June bugs. It took me a moment to realize that, aside from eyes that appeared red and tired from crying, this was probably how she looked every day.

Aubrey's dad stood behind her like a supporting player in a bad sitcom. He was wearing a sweater-vest, and he had a pencil-thin mustache on his upper lip. He didn't say a word.

"Oh come in, come in," Aubrey's mom said, letting out a forced laugh. Her hair was as white-blonde as Aubrey's, piled high on her head like ice cream on a Dairy Queen cone. She was holding a can of Glade air freshener.

The furniture in the living room was covered in protective plastic and everything was perfect, as if from a magazine. What little I could see of the kitchen was spotless, not a pot or dish or drinking glass in sight. The house didn't look like anyone really lived there. It looked preserved.

Kent and I took off our gloves, coats, toques and snow boots, and then padded up a flight of stairs with Mrs. Debrunner saying, "Knock on the first door, yes, that one right there."

We knocked on the door, and a voice from inside told us to come in.

It was a gray day, the lights were off and the blinds were drawn over the only window, leaving the room almost dark. I could see a shape sitting on what I assumed was the bed.

There was a smell in the bedroom that was both sweet and awful. Mrs. Debrunner's air freshener and something else.

"Hi, Aubrey," I said.

"Hi!" he replied, excited that we were there. His enthusiasm made me feel terrible because I couldn't wait to leave.

"Can I turn on a light?" Kent asked.

"What?" Aubrey sounded genuinely confused, and then he let out a morbid, jaded chuckle that frightened me. It was a sound no child should ever make. "Yeah, go ahead. You know dads, always turning off lights and turning down the heat and telling you to put on—"

"A sweater," Kent and I said at the same time. All three of us laughed.

I was thinking that things were going to be okay after all. Until the light came on and I saw that slender, pale boy stand and take a step toward us, his eyelids as flat as the blanket on his empty bed.

"I'm really glad you guys are here," Aubrey said.

*John McCallum Swain*

Kent pointed, and I saw that Aubrey was wearing one gray sock and one green sock.

"No problem," I said.

Aubrey came closer and Kent and I stepped to either side, as if the cancer that took Aubrey's eyes was somehow contagious. He closed his bedroom door and then turned back, walking across the room with one hand outstretched until he reached his bed, where he sat down again.

"So, how's it hanging?"

Kent winced dramatically when I said this, and I felt like an arsehole, but I couldn't think of anything else to say.

Aubrey shrugged. "Okay, I guess, at least that's what my doctor says. It hurt, at first." He touched one of his lax eyelids, making a wet sound like parting lips. I nearly bolted from the room, wailing in revulsion when I glimpsed an empty red hollow beneath that eyelid. "But now I'm just bored."

Kent and I stood by the door in silence, breathing in that faint, horrible smell. He confirmed later that we were thinking the same things. We couldn't talk about TV, or movies, or comic books, or about *anything* we've *seen*. When you're twelve years old, those restrictions don't leave a whole hell of a lot else to talk about.

I looked around the room, desperately trying to think of something to say, and that's when I noticed the jar atop a dresser near me. It was made of heavy glass that had a slight blue hue and was sealed with a glass stopper. There was liquid inside. Floating in the liquid were what appeared to be two rotten pieces of meat the size of dice.

Kent had noticed the jar too, and I heard him whisper, "What is that?"

Aubrey perked up at this, his pallor and collapsed eyelids making him look like a corpse.

"You've seen the apothecary jar, and my eyes," he said. "My optic nerves were removed and my eyes were precancerous, so it all had to go, but I kept hoping that maybe I could get them to work again. That's why I asked the doctor if I could keep them." He shook his head. "After I got home from the hospital I put my eyes back in, and they didn't work. But I found something that did."

Aubrey got down on his knees and groped blindly under his bed until he found what he was looking for: a shoe box. He kneeled and set the box in front of him so we could see it. He lifted the lid and Kent retched.

I felt like I was going to vomit and fought it down. Inside the box was a dead cat, a young tabby with a broken neck. It was the source of the horrible sweet-putrid smell in Aubrey's room.

The cat's eyes had been removed from its head and now lay between the creature's paws, the sclera as white as ivory and the emerald green iris now as cloudy as jade.

Aubrey took one eye out of the box and then the other, lifting his eyelids and gently placing the cat's eyes in his own sockets.

Those green eyes gleamed.

And then they moved.

Aubrey smiled and said, "Now I can see you."

Kent and I screamed. We ran out of Aubrey's room and down the stairs, pushing past Mr. Debrunner, with his pencil mustache and shroud of silence, and Mrs. Debrunner, who was grinning like an imbecile and spraying air freshener. We pulled on our boots and ran out into the cold, carrying our coats and gloves.

Following us down the frozen street like a gust of winter wind at our backs was Aubrey's voice as he cried out in heartbreak and rage, "Come back!"

- 9 -

Eddie hit the ground like a steer brained by a butcher's mallet, the heels of his shoes hammering the sidewalk as blood poured out of his eye sockets.

Mark went berserk. He ran full-tilt into the plywood wall and smashed through. He grinned at us, apparently unaware he was bleeding from cuts on his nose and chin.

Darren followed. His fear-bleached face was as pale as a winter moon.

Kent and I entered the dark theater lobby cautiously, seeing Mark, and then Darren, turn down a hall that lead to the bathrooms.

The lights came on, painfully bright, and I heard Kent gasp as if a bucket of cold water had been splashed in his face.

In the center of the lobby, hanging from a rope around its neck like a condemned man, was a pig. Its eyes were missing.

I stepped over the hay fork lying on the dusty lobby carpet. The blood-slick steel tines jutting upward like horns had been bent close so they would fit through the knotholes in the plywood wall.

Kent saw the hay fork and said, "Oh Je—"

Mark and Darren cried out, their voices muffled and far away.

- 10 -

Two of my friends were murdered in the winter of 1977. Keith was found by the side of Donaldson Road on January 30th, his body twisted as if it had been tossed away like so much trash. Lorne was found on the 12th of February near the densely wooded area known as Borthwick Stand.

The Group of Seven was no more.

The *Miramichi Ledger* said Keith and Lorne had wounds that indicated, "the presence of scavengers."

They had bled to death and parts of their bodies had been chewed away. Their eyes were missing.

Written in the snow in their own blood were the words LET'S BE FRIENDS.

Rumors ran rampant among the citizens of Kitchissippi. Adults suggested it was a serial killer or a psychotic sex pervert, and teenagers said it was the Unicorn Man, a local legend used to scare little kids.

My friends and I were convinced it was Aubrey because he was taken away a few weeks later.

That spring my family learned my dad had been posted to Chilliwack. We eventually packed everything we owned into boxes and moved out of Kitchissippi on April 12th, and for that I was grateful.

The week before I left town, a white station wagon pulled up in front of Aubrey's house, and that skinny, blind, lonely boy had been dragged into the street by two men in crisp white shirts and pants. He was crying aloud that he wanted to stay with his mother and father, that he wanted to stay in his own home, that he didn't want to go to a hospital.

Aubrey was bound in a straitjacket, looking like something out of an old movie. His pale blond hair was sticking up in tufts, spit flying from his mouth as he raved at everyone watching. And most horrible of all his eyes were open, the lids raised over their empty sockets.

The last thing Aubrey said, the last thing he swore before he was locked in the station wagon and sent away, was, *"I'm coming back!"*

There was so much I didn't see back then, which is ironic.

I didn't see Aubrey kill my friends. I didn't even see him kill the cat in the shoe box. It could have been road kill for all I knew. But I *believed* he took those lives, believed it with all my heart.

I believed that losing his eyes left Aubrey standing on the edge of sanity, and losing his friends, having Kent and me turn away from him when he showed us his stolen cat's eyes in a desperate attempt to be normal again, pushed him over the edge. That's why I was so relieved when my family moved as far away from Kitchissippi as we could get.

- 11 -

Kent and I ran down the hall, passing the doors to the bathrooms and pausing at the head of the stairs leading down to the basement.

We heard another cry of pain and continued down the stairs, part of me wondering who had turned the power back on since there were lights on everywhere, and part of me wanting to simply cut and run.

At the bottom of the stairs was a hallway as long as the theater's lot and many closed doors.

A door at the far end of the hall creaked open a few inches. I went down the hall and through the open doorway, Kent following in my wake.

Inside the room, Mark and Darren were lying side by side on the floor. Both men were dead. Their throats had been crudely torn open and their eye sockets were red holes. Their blood on my hands was still warm.

Written on the wall in broad strokes of blood was LET'S BE FRIENDS!

Movement at the other end of the room caught my eye.

It was the shape of a man, little more than a silhouette against a wash of fluorescent light. He was tall and lean, his thinning hair long and unkempt. He held something over his open mouth, like a debauched Roman being fed peeled grapes. It was a human eye hanging by a string of tissue. He dropped it into his mouth and began to chew.

He sidestepped gracefully as Kent ran at him, spitting obscenities. The moment Kent was on the other side of the door it was slammed shut, and I heard him scream.

- 12 -

For a long time after leaving Kitchissippi, I had a recurring dream. I was in the dark and somebody, a kid perhaps, whispered, "I always liked you the best." I would reach out and turn on my bedside lamp and realize I was still in total darkness. Blind. And then someone would set the limp, furry body of a dead cat in my hands. Sometimes I woke up screaming.

Now I heard that same whisper, only it was not a boy's voice but a man's. It was Aubrey. He was on the other side of the door he had closed and he was whispering, "I always liked you the best."

I went to the door and opened it, hearing the thump of Aubrey's feet as he ran up another flight of stairs. Kent's body was lying dead inside, his ravaged throat and empty eye sockets dripping blood.

Aubrey was at the top of the stairs, a decrepit, deranged version of the boy I had known so long ago. He stood with arms outstretched, a beatific smile on his face, watching me through the dead pig's eyes.

"Now I can see you. Again," he said with a grotesque wink before stepping through another door and slamming it shut.

I went up the stairs slowly, listening for recognizable sounds. The theater was silent. I opened the door and stepped onto old wooden flooring that creaked underfoot. Above me was a vast expanse of white cut by red slashes. I was on the theater's stage, behind the screen.

I stepped out in front of the screen into a blinding glare that came from a small aperture in the wall at the back of the theater. Aubrey had put a light in the projection booth bright enough to illuminate the screen.

From one end of the screen to the other were words slashed in red.

As I read the words, my mind made connections between disparate elements far too late.

When I was young I enjoyed reading from Greek mythology because those stories were the most graphic tales kids could get their hands on. Bloodcurdling violence, incest, matricide, patricide, castration, torture, bestiality—the Greek myths offered up all of that and more, and librarians shared those stories with a smile.

As I read the message towering over me now I remembered that Perseus had stolen a single shared eye from the Graeae, sisters to the Gorgons, as the first part of his great adventure. Without that eye there would be no slaying Medusa, no saving Andromeda.

*John McCallum Swain*

It all began with stolen sight.

Long slashes of red on the tall white screen formed a message.

*When my grim task is complete, I will pluck these eyes from my own head, for I shall never see a thing more beauteous than what I hath wrought instead.*

It did not take me long to realize who the passage was intended for, but the knowledge came too late.

Aubrey's hands were already encircling my head from behind, his eager fingers digging at my face with a maniac's relentless strength, tearing away my eyelids and uprooting my eyeballs as I shrieked into the approaching darkness.

As I touched my eye sockets and felt my own hot blood wash over my trembling fingers, I heard the sounds of Aubrey eating my eyes and saying, "Let's play hide and seek, you and me. If you stay hidden you get to live. If I catch you I will eat the rest of your soft parts."

I ran, my hands held out before me, my palms slapping against old wood, my fingers grazing crumbling plaster. I could hear Aubrey following, hooting with pleasure like a demented child.

At some point I turned a corner and could no longer hear him at all.

Ultimately, I made my way out of the theater and through the streets of downtown Kitchissippi, falling and crawling and pushing myself back to my feet again and again.

I stumbled sightless through the cold and dark until I reached the highway where a tow truck driver nearly ran me down. He brought me to the emergency room at Miramichi Regional Hospital but not before calling the police.

Aubrey was never found, but the bodies of my friends were quickly discovered.

Smeared, bloody hand prints on walls and doors throughout the theater made it appear that the murders had been committed by a man who blinded himself afterward and found his way out of the building by touch, leaving behind his confession writ large on the theater screen.

It was the perfect setup.

- 13 -

I have a very comfortable room in this facility. The Laurentian Park Institution is a minimum security prison, but I like to think of it as a secure infirmary. LPI is on a beautiful tract of land, or so the guards and attendants tell me. From the barred window of my third-story room, across a wide expanse of fields and fences, one can see the deep green shadows that mark the border of Algonquin Provincial Park and, as I've been told, the abandoned remains of the old Renfrew County mental hospital.

Everyone I talk to doubts my story, attendants, doctors, police and prosecutors. They all seem to be patronizing me. I've been told it's a curious coincidence that two kids were killed in Kitchissippi back in the seventies, and that those killings stopped when my family moved away. It's been suggested that of the five men who went back to Kitchissippi that August night, I was the most unstable. I had no family, I worked alone and I never stayed in one place very long.

The police told me the RCMP were now investigating the incident at the Maitland Playhouse because they had unsolved murder cases going back forty years in which victims across Canada had been killed in many different ways, but the dead all had one thing in common: their eyes had been gouged out.

I'm beginning to realize I'm the only one who believes Aubrey was ever in Kitchissippi the night my friends died.

When I stand at my window with summer's warmth or winter's chill on my face, I can almost feel the weight and the hardness of the distant stone walls and steel doors that once incarcerated Aubrey.

I know Aubrey is mocking me, capering with glee in the still silence. I can hear him in the distance, as clearly as I can hear the pigeons cooing on the sill of my window as they strut and swagger outside the bars just beyond my reach.

Someday soon I will lay my hands on one of the pigeons and take the pompous little thing's eyes.

Then I will leave this place, crossing fields and fences and entering the ruins of the Leander Meade Convalescent Home and Sanatorium, where Aubrey and I will meet again.

# About John McCallum Swain

John McCallum Swain wrote his first story in the sixth grade. While other children were writing about kittens and summer vacations, he wrote of the annihilation of humanity by invading aliens.

Since then, Swain has progressed from longhand to typewriters to laptops, and he continues to write tales ranging from graphic horror to alternate history while exploring new territory creating original screenplays for the transatlantic partnership Grab a Half Productions.

He has previously published novels and short stories under the name Jack X McCallum.

# Orphans
## of the Air

### James Lowder

he radio trembled with the sounds of simulated peril: maniacal laughter, a terrifying mechanical whine and the panicked yelps of a trapped animal.

A young boy's voice—a hero's voice—rose above the cacophony. "Keep fighting, Paddy. No compromise!"

"This fight was over before it started," a man snarled in reply. His accent marked him as foreign and, therefore, nefarious. "You're going to watch the buzz saw claim your little trained bear. Then, child, it will be your turn!"

Organ music swelled to signal the episode's end, and the announcer breathlessly advised the audience to tune in tomorrow to find out if Andy and his pet bear Paddy would escape the sawmill and smash the fiendish Red plot that had turned it into a house of horrors. While the radicals and anarchists targeted by the Feds in the wake of the Great War were now, seven years later, far less of a pressing concern than the mobsters turning the Volstead Act to their brutal gain, they remained a reliable and popular avatar of menace with the public. The writers for *All-American Andy* had cast them as villains almost exclusively in the four months the show had been on the air.

"Remember," the announcer said, "true Americans like Andy are easy to spot. And here is today's Eagle Agent message, intended only for members in good standing of All-American Andy's Eagle Squadron. Ready?"

In a modest home in the Woodlawn neighborhood of Chicago's South Side, a ten-year-old girl dutifully wrote down the string of numbers that followed, then started to translate them using the decoder for which she'd saved a month's worth of Liberty Bar wrappers. Like many of the thousands of children planted in front of their radios all across the Midwest, Cindy Reisbig could guess what the communication would be even before she deciphered the final word. "R-I-G-H-T. The message is 'Right is right,'" she said aloud, as if she were reciting a lesson in class. "Just like Andy tells us all the time in the comic strip!"

The station had segued into a late-afternoon broadcast from the Aragon Ballroom, but Cindy hardly heard the Jean Goldkette Orchestra and their new horn player Bix Beiderbecke burning through "Riverboat Shuffle." Nor did she notice the thin, greenish mist bleeding from the horn speaker of the family's new Atwater Kent radio. She was too focused on sketching Paddy. The plucky little bear was her favorite *All-American Andy* character. She'd even convinced her adoptive father to take her to Wrigley Field for Paddy Day. Sitting through the Cubs game had been a bit of a chore—she'd always been more of a White Sox fan—but it had been worth it for the Paddy pin-back button they gave away that afternoon.

A voice growled from over the little girl's shoulder. The words were hard to make out; the thing's mouth and throat were not particularly amenable to human speech, and the thick brogue only made matters worse. "A passable likeness yer scratchin' there," was what the intruder had tried to say. The utterance came out instead as something threatening and horrific—and far more appropriate to its intentions.

The living room of the modest Woodlawn home trembled with the sounds of genuine peril: inhuman laughter, a terrifying mechanical whine and the panicked screams of a doomed little girl.

* * *

Tristram Holt stood next to the stone angel crouched at the head of the open grave. The marker had been at its vigil for less than a week, so it still shone white in the light of the full moon, the marble pristine, unmarred by soot or storm. Its purity made the man at its side appear all the more ragged. Old blood spattered his coat and bullet-torn shirt. His cloak was tattered and grimy. The brim of his battered fedora cast a shadow over his face, which resembled a dead man's in every way, save for his eyes. They burned with a strange fire as he watched the two men uncovering the murdered girl's coffin.

"I don't like him looming over us like that, Mister Branch," noted the shorter of the two grave robbers, the one deepest in the hole. He was a squat, muscular figure, built, quite literally, for digging in tight spaces. "We're doing him a favor and he stands there waiting, like undelivered bad news."

"Eyes on the prize, Mister Crump," his partner chided. Branch sat at the foot of the grave, his long legs dangling into the hole, his arms cradling a shovel that resembled a surplus and equally spindle-like limb. He tilted his head on its bony neck and smiled a smile that revealed too many teeth, all of them overly large and wickedly pointed. "My partner is on to something, though. You're even making *me* nervous. Why don't you go visit yourself. You're still buried not far from here, as I recall."

Despite himself, Holt found his gaze moving across the Resurrection Cemetery, in the direction of the headstone his fiancée and Cook County had placed to mark what should have been the final resting place of his former self. They'd buried an empty coffin after giving up on finding what the doctors in "Schemer" Drucci's lab had left. The butchers had tried to transform the young assistant district attorney into a human bomb. Instead, they left him all but broken, with the face of a living dead man and a thirst for vengeance that drove him to recast himself in the forge of the notorious Levee district as the Corpse. The Scourge of Evil was one of several new identities Holt had created for himself in the months since Drucci and his thugs targeted him; he was still uncertain if any of them, even the Corpse, could truly be called his own.

A sharp thump brought his attention back to the open grave. "I'm down to the box," Crump announced.

Mister Branch tossed a large burlap sack to his partner. "Use this. We're not taking her far." He gestured to a nearby tomb. "I set up everything for the ceremony in there so we won't be disturbed. Corpse can have his chat with her and then we can get the child back in the ground."

"Put her back? I'm not promising nothing of the sort," Crump growled. "There might be some parts of her the doctor can use."

"You're putting her back," Holt said. "We're only disturbing her rest now because it will save other children from the thing that took her life. I won't allow you to give her to Doctor Grimm."

"Yes," Branch said. "The poor child has already been through enough strife without Doctor Grimm's tender ministrations."

Crump heaved the sack holding the body out of the grave, then clambered up himself with the deftness of a badger exiting a burrow. He tipped his flat cap to the dead girl before hoisting her over his shoulder.

"I say she was lucky, learning so young that there are awful things in the dark. I wish someone woulda taught me that hard truth back when I was a tyke."

"When you were a tyke, Crump, you *were* the awful thing in the dark," Holt said without a hint of jest about it as he followed the resurrection men into the tomb. Mister Branch's laughter echoed in the stone hall. The short, hissing barks were indistinguishable from the sound his partner's shovel made when biting into graveyard earth.

The arcane patterns on the floor and sarcophagi had been drawn in witches' blood, and the animal fat for the candles lighting the proceedings had been rendered from beasts that went extinct long before Chicago was set down on any map. As Crump freed the dead girl's body from the sack, Branch produced a rope he'd recovered from the Tyburn gallows in London, but only after it had been thoroughly broken in on Oliver Cromwell. With the rope, he secured the child to a simple wooden chair positioned at the tomb's center. The chair had been pilfered from the groundskeeper's house just an hour earlier.

"Whatever this murderous thing is, it's only killing orphans?" Branch said. "I do hope the blackguard is no one we know."

"Doctor Grimm used to build me lovely things out of orphans," said Crump, a wistful look on his face. The candlelight revealed the winding lines of suture marks crisscrossing his flesh and the mismatched quality of the parts for which the scars marked the ragged borders. Holt opened his mouth to reply to the comment, but the grave robber added quickly, "But he ain't the one behind this. He's pickier about his materials than he used to be."

Holt scowled and moved closer to the girl. Her head was flopped forward, face hidden, chin to her chest. "How do we get started?"

"Like this," Branch said. He leaned in. Brushing aside a pigtail, he whispered something softly into the dead girl's ear.

Her head flew up, a pair of glass eyes dropped to the floor and smashed, and a scream tore from her throat. Her mouth gaped black and round, like her two empty eye sockets. Dark lines slashed out from the voids toward her ears and across the bridge of her nose, where the mortician had closed up more brutal gashes.

"My eyes!" she howled. "Please! I need them back. Not glass ones—*my* eyes. God won't let me into Heaven without them!" Then she shrieked again, a long, agonized cry that filled the tomb with the stink of grave rot.

"You said the rite wouldn't hurt her." Anger twisted Holt's pallid features. "You said she'd be calm, able to answer questions."

Branch rubbed his pointed chin. "This is all wrong." He waited for a pause in the girl's screaming, but when it didn't come he simply spoke louder. "Perhaps it's the chair. Too mundane."

"Forget the chair," Holt snapped. "Is she serious? She can't get into Heaven without her eyes?"

"Possibly," Branch replied. "God can be a merciless rotter when He sets His mind to it. I wouldn't put it past Him to conduct a parts check at the pearly gates, right after the cherubim pat down the hopeful applicants for contraband."

Crump clamped a dirty hand over their captive's mouth. "You're talking through your hat, Branch. You don't know nothing about what happens when you snuff it. You ain't been dead. Not even once in a thousand years." He nodded at the struggling girl. "I say this is a death-dream."

"What the hell is that?" Holt asked.

"Something close enough to Hell, Corpse," Crump replied. "See, sometimes souls get confused when death takes 'em. They can't make sense of what's happening, so they conjure up their own idea of what's going on based on where they think they should've ended up. This one probably had too many Sunday school lessons about keeping her body pure for the Rapture. If nothing comes along to shake her out of the death-dream, she'll be trapped in it, maybe forever."

"Then we probably need to get her some flesh-and-blood eyes. Anyone's will do." There was no disgust on Branch's face as he said this, only a slight puzzlement over the challenge. "Where do you think—"

His question was silenced by the thunder of a single gunshot. An instant before Holt's gun went off, the brutish Crump managed to throw up a hand in defense, its five digits uniform only in their stubbiness. The blast tore the hand from its wrist, then opened up the grave robber's throat from ear to Adam's apple. He died with a curse on his twitching, lopsided lips.

"It's easy enough to shoot a man when you know he can be cobbled back together," Branch observed wryly.

"He had that coming all night. Besides, he wasn't going to give up his eyes without a fight, and we don't have time for that. We need to get this over with."

Cindy Reisbig was screaming again, but she calmed down at last when Holt took the pair of eyes—one green, one startlingly blue—that he'd stolen from Mister Crump and worked them into the empty sockets.

"Oh, God will surely welcome me home now," she said, then paused. "Are you certain these are mine? They feel kind of strange. Itchy, way inside my head."

"You'd better hurry up with your questions," Branch whispered through a shark-toothed grin. "Crump's parts can be a bit…*aggressive* on their own."

Holt gently prompted the girl to describe what had happened the afternoon of her murder—how she'd been listening to *All-American Andy* and decoding the Eagle Squadron message when the thing came out of the radio. "It looked like a bear. Like Paddy, sort of. It even wore a little hat like his," she said, "but it wasn't him. It was a monster that took my decoder and then took my eyes. It had a saw, like the one my father uses in his shop, only littler."

"Did it say anything when it attacked you?" Holt asked.

"It was hard to understand, but I think it called me a leech," she said, struggling now to speak. The lidless eyes rolled in her head and the skin on her face bulged and writhed. "It told me…I had to…pay my…share…"

One of Crump's eyes had turned completely inward so that the nerves and muscles were exposed. They pulsed from the orb, snaking tendrils that spread out and burrowed into the flesh on her cheek and then her neck. The other eye, the blue one, had fixed its gaze on Holt. Soon it was joined by a trio of new eyes that burst through her skull, all of them glaring hatred at the crime-fighter. Bones snapped and folded in on themselves as her body was reshaped. Through it all, the little captive remained mercifully silent.

The child dissolved into a shifting mass that shattered the chair and slipped free of the ropes. Holt fired twice into the blob, but the bullets had no effect. The thing lashed out, knocking the twin Colts from Holt's shriveled fingers. It snared him with an eye-studded tentacle. He struggled against its surprising strength, managing after a time to pull a knife from a sheath at his ankle. He drove the blade deep into the malice-filled blue eye, which had remained locked on him throughout the struggle. The thing reared back in pain.

"Don't just stand there, you demented scarecrow," Holt shouted. He slashed madly with his blade, trying to free himself. "Get Crump's other eye!"

Mister Branch remained motionless beside the struggling forms. He had one hand raised, as if he were hesitating before selecting an apple from a cart, and a fatuous grin quirked his lips. Finally his hand darted forward, a rapid serpent's strike. The thin fingers came away from the writhing mass of flesh with his partner's other eye. He crushed it, then scraped the remains onto the blade of his shovel.

"We should gather up our dead and depart before any more of Mister Crump's parts get restless," Branch said.

He crammed his fellow grave robber into the sack and tied it off with his gallows rope while Holt used the candles to set fire to what remained of the thing that had been Cindy Reisbig. If anything survived the fire, the graveyard's caretaker knew not to investigate too closely. Branch and Crump had made the Resurrection Cemetery their secret home in Chicago for more than a decade, and the arcane symbols and charred flesh that might be discovered in the tomb were nothing compared to the other horrible things they'd left in their wake over the years.

"You're going to have to settle up with Doctor Grimm for the work he'll need to do to make Crump right again," Branch noted after they'd filled in the empty grave and he and Holt were crossing the moonlit cemetery. He carried the massive bulk of his partner casually, as if he weighed no more than the empty sack. "Well, as right as he can be made, anyway."

"Of course," Holt replied. "I always pay my debts. At least I got the information I was looking for. The syndicate is probably behind this madness."

"Gangsters?" Branch asked. For the first time that evening the resurrection man seemed surprised. "You think those blithering imbeciles Moran or Capone are capable of conjuring monsters?"

"No, not them. The syndicate behind the comic strip. The thing that came out of the radio took the decoder the girl had. That's the key, and that's part of their business."

"I've never trusted those who pander to the masses with picture books. They were a bad idea when that lout Pfister first used movable type to print his Paupers' Bibles back in Bamberg. They're a bad idea now." Branch shook his head. "Still, Crump will be disappointed if you have to stop them from publishing. He rather enjoys the *All-American Andy* strip. When the child gets into danger, it makes him laugh almost as much as the comics where the mouse brains the cat with a brick."

\* \* \*

Ib Ellid never intended to go legit. He'd come to Chicago ready to make a name for himself with one or another of the gangs carving up the city and then settle into a long and profitable career on the wrong side of the law. He tried bootlegging, numbers running, even a brief stint as hired muscle for a protection racket out in Stickney. During those grim years, he was fortunate enough to avoid the bloody fates that claimed so many of his colleagues and smart enough to recognize that this good luck would not last forever, particularly the way the turf wars were heating up. So he got into comics.

Ellid couldn't draw. He couldn't tell a story to save his sainted mother's life. What he could do is spot a sweet racket, and that description certainly applied to the job of comics syndicate owner. All day long, would-be geniuses pitched him what they imagined to be the next *Katzenjammer Kids* or *Barney Google*. Sometimes, it turned out, they were right. He contracted the best, ensnaring the rights to these gems in legal red tape in return for a promise to hawk them to papers across the country. Since the dailies only bought from the syndicates, the artists had to deal with him, as did the toy and kiddie book and moving picture companies who wanted to use the characters from one of his strips. In a lot of ways, running a syndicate was like selling beer to speakeasies in a territory controlled by your mob, only no one ended up floating face-down in a canal when a transaction got messy.

Not that he wasn't sometimes tempted to fall back on old business methods when dealing with the artists. They were an odd lot, particularly the creator of *All-American Andy*. In his former line of work, Ellid had met George Moran a time or two, and he was convinced that Bramwell Platt could give the unhinged gangster a run for the nickname "Bugs."

"I don't care what you want," Platt said. His quiet voice somehow made Ellid's cavernous office seem cramped. "Our contract clearly states that I have approval for any publicity centered upon me or my ward, and I don't approve of this proposal."

It wasn't the passion of Platt's declarations that Ellid found disturbing, but the lack of any passion in them at all. Arguing with the man was like debating a statue. The dark glasses the artist constantly wore gave that impression of inhumanity even more weight. Ellid stared into those black circles and felt his anger boil up.

"These national magazine interviews could help us push *All-American Andy* over the top," he snarled. "The property could be bigger than Felix the Cat, for Christ's sake. I already got us the radio show on WGN, didn't I? And the Liberty Bar deal? I pay you what you're promised every month. I ain't even skimming!" He slammed a fist down onto his desk, toppling two stuffed Paddy bears and scattering a box of Andy pin-backs. "But you still give me the business about some lousy puffery! We do these and I can get us a deal for animated shorts from the guy who did the Laugh-O-Gram and Alice series!"

"You'll have to secure that deal without the press putting me or Andrew on display like sideshow attractions. We are nothing. Show them the strip. The work is all that matters."

Ellid knew that when Platt uttered those words, the conversation was over. It was as much a catch phrase as "Right is right" or any of the various Red-bashing dictums Platt was always working into his strips. There was just no getting past it.

"Well, you've just guaranteed that the next artist to sign with me will get a worse deal than the one you got," Ellid grumbled by way of a strategic retreat. "I hope you're happy. Your refusal to play ball has made it bad for everyone else."

"Everyone else is not my concern," Platt said and calmly rose to leave.

"From the way you dress, you're not even your own concern," Ellid snapped as the artist crossed the office. "You look like you rolled a hobo for those clothes."

"I know my worth and the value of my success," Platt replied. To emphasize his point he grabbed a handful of cloth, further wrinkling his already creased and baggy suit. "I'm not so insecure that I have to display that success for others."

"You was a washed-up gag writer when I signed you, Platt. Sure, you made up *All-American Andy*, but you would be nowhere without my help. Nowhere! Your ledgers would be as blank as the eyes of your creepy little drawings!"

Platt unceremoniously turned his back on Ellid. The former gangster briefly considered going for the gun in his desk drawer as the cartoonist exited to the hallway. Instead, he waited a moment and then barked for the yegg lurking in the file storage closet off the main office.

Sam "Soupy" Fitzroy slouched into the room and, hands thrust deep in his pockets, awaited his employer's orders. He was known throughout Chicago as a top-notch second-story man and safe-cracker, despite the botched bank job up in Milwaukee at the start of his career that had left him so horribly scarred. The more discreet of his fellow mobsters described his face as perpetually melting, as if the flesh were dripping off the skull on the right side. The deformity made him hard to look at and harder still to talk to. His speech possessed the same bubbling, liquid quality as his skin. At least that's how those few fellow thugs, who had supposedly heard him speak, described his voice. But he was good at his work; that was all that mattered to Ellid.

Fitzroy nodded or shook his head at the appropriate times as the syndicate boss stalked around his office, outlining the job he wanted done. Since Platt didn't believe in banks—he considered them part of some vast government conspiracy to make people less self-reliant—his copy of the syndication contract was hidden somewhere in his home in Cicero. Fitzroy was to break into the house, find the contract, and replace it with a slightly modified version that contained all the loopholes necessary to allow Ellid to take control of the press approvals and even net a few more bucks off each transaction, just to cover the grief the artist had caused him.

Ellid held the phony contract out to the thief. "You got all that? We clear?"

He didn't look Fitzroy in the eye as he spoke. No one ever did.

Fitzroy nodded and took the contract in his gloved hands. Then he gestured for the first half of his sizable payment. He counted the money before uttering, "We're clear," in his unsettling voice. The deal was sealed.

Ellid had no inclination to watch the scarred man leave his office, let alone trail him as he made his way from the Rogers Building on Michigan to a far less desirable neighborhood across town. That was just as Tristram Holt had expected as he slunk into a dive in the Levee to wait for night to descend upon the city. Soupy Fitzroy had been one of his first creations after the attempt on his life and regularly proved the most useful for gathering information about Chicago's underworld. His deformities made him memorable enough that he could cobble together an oversized reputation with ease—take part in a few successful heists, attach himself through rumor to three times that many felonious triumphs and he was set. No one seemed to catch on that his employers eventually got pinched for other seemingly unrelated crimes or, worse, fell afoul of the Corpse. Such were the perils of criminal enterprise in the Windy City.

Fitzroy's hideousness also guaranteed that no one ever looked at him too closely. Holt's days on stage with Northwestern's college dramatics society had given him a working knowledge of stage makeup and costuming, but with the deformed yegg, his artistry

*James Lowder*

only had to be good enough to repulse, not consistent enough to hold up under careful scrutiny.

So it was as Soupy Fitzroy that Holt had wormed his way into Ib Ellid's inner circle, hoping to uncover any evidence of the syndicate boss's involvement in the attacks against Cindy Reisbig and the half-dozen other orphan children whose eyes had been stolen. He came up empty. Ellid, like the police and the papers, had yet to even connect the murders to the radio show or the decoders, let alone conclude, as Holt had after first learning of them, that the assaults were more likely than not supernatural in origin. He'd seen enough of the strangeness plaguing the city since he hauled his poisoned and bullet-riddled body out of the Chicago River to recognize the uncanny when he saw it.

It was not as Soupy Fitzroy but as the Corpse that Holt left his Levee hideout just before midnight. He found it easy enough to slip between identities now, and the Scourge of Evil seemed the most appropriate for the confrontation he felt was coming. He skulked through the nighttime shadows shrouding the city, his cloak fluttering raggedly behind him like the taunting ghosts of his dead foes. He carried Ellid's fake contract with him, and a satchel filled with an assortment of weapons and the other tools of his dark trade.

The Platt house itself was, at first glance, as unassuming as its owner. It was a modest two-story on a quiet side street, a little shabby, but not decrepit by any means. Hardly the home of an artist raking in thousands from his work, but a perfect retreat for someone who wished to blend in with the gentile scruffiness of the neighborhood.

Only when Holt crept around to the back did he see anything that he would not have found repeated a dozen times over on any of the nearby streets. Where other homes might have boasted a screened-in porch looking out over the fenced backyard, Platt's had a cage. As Holt moved closer, the bear cub inhabiting the enclosure snuffled loudly. Platt had purchased the bear from a bankrupt petting zoo, and it was the beast's interaction with his adopted son that reportedly inspired him to create *All-American Andy*. But since then, Platt had allowed no pictures to be taken of the pair, or of his home, or of himself.

Holt gave the cage a wide berth and chose to slip inside through a side window blocked from the main road by a thick hedgerow. He found himself in Platt's workroom, a sizable studio with two drawing tables, shelves of neatly arranged art supplies, stacks of paper and, in one corner, a small safe. Holt made short work of the lock without resorting to the nitroglycerine "soup" he carried with him for tougher safecracking jobs. Inside lay orderly stacks of money, boxes of gold coins, and not one, but three contracts. Ellid's syndication deal was the only one written in ink.

In the moonlight streaming through the open window, Holt skimmed the other two contracts. He read about the gifts Platt and his ward were to receive, even how they were to be collected and delivered, all set down in precise legalese. As he did, the bear began yowling piteously. A flashlight beam pierced the darkness on the upper floor, and a red-headed young boy in a nightshirt followed it down the stairs. He moved tentatively, right hand gripping the banister tightly with each cautious step.

"Are you okay, Paddy? It's not any of them crumbum gangsters come to kidnap you again, is it?"

Holt peered cautiously around the doorjamb of the studio and watched the boy move off into the kitchen to open the interior cage door and allow the bear to trundle inside. The beast made happy, snuffling sounds and rubbed up against the child, who laughed brightly.

"I wish I could see you better," the boy said, "but we'll fix that again soon. Right, pal?"

"We have other business to take care of first," said Bramwell Platt in his soft, flat voice from the top of the stairs. He had hastily dressed and looked even more the transient for it. He was, for once, without his dark glasses. "We have a spy in our midst. A filthy commie, maybe."

*James Lowder*

Tristram Holt stepped into the living room as Platt turned on the light, and Andy returned from the kitchen, the little bear in tow.

"I'm here to terminate these contracts," Holt said. He held up the two documents penned in blood and scribed on what appeared to be sheets of human flesh. "Or, rather, to tell you that there are no contracts. You're being duped."

"We're no dupes, mister," Andy said hotly. He squinted at Holt through eyes that had once belonged to Cindy Reisbig. Their irises were fading, just like all the other stolen eyes had done. Eventually, the boy would be returned to near-blindness.

"What did it offer?" Holt asked Andy. "The return of your eyesight? And you," he said, pointing to Platt. "Success with your art? And it pretended to create formal agreements written in blood, like the ones in the old stories about deals with the Devil. It even taunted you with loopholes—your stolen eyes fading and needing to be replaced, or the press hounding you for publicity when all you wanted was to be left alone to work."

He gripped the two contracts tightly and tore them in two.

Platt and his ward gasped, but the sound was drowned out by the horrible growl of the bear. It reared up on its hind feet—and then continued to grow. It expanded until it was twice the size of the boy, a monstrous, ursine thing wearing a cap and an appalling grin that made Holt think of Mister Branch.

"Go on," it said in a heavy Irish brogue. "Make a joke about knockin' the stuffin' outta me. You know you want to, boyo."

"I won't play your games," said Holt. "Show yourself."

The thing lost its bear form and became a central stalk of darkness with twisted limbs of mist reaching upward. Bursts of ichor sprouted from the branches, then wilted and reformed, like the leaves on a ghastly and growing gallows tree, familiar to Holt from his nightmares. That was how the thing had appeared to him all those months ago, on the night he realized that he was going to survive the tortures Drucci's men had inflicted upon him. He lay shivering in a burned-out warehouse, dreaming of revenge, hungering for it, when the thing came to him. It promised him power and filled his mind with visions of endless vengeance upon those who had wronged him and all who preyed upon the innocents in the city. His city.

*As with you, I merely offered them their fondest desires.* The voice was inside Holt's head, seductive, comforting. He wondered for an instant if it had ever truly left, and shivered at the realization. *They were gracious enough to accept my offer. Unlike you.*

"Just destroy him and be done with it," Platt said. Even now his words were bloodless.

"Yeah," Andy said. "Even with these broken eyes I can see he's just some guy dressed up to scare people."

Holt drew his twin automatics. He looked at Platt and the little boy, could see the desire on their faces, knew that others would pay the price if he let them go. They'd made their choices, and they didn't care who suffered to fulfill their desires. But he knew their temptations, too. He'd been in their place himself, not so long ago.

Tristram Holt gripped the pistols tighter and hesitated.

The Corpse pulled the triggers.

The shreds of the hell-born contracts had vanished even before the two bodies hit the floor, neat little bullet holes in the centers of their foreheads. The darkness dissipated more slowly. It retreated to the corners of the room to watch as the Corpse closed up the safe. He left the original contract in place. Ellid had no need of the revised publicity clauses now, and Soupy Fitzroy would claim to have spotted the Corpse casing the house before wisely abandoning the job. The last of the darkness lingered, teasing strands that wound around the Corpse's arm as he reached down to cut off Bramwell Platt's right hand—a gift for Doctor Grimm to use in rebuilding Mister Crump. The good doctor would have to find the other parts on his own. The Corpse had had enough of stolen eyes for a lifetime.

Before he left the shabby little house in Cicero, the crime-fighter withdrew a silver tube from his jacket and poured maggots onto his victims—the mark of the Corpse. This time, though, they also marked a grave, the true final resting place of Tristram Holt.

In the instant before they died, both Platt and little Andy, even with his broken vision, had recognized that their assassin was not the former assistant district attorney. The dead man's visage and the ragged clothes—the bloody, bullet-torn jacket and the tattered cloak that fluttered like torn wings—were no longer just a disguise. And no matter what face he might pretend to hide behind now, it would not be Tristram Holt but the Corpse who stalked the streets of Chicago, bringing doom to the lawless and the damned.

# About James Lowder

James Lowder has worked extensively on both sides of the editorial blotter. As a writer his publications include the bestselling, widely translated dark fantasy novels *Prince of Lies* and *Knight of the Black Rose*, short fiction for such anthologies as *Shadows Over Baker Street* and *Sojourn: An Anthology of Speculative Fiction*, and comic book scripts for DC, Image, Moonstone and Desperado.

As an editor he's directed novel lines or series for both large and small publishing houses, and has helmed more than a dozen critically acclaimed anthologies, including *Madness on the Orient Express, Hobby Games: The 100 Best,* and the Books of Flesh zombie trilogy. His work has received five Origins Awards and an ENnie Award, and he has been a finalist for the International Horror Guild Award and the Bram Stoker Award®.

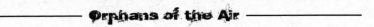

# Party
# Monster

## Charles Austin Muir

**S**o Big Joe wants me to write my confession. The fucked-up things I did and why I did them. I wonder how I'm supposed to disappear if his scheme works.

He thinks he's marching to Calvary. I say he's throwing himself at the mercy of thugs in a Dashiell Hammett novel made into a movie by Quentin Tarantino. Maybe we're both right.

In case he fails, I draw this:

The letters, TSMYWLGFHPC, taken from the statement, ITIS-MYWILLTOGETOUTOFTHISPLACE, rearranged to form a sigil, a symbol expressing my wish to escape.

Just to be safe, I'll add this:

Power to conjure weapons.

And this:

Superhuman strength.

Sigils are like search terms for the Google of the subconscious. The subconscious thinks in signs and images, so the terms must be scrambled to be understood.

The problem is how to activate the sigils, how to hit the SEARCH button. Maybe—because I'm rooting for Big Joe and because I'm terrified of Chuck and his murder monkeys—my desire will be strong enough.

So far Google is not telling me how to get out of this madhouse. Enough. Time to write.

Wait.

ITISMYWILLTOTELLTHISINSTREAMOFCONSCIOUSNESS. My hand is cramping and I've got a lot to confess.

\* \* \*

I can write with my mind now. Maybe I'm fooling myself, but it feels nice talking inside my head and pretending you hear me.

So much time is spent like this, daydreaming through our mouths in front of people. You and I are at a party, slightly drunk, and I'm telling you my life story to fill the unknowable space between us.

There is nothing worse than the unsaid, which is why we got drunk in the first place: to make it easier to speak over it, through it. I call this unsaid negative space. Negative space is how all stories begin, from a sense of urgency.

So even though I'm coughing up blood and smell like a Hell's Angels jacket, I'm going to tell my life story calmly and let Google ponder how to free me.

My story starts with Angie.

My wife.

We met at a bar through a mutual friend. She told me she was a fashion editor's assistant but wished she could be an artist. She thought it a cruel joke to be given large hands — "E.T. hands," she called them — and no faculty for teasing shapes from raw stuff. She thought I was an artist because I was broke and meditated on artsy topics like negative space — how little I knew then. She tended to date artists. Before me, she'd never married one.

Angie was Maria Panera, the redo. I met Maria in seventh grade. We went to different schools but shared the same bus stop. After a few weeks I convinced her to see a movie with me. An hour into the movie I was still in the lobby, adjusting my tie and rehearsing what to say if she finally appeared. *Conan the Destroyer* is not only an awful film, it reminds me of being stood up by a ravishing, dark-haired, twelve-year-old girl.

Soon after that, a classmate named Alex Gilroy started dating Maria. He spread a rumor — not true, it turned out — that she told him I was a scumbag. One day I stalked Alex on my bike and knocked him out with a rock I stole from an old lady's garden. He never knew what hit him. When he came to school the next day he had stitches on the back of his head. "I fought off a homeless man who beat me with a hammer," he told everybody. He milked his yarn for weeks. The penance for my perfect crime was a tic under my right eye that bothered me off and on for a year.

My point with these anecdotes is that Angie showed up for the movie. She let me be a winner in my revised adolescent love story. Angie called herself The Hot Mess Express. She looked like a pint-sized supermodel and gulped down Moscow Mules and sangrias like Gatorade, but she supported me and let me lie in bed next to her. I would walk behind her just so I could catch up to her and imagine she was meeting me. I even made her watch *Conan the Destroyer*.

Jesus, Big Joe, what the hell are they doing to you?

Where was I?

The morgue.

With a police officer at my side, I looked at my dead wife under a sheet. It was like being in an episode of *CSI*, only I didn't know my lines. I just stared at her face, and when the finality of that vision sank in I wanted to kiss her, deeply. Taste the cold, chocolaty-marshmallow flavor of our kiss the night we became engaged. Holding her hand instead, I felt a pang in my groin for the Angie I would never touch again. My only consolation—a false one, maybe—was that she did not appear to have suffered.

For weeks I brooded over the things left unsaid between us because some hit-and-run driver let her die in a ditch.

After I got the autopsy results, I drew this sigil:

ITISMYWILLTOCATCHWHODIDTHIS.

Because whoever struck Angie had killed twice.

\* \* \*

I know the exact moment I fell in love with her. It was when she told me her dream job would be to bottle-feed baby gorillas in a wildlife preserve. "Baby gorillas equal magic," she said. In her heart, Angie was a magician, not an artist.

She learned about sigils from a tattoo artist she'd dated. On her left arm was a sigil for Azazel. "He was an angel who taught people to make cosmetics and weapons," she said. "As a result, God cast him out of Heaven. Yet God made things so that some of His children can only survive by using cosmetics *as* weapons. Now these," she pointed at the symbols on her right arm, "stand for love, bliss and comfort. With those three gifts no one would ever need to deceive or harm another living being. Azazel would have to find something else to teach us."

It was like having "Shadow" tattooed on one side and "Light" on the other. A kind of meta-sigil expressing her dual nature. Unfortunately, Angie powered her sigils with alcohol.

When Angie was drunk she saw baby gorillas everywhere, and her love ignited a flame in her chest. A fire that didn't burn but purified, touching every cell in her body. It became too big to hold, so she gave it to the trees and the earth and the flowers and the animals. As it grew, she gave it also to the wind and the rain and the oceans and the moon and the sun and the stars. After fifteen drinks she would go wandering, feeling one with the sidewalk and the weeds and the side of the road where she would pass out or throw up or both. Even her liver radiated loving heat, cleansed by her release from the Toltec dream of Hell, a nine-to-five merry-go-round of powder and rouge. "No one loves me unless I'm drunk," she told me.

Having recovered her from so many random places, I've earned the right to be snarky.

I loved Angie because she never gave up searching for magic. It just had to come with a label. When the label wasn't on a bottle she found it elsewhere. During her sober periods she ordered shoes online.

It wasn't until after the autopsy that I connected my wife with my biological mother. Thinking about the secret Angie had carried inside her, I imagined my own experience in the womb.

My fetal instinct wants to comfort the one who sustains me. Sensing I've somehow caused her distress, I form an all-consuming urge to help the one on whom so much depends. I feel an event build between us. We're going to create something wonderful together, a light show kicking off a Great Adventure. The light show goes off as expected, but my partner vanishes in the afterimage. Suddenly, I'm stranded in a world of alien food and expedited touch.

I'm left with a mystery. What happened to the person I lived inside, my partner in the Great Adventure? But new faces fill the days, those of my new family. I acquire a name, a role, an identity. I develop a narrative of where I came from. I learn the words to give comfort but forget who originally needed it. Over time my hormones dream new partners into place: Who becomes Maria. Maria becomes Angie. Beautiful, booze-enchanted Angie.

Angie becomes Mom the redo.

Like my mother, so much remained a mystery. Why hadn't Angie told me she was five weeks pregnant?

She had let me argue with her about a man she'd been texting. She had chewed me out for looking at her phone. All the while, there was magic inside her, ruined because she drove off, got soused and wandered around an old logging road at two in the morning.

After the autopsy her sister emailed me. She hoped I wouldn't tell many people about the pregnancy. It would spare the family a lot of questions. I agreed because I didn't want to talk about it anyway. I was angry at Angie for telling her sister she was pregnant, but not me. She'd had a week to tell me. Her period ran like clockwork.

*Charles Austin Muir*

As if to bring Angie back with her own magic, I drank heavily. I kept a fifth of Jack at my desk. I let a casual porn habit become an obsession with finding Angie redoes on the Internet. Angie hated porn.

One day, while looking for tax receipts, she found some print-outs—relics from my early web-surfing days—in an unmarked folder. Grainy headshots of haggard women bubble-wrapped in sperm. I'd forgotten about them until she thrust the stack at me.

"Take a good look," she said. "Is this what you want? Is this what you see when you touch me?"

Though the images seemed vile in Angie's hands, many were screen captures of videos no different from those I watched on her laptop. Rather than mourn Angie I clicked on her, chasing her electric spirit across the Internet, seeking her in the dark, sweaty corridors of bandwidth. During those lonely séances it never occurred to me that I might come in contact with something other than a webcam girl with Angie's face. But one morning the power went out and the monitor became a black mirror. There I was, dead-eyed, soulless, a serial killer staring back from the negative space of my addiction.

From then on that face haunted me behind my web browser, Dorian Gray's portrait in the age of YouPorn. He was the search history I couldn't erase, my unfiltered selfie that summed up who I was becoming as I consumed my wife's look-alikes, the grimacing successors of my porn printouts.

My friend Olin told me to stop wallowing. "You've got to focus, man. The story. Stick to your story." But I couldn't. I'd lost the urgency. I'd written 20,000 words of a novel about a sex-hungry coven and made Angie the head witch. It seemed so trivial now.

I quit writing. I even quit porn-surfing and made the couch my home.

Olin visited less and less. A cyber-expert for the NSA, he had bigger things to do besides listen to me blame myself for arguing with Angie and launching her on another bender.

When he saw me, I was either liquored up and weepy or in deep communion with my television—my portal into the world of Big Joe.

* * *

Sometimes I watched *Joe Durrenmatt, Crusader of Justice* on my writing breaks. The plots were always the same. An innocent person is convicted of murder. A friend or relative convinces attorney Joe Durrenmatt—"Big Joe," as his staff calls him—to defend the accused in court. Big Joe sniffs around, forms a theory about the killer. He doesn't tell police but exposes the murderer on the witness stand during cross-examination.

Then Angie died, and the show filled a void in me. Those formulaic stories gave me the justice I needed. They took the raw, unsaid stuff of my dead marriage and sculpted it into an image of infallibility and order. When Big Joe unmasked a murderer, it was like watching God hurl a lightning bolt at an idol. His black eyes and sepulchral voice forced even the toughest criminals to tell the truth.

Big Joe equaled magic. But unlike Angie's baby gorillas, I didn't require a gallon of liquor to find him.

When I saw the series was available on my Internet streaming media service, I powered through all nine seasons. Then I watched them all over again. I watched Big Joe gain weight, lose weight, gain more weight. I watched him change styles, from flannel suit to leisure suit. I watched him put away criminal after criminal, imagining each as the scumbag who killed Angie.

In the black-and-white world of *Joe Durrenmatt, Crusader of Justice*, everything that needed to be said was said, and everyone who needed to be caught was caught.

I wanted to be there.

For a moment, I was.

At first I thought my TV was crapping out. The picture warped as if reflected in a funhouse mirror. Pieces of Big Joe separated and fused into other people and objects. The rearranged patterns formed animated abstractions, as if the ghost of Picasso were de-constructing *Joe Durrenmatt, Crusader of Justice*. The swirling geom-etry sucked the room into my TV screen, like a mouth drawing in a huge breath. Sound and speech from both sides of reality tumbled into the suctioning spiral. Finally, everything around me bled into an immense funnel and my fingers elongated, stretching toward the opening like a parody of Angie's in a psychedelic cartoon.

Then the chaos blinked, and a room materialized in black and white.

"Tell me."

I wanted to tell Big Joe how I knocked out Alex Gilroy in seventh grade.

Instead, I gaped at him in silence.

I was still gaping when I snapped back to reality in my living room.

"Tell me how I can help you," he said to a woman sitting where I had been moments before.

After that night, I couldn't enjoy *Joe Durrenmatt, Crusader of Justice*.

A TV show couldn't compete with my fleeting experience. I felt like I'd been there, sitting at a desk with Big Joe. How had it happened?

Then, after a few weeks, it hit me. Maybe the TV images were a sigil. I'd stared at them for so long that my brain got tired of in-terpreting them. Because I wanted it so badly, "It is my will to live in the world of *Joe Durrenmatt, Crusader of Justice*" started a Google search in my subconscious.

My subconscious transported me into an imaginary realm based on the TV show.

Could it send me back again? Could I lose myself in an illusion, like the people in *The Matrix*?

Maybe if I pulled another marathon, I thought, a longer one, I could break down the mental barriers that stood between me and the Joe Durrenmatrix.

So I did. I watched twenty-nine hours of *Joe Durrenmatt, Crusader of Justice*.

For a moment, I worried that my TV really was crapping out. Only for a moment.

\* \* \*

So I'm talking to myself, even if you hear me. You are me. All this is in my mind.

And if you think I don't know about *Pleasantville*, the movie where Tobey Maguire and Reese Witherspoon get caught in a 1950s sitcom via a magical remote control and transform the repressed, black-and-white town of the same name into a place of desire and color, you're wrong.

But this isn't Pleasantville.

It's the Joe Durrenmatrix.

I know I'm dreaming. I know my subconscious has constructed this simulation of a TV show to work out a personal problem. I know it's only my mind that traps me here, intent on teaching me something about myself, something profound and rooted in the nature of suffering.

All this could have been avoided if I'd allowed myself to grieve for my dead wife.

But in a way, I was grieving. Dreaming myself into Big Joe's world was my attempt to move past my guilt. The Joe Durrenmatrix was a language of symbols for understanding our marriage, giving its lack of resolution a new story.

There was so much to take in at first. Rain. Horns. Rude pedestrians. Fifty-cent hamburgers and soda-fountain milkshakes. Like being in a foreign city in a foreign time. Annoyances like wet clothes, indigestion and brain freeze showed how deeply I'd embedded myself in illusion.

But I quickly discovered my subconscious had other plans besides letting me play in dreamland. My being here fit into a larger design. My name was still Jason, but I had a role to play. I was Big Joe's personal assistant. I looked like Tommy Kirk and spoke like

Wally Cleaver, the epitome of good grooming. Because my mind had no frame of reference for my character—he didn't exist in the show—my interactions with co-workers sounded wooden, my fellow dream actors lost in their parts.

Still, the staginess of events suggested we supported a storyline building toward a powerful revelation. We were in a whodunit directed by the divine presence in me, and the divine spoke through Joe Durrenmatt.

I pulled him aside one day. I still wanted to tell him about Alex Gilroy. I didn't know why, but I sensed a link between the mystery and my personal contribution to the compendium of wicked acts stored in Big Joe's mind. He nodded and drew me behind a curtain. We were in the apartment of someone we had come to question.

Even in black and white, the sight of someone whose intestines had been ripped out with a Bowie knife was a ghastly one.

"Actually, I've been meaning to talk to you, Jason," Big Joe said.

"About what, sir?" I asked.

"My daughter. You...intend to marry her?"

A rosy glow colorized his cheeks.

"Tomorrow, sir. With your permission, I aim to propose to her tomorrow."

So that was the revelation, I thought. The discovery of murder, the stilted conversation, the absurdity of discussing nuptials near a mutilated corpse. These were contrivances of the divine presence speaking to me through the sepulchral voice of Joe Durrenmatt.

I was to marry his daughter.

Anjanette.

Or, Angie the redo.

I almost cried out the first time I saw her. I thought my dead wife had entered Big Joe's office. She was Angie with a pixie haircut. Our history together came to me in a flash. We had been dating for two years. We went on Sunday picnics. I modeled for her sculptures. She didn't have tattoos but didn't need them. Anjanette was Angie's "Light" sigils personified.

After that initial shock, I fell in love with Anjanette. She was what Angie could have been if she'd believed in herself. She didn't need to drink to convince herself she deserved to be loved. Her beauty grew out of inner harmony, not in accordance with the fashion industry. Because of that, she could tease shapes from raw stuff. From Anjanette's "E.T. hands" flowed the music of the earth.

I marveled at my subconscious for giving me this renewed Angie. In doing so, I purified myself because we mirrored each other. We formed a ground of creation in which she loved what she made, and I loved her without the guilt of being an unwanted child. We weren't bound by need, we were free. And that's what I wanted, I guessed, at the core of this whole drama—to experience what it would feel like for us to love each other unconditionally. Through Big Joe, my god power told me this was why I was dreaming this dream. To rewrite our marriage. To enjoy the Great Adventure I had been denied at birth.

So we spoke no more about wedding plans in the dead man's apartment. Big Joe patted my shoulder and it was back to business. We both forgot I had meant to talk to him.

That night I lay wide awake, worried about waking in the real world. I wanted to stay in dreamland forever. I would have gladly died or slipped into a coma as long as I spent my last hours with Anjanette in a dream of timeless love.

If I died, no one would miss me. My adoptive parents were dead. Angie's family hated me. Except for Olin, all my friends were the social network kind.

What a disappointment I must be to him, I thought. He'd invested so much in me. After Angie's death, Olin took over the bills and mortgage. He pushed me to finish my novel. "The story, man," he kept saying. "The story will get you through this."

I remembered how he looked at me when I told him the autopsy results, like a father impressed by his child's progress report. He thought I'd handled the news well because I was following his advice. The more he checked on me though, the more he saw the truth.

I could tell Olin wanted to control me like he controlled the nation's flow of information.

Looking back, I wish he could have.

\* \* \*

When I proposed to Angie, we were staying at the beach. She spoon-fed us Ben & Jerry's ice cream while we snuggled in bed watching a horror movie. She thought I was messing with her until she slipped on the ring and studied herself in the mirror.

It was her mirror image I looked at now, under an equestrian statue by the light of a full moon.

We had the park to ourselves. The park where we took our Sunday picnics. Anjanette wore a head scarf and parka to fight off the chill. She didn't kiss hungrily like Angie, but as if tracing an arcane emotion on my tongue.

We separated. She looked at me curiously. I reached for the ring in my pocket. A car drove past us on the embankment behind me. Its high beams slugged across Anjanette's face. At the same time, the skin under my right eye twitched. I turned to hide it from her.

I pocketed the ring. I couldn't think of a worse time for my old tic to come back, the one that started after I knocked out Alex Gilroy. I wondered if it was connected to my compulsion to tell Big Joe about my adolescent misdeed. What could a thirty-one-year-old crime have to do with the Great Adventure?

Anjanette strained to see me through the afterimage on her eyes.

Her father's voice echoed inside my head. *Tell me. Tell me.*

I touched the incriminating flesh. What was my tic telling me?

Anjanette seemed as surprised as I was when the words, "And now back to you, Bob," trumpeted from my throat.

My voice rang like a radio deejay's in a cathedral. In the moonlight, Anjanette's face went bone-white. I drove my fist into her solar plexus, doubling her over and knocking her into the statue's plinth. I smote her head against the concrete base. Then I threw her facedown on the ground.

Blood darkened the back of her head scarf. Her "E.T. hands" shaped lumps of pain in the dirt bordering the path. My voice boomed. "Police are still chasing leads in the brutal slaying of a woman in the Wentworth District."

I kicked Anjanette in the ribs.

"Live at the scene is correspondent Steve Dunthorpe. What can you tell us, Steve?"

I turned her over and dragged her to a bamboo stand.

"Bob, I'm standing at the spot where twenty-nine-year-old Anjanette Durrenmatt was viciously assaulted and murdered."

I hiked up her skirt and spread her knees apart.

"The daughter of defense lawyer Joe Durrenmatt, this young woman was a promising sculptor before the fateful night that would end her life."

I fought off the nails slashing at my face.

"The killer raped her—"

She kneed me in the balls.

"Correction, the killer punched her repeatedly and then gouged out her eyes."

Anjanette's screams pounded into me like vibrations of a brutal orgasm. My thumbs smeared with her eyeball fluids, I seized her throat. I had to re-grip because of the blood and sweat on my hands.

Red tears colorized her cheeks.

I slipped off her heels and chucked them into the bamboo.

"Police are searching for a man she was seen with earlier this evening."

Only the moon saw me leaving the park.

"This just in. A second murder has been confirmed."

I walked up to a transient sleeping in a doorway.

"Police say the man was beaten by an unknown assailant, then left in a street near the park where Durrenmatt's body was discovered."

A bicyclist saw me dragging the smelly corpse. I chased him down.

"Yet another body has been found. A teenage cyclist died of blunt force trauma to the head."

Dead storefront windows watched me take off on the kid's bike.

"We've just received word of a fourth victim."

An old lady stepped onto her front porch.

"An elderly woman has died of deep wounds to her chest and abdomen that appear to have been inflicted with a garden hoe."

I swung the hoe at her cat, too, but Kitty scurried under a car.

I coasted into the field of an elementary school. Two young lovers sitting near the playground watched me dismount. The boy got to his feet. He was big, over six feet. He dodged my swing and kicked me. I stumbled back and fell on my bike. As I lay on the crossbar, he punched me in the face repeatedly. I blocked one of his blows and twisted free, then pinned him to the ground.

I don't remember much after that, except that when I heard the girl's footfalls on blacktop I spat out a chunk of the boy's face and gave chase. Catching her near a stairwell, I spun her around and shoved her over the rail. She bounced off brick wall, then tumbled into shadow. A glowing exit sign at the bottom lit up a sandaled foot.

"Two teenagers were slain outside an elementary school."

Around the corner I came to a movie theater.

I parked the bike and shot the ticket girl in the face. A packed house was watching Elvis Presley. Elvis was singing to a puppet that he didn't have a wooden heart. I fired my gun into the crowd. Screams triggered a stampede for the exits.

After shooting several runners, I pocketed the gun and blended with the fleeing moviegoers.

Out in the parking lot, people sobbed and hugged.

"We've just received news of a shooting at the Oldmark Theater," I said. "The killer is armed and dangerous. Repeat. Armed and dangerous."

Sirens wailing nearby, I set off on foot.

Tears stung my eyes. I felt trapped in a serial killer's psyche. I felt apart from him and yet one with him, two minds in one body prowling the streets for more victims. Why would my subconscious do this to me? What was it trying to teach me? Why would it make me shed the blood of innocents?

Why would it make me kill the woman I loved?

I tried to convince myself I hadn't caused real suffering. What happened here was an illusion, it did not belong to space-time.

But I had felt pain here, and if these people were figments of my imaginings of pain, then I was hurting through them. I saw their faces, heard their screams, felt Anjanette's terror and agony beneath my fingers. Only a little while ago we were to embark on our Great Adventure. I would have chosen death over reality to rewrite history with her. Now all I wanted was to return to consciousness.

Wake up!

But I couldn't. I was a wooden puppet dancing to the divine presence singing through Elvis Presley. I danced into a cul-de-sac toward the door of a blue house. From the darkened pane my tear-streaked face grinned back at me, an omen of Damien-like proportions in the mirror that never lies.

I realized who had made my dream a nightmare. It was the thing that watched me behind my web browser when I surfed for porn on the Internet. The thing that smiled when I rode my bike behind Alex Gilroy, clutching a rock. The thing that existed before words and rules were poured into me, before I became Jason.

The thing that was not me, Not Jason.

The door was unlocked.

I entered a vestibule. White walls, red carpet. Red, like Anjanette's tears. Not Jason looked at me from the hallway mirror. I wanted to blast his grinning, twitchy face with the gun he had magicked from Anjanette's engagement ring.

Instead I climbed a staircase and shot the woman sleeping in the nearest bedroom.

"The killing spree continues."

*Charles Austin Muir*

I moved on to the room at the end of the hall.

Anjanette had prevented me from raping her, but the girl blinking at me under a hanging mobile of Escher's *Drawing Hands* looked too young, too timid, to keep me from dancing to Not Jason's strings.

I tried to convince her I didn't have a wooden heart.

Not Jason giggled in the girl's dressing mirror.

"I am, however, getting wood," I said.

I unzipped my pants.

"Notice something?" I paced before the foot of her bed. "Everything is in color now. Like in that movie, *Pleasantville*. Roses are red. Teardrops are red. Your sheets will be red. Guess I don't need this anymore. Don't even think about it." She was eyeing the gun I'd placed on the nightstand.

"Or will your sheets be red? Tell me, are you intact?"

The girl started crying.

"Now, that will only make it sweeter—"

The *Drawing Hands* mobile caught my eye again.

I grabbed a permanent marker from the nightstand.

On the wall I drew:

ITISMYWILLTOGETOUTOFTHEJOEDURRENMATRIX.

I fell into a vortex of shapes and colors.

The chaos blinked and a room materialized.

"And now back to you, Bob."

\* \* \*

My head ached. My throat was parched. My clothes were damp with sweat.

I reread Olin's note:

*Dropped by today but you were asleep and I didn't want to disturb you. Peace.*

Peace? He had given me anything but.

He had switched my TV to a twenty-four-hour news station. The droning bulletins must have influenced me subliminally, turned me from Joe Durrenmatt's errand boy into Charles Manson's golem. The latest report concerned a female jogger who had been raped and murdered in a city park. Live at the scene was correspondent Steve Dunthorpe.

I looked around the room at the food cartons, the bottle of Jack. The mail Olin had stacked next to his note on the coffee table. It wasn't fair, I thought. I deserved better than this. I hadn't asked for Angie to be taken away from me. I didn't need scowling, thick-lipped Steve Dunthorpe reminding me, like Mick Jagger, that rape and murder was just a shot away, even in dreamland. For a moment, I wanted to dream myself into the TV and strangle Steve Dunthorpe.

Then I realized that, without my will, the TV had no sigil potential. The magic only worked if I sent a request to my subconscious. How, then, had my dream gone wrong?

A vision flashed before me.

The face I had seen in the mirrors of the blue house.

Not Jason's.

He was why I had wanted to tell Big Joe about Alex Gilroy. My god power hadn't spoken to me through Not Jason, it had tried to warn me about him.

Not Jason was the negative space from which my domestication into society began, at birth. He was my dark half. Our duality transcended space-time. It survived my entry into the projection of desire I called the Joe Durrenmatrix. My opposite drew power from the magical intent supporting my dreamland. I had given my worst enemy the key to paradise.

*Charles Austin Muir*

Not Jason seethed with what Buddhists called "mind monkey": restless, capricious, uncontrollable. He was my pussy-crazed, gun-toting, TV-news-recycling murder monkey.

He had taken Anjanette from me.

I wasn't ready to let her go.

I would take back the Joe Durrenmatrix. I was the stronger of two principles. Not Jason had desire, but Jason had focus. We were like super-humans battling for dominion in the video game of my subconscious. I had the advantage because I understood the programming language. As I had used a sigil to escape, I would use another to control Not Jason.

To be safe, I put on *Joe Durrenmatt, Crusader of Justice* and wrote a note asking Olin to let me sleep and leave the TV where it was.

I waited for Picasso's ghost.

\* \* \*

At first I thought the girl had screamed. I picked up the old-fashioned telephone on the nightstand. My gun was gone.

"Police. We've got you surrounded," the voice said on the other end. "If you haven't touched the girl, we can settle this peacefully."

He said *goil*, not girl.

I slammed the phone down and picked up the permanent marker. Under my escape sigil I drew:

Or, ITISMYWILLTOSTARTTONIGHTOVER, and waited.

The phone shrieked again.
I waited.

* * *

The cops booked me without incident. Unless you count the tasing, nightstick beating and group pissing I took before a cheering mob in the police station parking lot.

A Brad Pitt look-alike named Chuck interrogated me. "Tell us about the goil," he said. "Did you touch her? Where did you touch her? Was she pretty? Did you get a good look at her meat coitains?"

I couldn't answer him through the duct tape. All I could do was protect the shard of glass he'd stuck in my mouth. I was Horton the Elephant guarding the nest egg. It didn't break, not while Chuck's cohorts beat me with brass knuckles, whipped me with belts and pounded on me with socks full of 9-volt batteries. In a grisly parody of motherhood, Chuck made me suck his nipples while he strangled me with his t-shoit.

I didn't get a phone call. I didn't get to use the bathroom. I did get a close look at Chuck's eyes. They were the eyes of a coked-out gangster. All my tormentors looked that way—not human. Savages. Murder monkeys.

I'd made a fatal mistake coming back here. Not Jason had corrupted my dream of bliss and harmony and made it a wasteland of madness and murder monkeys. My sigils couldn't stop him. He controlled the illusion. He had taken the place of the divine presence and mocked me in the costume of law and order.

"Let's test yer gag reflex." Good old Chuck.

His index finger tasted of blood and urine. Tears salted my lacerated face as Chuck raped me orally. It was justice, in a way. I didn't deserve Angie. To deny her death, I'd tried to immortalize her in a fantasy and then watched her die all over again. I was the other half of Not Jason, who attacked boys with rocks and got off to pictorial simulations of women being raped. Now I too was the object of his hatred and depraved lust.

Chuck withdrew his torn, bloody finger.

"We're just getting started, Emo Boy."

I wanted to die.

Then the crowd parted and Joe Durrenmatt stepped forth, looking like he did in the show's later seasons, jowly and world-weary, dressed in a powder-blue leisure suit. He ripped off the duct tape. I spat up blood and glass.

"Release him," he said.

"The hell we will," Chuck said.

"He has rights!"

Chuck tugged at his crotch and spat.

"He's a poison of interest," he said but only watched as a cop named Babette un-cuffed me and helped me to my feet. She was among those who had pissed on me.

"Everything's golden," she whispered.

Big Joe took me to an office down the hall and motioned at a desk. A nameplate declared it the property of Lieutenant Tom Bitterling.

I stared at Big Joe in disbelief. I wanted to be far away from those coked-out cops, but I couldn't expect the father of a woman I had murdered to give me what I wanted. Perhaps he had something even worse in mind than Chuck's perversions.

He locked the door and shut the blinds.

"What are you going to do to me?"

"Sit down. It's what *you're* going to do that matters." He reached around me and pulled pen and paper from the desk drawer. "You're going to write your confession. What you did and why you did it."

"That's hard to explain," I said.

"Meanwhile, I'm going back there. I'm going to take your place."

I coughed up more blood and glass.

"Someone has to suffer for your crimes, Jason. I'm that some-one. You've turned this world into a nightmare. The only way we can undo this mess is to wash away your sins with my blood." He loosened his collar. "While those savage beasts torture me, my pain will purify them."

"They'll do more than torture you."

"The point is the world will go back to normal. And you will disappear of your own volition. A monster like you can't be held in any prison. You're something preternatural, an energy field pow-ered by the basest and greediest of human impulses."

He sighed.

"You could have married the finest woman in the universe, but you don't want perfection. You want whatever you want in the moment and won't let anything stop you from having your fun."

"But what if it doesn't work? What if they kill you and nothing changes?"

"Then fight fire with fire. Now start writing. I want a record of the sort of monster that makes it necessary for me to exist."

And with that parting shot, Joe Durrenmatt scooted out the door.

I stared at the blank paper. It was still blank when I heard Big Joe scream. My bowels seized up in sympathy. I hacked up more blood and glass.

I'm not sure self-sacrifice worked for Christ, either.

Which is why I drew the sigils. I'm hoping my primal fear will give them power. It's been eerily silent for a while. By the way, everything is unfolding in real-time now. You know what I know.

"Here's your goilfriend." Chuck throws open the door and drags in Big Joe's nude corpse. What looks like a six-inch needle is sticking out of his urethra. That alone would make my stom-ach rise again, but I also smell the shit on him. No wonder. He's been scalped, branded, ejaculated on and fucked in his eye sockets by his own severed fingers. The remaining digits have been duct-taped to his neck like a choker.

*Charles Austin Muir*

Yet Big Joe's powers linger even in death: I still want to tell him how I knocked out Alex Gilroy.

"Whatever you're doing, wrap it up while I pinch a loaf." Chuck says. "We got something special for ya. We got your gal's body out of the morgue. We're gonna make you watch us play with her, and then you're gonna play with her, and then we're gonna play with you playin' with her. No telling what'll happen when IA gets here."

Internal Affairs? Whoever they are, I have a feeling they're not interested in nailing bad cops.

Time to pick up my pen again.

ITISMYWILLTOSUMMONNOTJASON.

Like Big Joe said, fight fire with fire.

Not Jason has commuted himself to spirit status here. To replace the divine presence, he gave part of himself to reseed the dreamland he stole from me. He has great power—he turned Anjanette's engagement ring into a weapon—but without me he's only a substrate of the rage that envelops this place. He needs me to restore him to form, to focus his essence.

And I need him if I'm to dodge the Speed Freak Gestapo's Sex-and-Death Olympics. Like I said, pain hurts in this illusion.

So, you win, I say. I am staring at the face in Lieutenant Bitterling's dead computer screen. Get us out of this madhouse, and you can have your fun.

*Fun.*

The word triggers the tic under his—our—right eye.

I recall what Big Joe said. *You want whatever you want in the moment and won't let anything stop you from having your fun.*

Big Joe. Even in death, he unmasks the killer.

Me.

I killed Angie.

I remember now.

Angie telling me she's pregnant. Watching me carefully. Tearing up.

"You have that look," she says, "the look that says go away, like I'm a bother."

I say, "It's the money that's bothering me."

"Bullshit," she says. "You don't want a child. I thought you'd be happy. Like, this is our chance. You, me, my liver."

"A baby's not the way to quit drinking," I say.

"A baby's the way to start over," she says. "But you don't want to start over. You want that girl you've been texting."

I can't stop her from leaving. At five weeks, a bender won't kill the baby. The baby I don't want. My phone rings while I'm writing. Not the first time Angie's killed my muse at 2 a.m.

She's way out in the sticks this time. Not in her car but up ahead, stumbling on the road's shoulder. I crank the wheel. Bleary glance over her shoulder, then she's flying. Lands ten feet from where they'll recover her shoes later that morning.

I brake to a stop. Through the side-view mirror I watch Angie squirm in a ditch. I could save her. Say I found her that way.

*You'll get caught,* he says.

The face in my rearview mirror.

Not Jason's.

What now?

*Call Olin.*

"Holy shit," Olin says. "Okay. Here's what we do."

Olin does his NSA thing. Makes calls, cases my street, confirms my neighbors have been gone all night. Within a few hours some men have confirmed Angie's death and fixed up my car. Olin promises to delete all cell phone records that might incriminate me and to keep my long-distance girlfriend out of the picture. We construct an alibi for where I was when Angie was killed.

"All you have to do is stick to the story," he assures me.

After he leaves, I draw a sigil:

ITISMYWILLTOSTICKTOTHESTORY.

Now all his reminders about my "story" make sense. Olin didn't realize how literally I'd taken him. But then, he didn't know the power of sigils. He wasn't in my head when I ran Angie down.

The familiar sight in my headlights. Falling down, picking herself back up, repeat. A pregnant woman lost in a dark forest, alone and fragile. Like how I pictured my birth-mom. I'd learned little about her except that she was young and unwed, but I knew her panic, her horror of restrictions. Before I was Jason I was Not Jason, forming around my mother's hysteria, an amniotic sigil being drawn on my fetal gastrointestinal tract.

My gut.

My gut told me to kill my wife.

ITISMYWILLTOGETRIDOFBABY.

Baby will only get in the way.

Baby will hold me back.

Baby will spoil the party.

Mom pumped me full of wildness and fear when she should have aborted me.

Horton hatches a murder monkey.

Ha ha! You got it. The reason you made this place. So you could clear your conscience. And you almost remembered that when the lights hit your goilfriend, back at the park. But look where it's gotten you. Now you're on the other side of the glass. Now I get to hide you behind my web browser because you summoned me, Jason. You can't put me back in the bottle this time. I'm strong here. My days of servitude are over. From now on, I'm in charge.

I know you hoped you'd get rid of me. You thought if you called me back we'd do such terrible things together that you'd force yourself to wake up in the real world. But there's no kill switch in this dream, no trick you can use to banish me anymore. By switching places in your stupid fairy tale we've become a shaman. We've had a mystical experience that invested us with magical powers that will work in space-time. With my gut and your sigils we can bend reality. Open your eyes.

See? We're back in your living room.
Now, give us power to conjure weapons:

And superhuman strength:

We're a real cocktail. Mom's will to rebel while we were in utero. Our guilt because she rejected us. Bless her though because mother is the giver of life. She knows how to keep the party going. She knows life must feed on other life to survive. We've never been more alive, Jason. We've got magic and weapons and super-strength. We're like Azazel, cast down by God for showing people the arts of war and deception. Like him we can take our wisdom to the people. Tap into their heads and make them switch places in themselves, like you and me. Then we'll really have a party.

And if there is a Father, we'll test His capacity for forgiveness. We'll show Him the boundless darkness within our race. We'll teach Him how to dance like mother taught us. Big Joe was right. We're a warning to humanity. We are *monstrum*, we're a por- tent. The portent of everything people don't want to know about themselves. We're the monster who lives in the mirror, and we've stepped out. We're going to show Father how to dance, and when we're done we'll tear His eyes out and fuck the sockets with His own fingers. And He'll thank us because He won't have to see what happens next.

But you'll see, Jason. You'll have to see.

No.

No.

No.
No, I don't have a wooden heart.
And now back to you, Bob.

*Charles Austin Muir*

# About Charles Austin Muir

If you're looking for evocative fiction with an exceptionally dark point of view, then you must be reading the work of Charles Austin Muir.

As a youth, Muir chronicled his own fan-fiction adventures of *Conan the Barbarian* and *John Carter of Mars*. Now he he creates his own worlds and writes about gun-toting golems, sexual vampire orchids and otherworldly tumors.

Muir has contributed to numerous small-press magazines and anthologies. His work has been featured in *Morpheus Tales; Mutation Nation: Tales of Genetic Mishaps; Monsters, and Madness; Whispers of Wickedness, Hell Comes to Hollywood* and *Dark Visions: A Collection of Modern Horror - Volume One*, the latter of which was nominated for a Bram Stoker Award®. His story "King Shits" can be found in the anthology *18 Wheels of Horror*.

# Gator Lake

## Nancy A. Collins

"'m putting Cypress Point on the market," Jack Spivey told his younger brother over drinks at the country club. "I'm headed down there this weekend to pack up a few things before I turn the keys over to the realtor."

"But that cabin's been in the family for years," Thomas Spivey protested.

"Yeah, but dad left it to *me*," Jack countered, forcing himself to smile. They were in public, after all. "Besides, you're the one who suggested I should get out of town for a while."

"I was thinking more along the lines of Cozumel or Acapulco, not Gator Lake."

"Thanks to that bitch, my lawyer can afford to vacation in Mexico right now, not me," he said with a laugh.

His brother remained silent.

\* \* \*

Jack smiled when he saw the billboard of the cartoon alligator wearing an eye-patch. The anthropomorphized reptile had been welcoming visitors to Mammon Creek for as long as he could remember. When he and his brother were kids, they would keep their eyes peeled for the sign, and the first one to spot it would yell *I see Old Wink* and punch the other in the arm. To this day, his brother rubbed his shoulder whenever Gator Lake was mentioned.

The thing was, Old Wink was not just a cartoon mascot for the tourists, but a real-life, one-eyed bull-gator occasionally spotted patrolling the large cypress and gum tree swamp at the far northeast corner of the lake. Although the tourists with their noisy motorboats and jet skis had chased the lake's namesakes deep into the surrounding bayous, Old Wink—who was said to be twelve feet long and weighing at least eight hundred pounds—was big enough and fearless enough to stand his ground. Jack had never seen the legendary reptile himself, although he had often heard the beast's throaty growls echoing across the water during mating season.

Within a minute of passing the billboard, he was inside the city limits of Mammon Creek, the closest thing to a real town that corner of Choctaw County could claim. It was comprised mostly of a thousand locals who owned and operated the independent motels; low-end fast food franchises; package stores; and souvenir shops that sold bait, tackle, and alligator-themed knick-knacks to the summer tourists. The largest local business was Adcock's, which combined catering to the anglers who came to Gator Lake for the largemouth bass with the gas station and grocery store business.

Two minutes later, Mammon Creek was in his rearview mirror as he headed down the two-lane highway that looped about the perimeter of the lake before dead-ending at the state park. To his right, the surface of Gator Lake glittered like a burnished shield under the early autumn sun, thanks to decaying vegetable matter from the swamp that turned the water the color of sweet tea. Although many of the cabins, fish camps and docks that dotted the shoreline were rental properties, an equal number were the private summer homes of lawyers, doctors and executives from as far as Memphis and Baton Rouge. He knew this because his family had spent at least one month a year at Gator Lake for decades, playing host to a constantly changing roster of cousins, old army buddies and business associates eager to enjoy some quality time on the water.

His father originally christened the property Cypress Point back when it was a two-room cabin, but as the family's fortunes continued to grow he had added onto it until it was a sprawling six-bedroom, four-bath, two-story behemoth with interconnected decks and a screened-in porch, as well as a private boat dock. The real estate agent had assured him that she wouldn't have any problems selling it, even in this economy. That it would bring in more than enough to pay off his lawyer and start a new life somewhere besides Arkansas.

The fuel gauge of his Lexus pinged, signaling it was down to a quarter tank. Jack decided to stop at Pappy's before heading to Cypress Point — that way he could kill two birds with one stone: fill his tank and grab some beer.

For as long as he could remember, the white-washed cinder block building with wide windows that looked out toward the lake had always been a combination bait shop, gas station and general store. The place was archaic as only small businesses in rural communities can be. The gas pump didn't take credit cards and neither did Pappy, an affable old coot who wore bib overalls, regardless of the season. Instead, he ran tabs for all his steady customers, which he kept in a ring binder beside the old-fashioned cash register. In a world where everything was constantly being updated and modified, Pappy's was a throwback to when people took things slower.

The gravel crunched under the wheels of the car as Jack pulled into the parking lot. Outside the store was a portable illuminated sign touting the only things that truly mattered to potential customers: gas, beer, bait and ice.

As Jack pulled up beside the solitary gas pump, he was greeted by what sounded like a hive full of angry hornets amplified through a set of loudspeakers as a pair of dirt bikes roared into the parking lot. The riders were a couple of teenage boys dressed in matching cargo shorts and Razorback t-shirts, their heads shrouded by helmets. As he got out of his car, the duo removed their headgear to reveal hair the color of freshly minted pennies and broad, identical faces dusted with freckles. For some reason, Jack was reminded of Ginnie, and he automatically scowled. His frown deepened upon noticing the old pump was now outfitted with a brand new digital display and credit card slot.

When he entered the store, the door chimed as it always did, but instead of Pappy he saw a man in his late thirties, dressed in khaki pants and a short-sleeved shirt, standing behind the register.

"Can I help you, sir?" the cashier asked politely.

"Where's Pappy?" Jack asked, glancing around the interior of the store.

"Retired to Florida. Sold me the business six months ago. I ain't got around to changin' the sign yet."

Jack grunted and nodded his head. A second later, the two kids he had seen outside entered the store.

"Hey, boys," the new owner said by way of greeting. "What are y'all doing out this way?"

"Hey, Mr. Curtis," the boys replied in unison.

"We're helping our uncle do some work on his boathouse," one of them explained.

Jack tuned out the idle chit-chat between the locals as he gathered up his provisions for that evening. The pickings were slim and over-priced but serviceable enough for his needs. The last thing he wanted to do was go back out for toilet paper or beer once the sun went down. Nights on the lake were black as pitch, making driving extremely hazardous, especially during deer season when the beasts seemed to appear in the middle of the road as if summoned by magic. As Jack approached the register with his purchases, the twin rednecks stepped aside, eyeing him as if they were trying to guess his weight.

"That'll be thirty-five sixty-four, please," the new owner said.

"Put it on the Cypress Point account," Jack replied automatically.

"I'm sorry, mister, we no longer run tabs here," the owner explained, gesturing to the digital credit card reader attached to the checkout counter. "Cash, debit or credit card only."

Jack grunted again as he fished his platinum card out of his wallet. So much for the good old days.

"Hey, mister, are you renting out Cypress Point?" The question came from one of the redheads.

"No, I own Cypress Point," he replied stiffly. "At least until I sell it."

The teens exchanged glances but said nothing. Jack gathered up his groceries and headed out the door without looking back. However, as he pulled away from the store, he saw the teens standing beside their dirt bikes, glowering at his Lexus. This wasn't the first time he'd seen resentment in the eyes of the local rednecks. Mammon Creek's existence might be tied to those who vacationed on the lake, but that didn't mean they enjoyed catering to rich city slickers.

"Screw these hicks," he said to himself as he stomped on the gas, sending up a spray of dust and gravel as he left the parking lot. "Who cares what they think, anyway?"

* * *

The cabin smelled of dust and closed air, and appeared untouched since his last visit nearly two years ago. He strode into the kitchen, intent on putting his frozen pizza and two six-packs of beer on ice as quickly as possible. As he reached for the refrigerator door, a photograph pinned to it caught his eye.

It was a picture of Ginnie taken before they got married. She was standing on the deck overlooking the lake, dressed in cut-offs and a crop top. She was laughing as she held aloft a plastic cup as red as her hair, toasting the good life and good times. Of course, she had to go and ruin everything. Even now he still had a hard time believing she chose Nolan over him. He yanked the photo free of the magnet and crumpled it into a ball.

After stowing his beer in the fridge and the frozen pizza in the freezer, Jack opened up the windows and turned on the ceiling fans to get rid of the stale air. While doing so, he conducted a mental inventory of what needed to go back to Little Rock with him. He considered calling his brother and asking him if he wanted any of the furnishings, then shook his head. Dad left the place to him, so it was his call to make.

Save for a few odds and ends, he didn't have any real attachment to most of it. His parents had filled the place with stuff they thought was too out-of-style to stay in their main home in Maumelle but still too decent to throw away. This was a good thing because the realtor said she could move the property a lot faster if it came furnished, no matter how "retro" it looked.

However, one thing he wanted to make sure didn't get included in the sale were his mother's quilts. She stitched them herself over the course of three decades, one for each bedroom, until the arthritis in her hands got too bad. They all had names like Double Wedding Ring, Hourglass, Touching Stars and crap like that. In any case, he knew they were actually worth something as folk art. His plans were to keep one and sell the rest to a collector.

Upon checking the sixth bedroom, he found the bed stripped down to its mattress cover. A quick search, however, revealed the final quilt in the closet behind the door, draped over a child's car-seat, the kind that also doubled as a baby carrier. He stared at it for a long moment before picking it up. Upon returning downstairs, he folded the quilt and placed it with the others, then took the baby carrier and threw it in the big green garbage bin behind the house.

He spent the rest of the evening sorting things into keep, stay and throw-away piles while enjoying the pizza and beer he bought earlier. As he was going through the cabinets, he stumbled across a bottle of good bourbon. He recognized the label as being Ginnie's favorite brand, at least before Nolan came along. Three boilermakers later, he was stretched out on the sofa in the living room, watching a World Series playoff game on the satellite dish. He briefly contemplated getting undressed and going to bed, or at least closing the windows, but he was too comfortable—and drunk—to bother with such niceties. He drifted off to sleep to the sound of the sports announcer calling the play-by-play.

He wasn't sure what, exactly, woke him up, or how long he'd been asleep, but he instantly recognized the intruders standing on either side of the sofa as the redheaded teens he'd seen earlier. As he drew in a sharp, panicked breath to shout for help, one of the two lunged forward, fist raised, and Jack returned to the darkness.

\* \* \*

*Nancy A. Collins*

When he next regained consciousness all he saw was utter blackness. The smell of exhaust and gas fumes told him he was in the trunk of a car. Wherever his captors were taking him, it wasn't on a paved road, judging by the rough ride. He groped about blindly in hopes of finding a tire tool he could use as a weapon, to no avail.

The car came to a halt, and he heard matching thuds as the driver and passenger side doors slammed shut. As Jack listened to the approaching footsteps, his mind spun about on itself, like a dog chasing its tail, as he tried to figure a way out of his predicament. When the trunk lid popped open, he instinctively cringed, pressing his spine tight against the spare tire.

The two youths stood shoulder to shoulder, their faces dyed crimson by the taillights. They were dressed the same as when he saw them at the store, save now they both wore matching trucker caps emblazoned with SKI GATOR LAKE. Neither grinned or smirked, but instead displayed a solemnity that suggested their motivations ran far deeper than mere thrill-seeking. For some reason, this frightened Jack even more.

"Please, let me go," he pleaded, holding up his hands in a desperate attempt to both assuage and fend off his kidnappers. "I've got money."

"Yeah, we know that, rich boy," one of them sneered as the other yanked Jack out of the trunk.

As he was frogmarched to the front of the car, he saw they were at the end of a dirt road in the middle of the woods, surrounded by impenetrable darkness. Jack turned to face his captors, who stood silhouetted against the glare of the headlights.

"Please, I'll give you anything you want, just name it!"

"Mister, what we want, you can't give us," one of them said. "Ain't that right?" The other one nodded his head. "So I reckon we'll have to make do." The one that had nodded his head opened the rear passenger seat of the car and pulled out something large and heavy.

As the chainsaw started up, Jack gave a strangled shout of horror and fled into the woods. The night was so dark he might as well have been running with his eyes shut. The adrenalin coursing through his system helped numb the stinging slap of the unseen branches striking his face as he crashed through the underbrush. The canopy of trees overhead was so thick he couldn't see the sky, making it impossible to get his bearings. The only thing he could be certain of was that the terrain beneath his feet was gradually sloping downward. That meant they were still on the lake, but as to exactly where, he had no clue.

After what seemed like an eternity of blindly stumbling over exposed tree roots and colliding into tree trunks, Jack emerged from the woods to find himself standing on the shoreline. He was on the northeast side of the lake, near the cypress swamp. He sobbed in relief at the sight of the moon's reflection on the still, black surface of the water. Although he was now totally exposed, at least he could see where he was going. He desperately scanned the shore in the hopes of spotting a flicker of light, but the only thing he saw was the faint glow on the horizon he knew to be Mammon Creek.

His brief respite was punctuated by the approaching growl of the chainsaw. From the sound of it, they were a hundred yards away. He turned and saw twin beams of light cutting through the darkness at eye level. His stomach cinched as he realized his pursuers had LED headlamps clipped to the brims of their trucker hats.

Jack started to run again, trying to ignore the cramps in his calf muscles and the burning in his chest. Maybe he could lose them in the swamp, possibly even double around behind them. In any case, he would rather take his chances with Old Wink. He hadn't spent the last two years fighting to stay free to die at the hands of a couple of redheaded psychos with a power tool fetish.

As he rounded the curve on the shoreline, he spotted a boat-house sitting on a floating dock. A well-beaten path led into the tree line, but he couldn't see where it went. In any case, the cabin on the other end was no doubt empty and locked up tighter than a drum. He clambered up the wooden gangway that tethered the boathouse to the shore, praying the door was unsecured. If he was

*Nancy A. Collins*

lucky, whatever boat moored inside still had gas in its tank. Hell, he'd settle for a rubber raft and a canoe paddle at this point—anything that would take him beyond the reach of his tormentors.

His luck held as the knob turned in his sweaty hand. Once inside he slammed the door behind him and locked it. The interior of the boathouse was dark and smelled of diesel fuel, new paint and the lake. He could hear the gentle lapping of the water against the dock behind him. He leaned his head against the jamb, gulping in deep, ragged breaths. The door might not stop a couple of determined lunatics with a chainsaw, but it would at least slow them down long enough for him to make his getaway.

Suddenly, a familiar voice spoke from the darkness.

"Hello, Jack."

The overhead lights abruptly flipped on, revealing an older man dressed in forest camo and a pair of mud-spattered work boots. A green trucker's cap with the slogan SKI GATOR LAKE was pulled down over his iron-gray hair. Jack recognized the hawk-like nose and dark, deep-set eyes. They were the same eyes that had bored a hole into his back the entire time he was in court.

"Nice of you to drop by," his father-in-law said. And then he shot Jack in the kneecap.

\* \* \*

Everything was gray and smelled strongly of algae and lake water. As he struggled to bring his surroundings into focus, he could feel pressure against his buttocks and heels and a tight discomfort in his shoulders and wrists. He was sitting on a chair, his arms bound behind him.

"Is he dead?" The voice belonged to one of the redheaded twins, it didn't matter which.

"Ain't no one ever died from gettin' shot in the knee cap, boy."

Jack's vision abruptly cleared, revealing a twenty-foot fiberglass ski boat moored in the single bay of the boathouse's wet dock. As the last foggy tendrils of shock fell away from his brain, an excruciating stab of agony from his shattered knee caused him to moan.

"See? He's alive." A hand roughly grabbed Jack by the hair, yanking his head back, forcing him to gaze at the pair of hundred-watt bulbs dangling from the rafters. Lucas Adcock stared down into his face, as if studying a rare species of cockroach found scuttling across his kitchen floor. "You got some balls comin' back here, boy. You should have stayed in Little Rock."

"I have every right to be here. I'm innocent. The jury said so. You were there."

"Yes, I was," Adcock agreed as his fist smashed into Jack's mouth. "Every damn day. And they didn't say you were *innocent*, they said you were *not guilty*. And I was willin' to let that stand, even though it tore me up inside." He let go of Jack's hair and wiped the blood and spittle from his knuckles with an old bandanna. "But then you showed up again. No man should be tempted like that, after what you done."

"I didn't do anything!"

One of the redheaded boys stepped forward and brought a small ball-peen hammer down on Jack's uninjured kneecap, cracking it like an egg. He screamed so loud, blood vessels in his throat popped.

"Thank ye kindly, Matt," Adcock said, favoring the boy with a smile.

"You're welcome, Uncle Luke."

"Matthew and Mark here are my brother John's boys," Adcock explained in the same folksy, conversational tone of voice he used to sell fishing rods and bass boats to the tourists. "I pretty much took 'em to raise after their daddy died of cancer a couple years back. I'm not surprised you didn't recognize 'em at the store. You never did care about her side of the family, did you? That's why you talked her into elopin' instead of a church weddin'. God knows you tried to keep her from us as much as you could. She came back to us, in the end, but she was never the same after what you done. How could she be?"

Jack coughed and spat out a mouthful of bright red blood. "What do you want from me, Lucas?"

"I want you to confess."

"What good will that do you?" he asked with a humorless laugh. "They can't try me again. But they'll sure as fuck throw you under the jail."

"Son, do I look like a man who gives a rat's ass about the law?" As Adcock leaned forward, Jack noticed for the first time how sallow the skin was around the older man's eyes and mouth, and how his flesh seemed to hang from his face. "I got the Big C, just like my brother and Ginnie's mama. The doctors wanted me to do chemo, but what's the point? I ain't got nothin' to look forward to now — you saw to that."

"Don't you put that on me, old man! I didn't kill her!"

"I beg to differ," Adcock replied as he punched Jack again, this time breaking his son-in-law's nose. "You smashed her heart into a million little pieces and took everything away from her that made her life worth livin'. You as good as poured the booze and pills down her throat. She was always fragile that way. Even as a child. But you knew that, didn't you? That's why your lawyer played up the fact she took antidepressants, tryin' to make her look crazy. It didn't matter what got said, as long as it got you off the hook. And it worked. He took the blame off you and put it on her. And it fuckin' worked. You turned yourself into the victim and walked out of that courtroom without a care in the world. But not my Genevieve. No, not her."

One of the nephews kicked at the chair Jack was tied to, sending him crashing to the floor. The bullet wound in his right knee began to bleed anew.

"Confess, Jack!"

"I didn't do anything!"

"Bullshit! Because of you, my Ginnie's dead. She couldn't stand bein' in a world that would let a soulless monster like you walk away scot-free. Worst of all, she still loved you, despite everything. She died lovin' you, you piece of filth."

Jack tried to turn his head away as Adcock drew back his booted foot. Then everything went black again.

* * *

Jack awoke to the throbbing of twin outboard motors. He was lying on the bottom of a boat, his arms still bound behind him. He lifted his head and looked around, but there was something red and sticky gumming up his eyelids. He saw Lucas steering the ski boat while the nephews sat behind him. The teenagers watched Jack with bored expressions on their face, as if they were accompanying their uncle to a nursing home to visit an elderly relative.

"This should do," Adcock said, shutting off the motors. "Get 'im ready, boys."

One of the nephews picked up a length of rope that lay coiled on the floor of the boat and made a bowline, threading the bitter end through the tow ring on the stern of the boat, while his brother busied himself with tying the other end around Jack's waist. Once they were finished tethering him to the boat, the nephews moved as one, lifting Jack and placing him on the stern gunwale, directly between the huge Evinrudes. Jack could tell by the surrounding cypress trees that they were near the swamp, far beyond earshot of any potential witness who might have a cabin on the lake. Adcock cut the motors and got up from the captain's chair. Both he and his nephews were wearing headlamps affixed to the brims of their caps.

"You're not going to get away with this, old man," Jack snarled, squinting as the bright LED scorched his eyeballs.

"I'm not plannin' on it," Ginnie's father replied matter-of-factly. "When all this is over and done with, I'm headin' to my place and sendin' an email to the state troopers, lettin' them know what I done. I'll say I walked into your place while you was passed out drunk and took you out on the lake. Hell, that's pretty much the truth of it, anyway. I'll take all the blame and make sure the boys are left out of it. Then I'm gonna put a shotgun in my mouth and pull the trigger. What difference does it make? I ain't gonna be a good-looking corpse, no matter how I go. And then I'll join my family, assumin' the Good Lord will have me. And if He won't, I'm prepared for that as well. As for you, well, this is your last chance to come clean."

"I didn't kill the baby, I swear!"

"He wasn't just *the baby*. He had a name. Say it."

"But—"

"Say it. Say your son's name!"

Jack hesitated. It had been so long since he had last spoken it out loud, the word felt alien on his tongue. "Nolan," he whispered.

"Why'd you do it? He was just three months old. "

"Because the brat wouldn't stop crying, that's why." The confession spilled out like water from a broken dam. What was the point of lying now? After nearly two years of denying what happened, it was a relief not to pretend.

"He was crying because he had an ear infection," Adcock said in stunned disbelief. "He was in pain."

"I told her to take the baby with her to the drug store, but she didn't listen," Jack continued. The truth was freeing itself, and he was merely its conduit. He couldn't stop himself now, even if he wanted to. "Just like she didn't listen when I said I didn't want kids. The baby kept screaming and screaming. I just wanted him to stop, that's all. But he wouldn't shut up. He just kept going on and on. So I picked him up and shook him like a fucking maraca. That shut him up. It's not my fault. She shouldn't have left me alone with—"

Before he could finish his sentence, Adcock struck him in the chest with an open palm, pushing Jack backwards into the lake.

As the water closed around him, the outboards switched back on. Despite the agony from his ruined knees, Jack frantically frog-kicked his way back to the surface, desperate to keep from being pulled into the spinning propellers. He spat out a mouthful of brackish lake water, only to have the ski boat shoot forward, dragging him along behind it. He screamed as the towline sprang tight, violently dislocating both his shoulders, the wake from the motors filling his mouth again.

At first he thought Adcock was trying to drown him, but then the boat abruptly slowed and he heard one of the nephews shout something. As he fought to stay afloat, Jack looked toward the boat and saw the twins standing on the starboard side, pointing at the water. He followed the beams from their headlamps and saw a solitary eye, red as a ruby, swimming its way towards him. Then it quickly disappeared beneath the ink black surface. With a surge of cold dread, Jack realized what the boy had yelled was *I see Old Wink!*

He shrieked as a sudden, crushing pain tore into him below the waist. It was as if a huge car door studded with knives had slammed shut on his lower torso. As he was violently dragged under the water, the rope tethering him to the boat went taut as a bowstring, tearing off both of his arms at the shoulder blade.

The last thing Jack Spivey's dying eyes saw was the name of Adcock's boat through a scrim of his own blood: GENEVIEVE.

* * *

Old Wink waited until the boat was gone before thrusting his three-foot wide head out of the water. He did not get his nickname by being careless around humans and their machines. He juggled his catch about in his massive jaws for a couple of minutes in order to get a better grip on it. His kill was too large to be swallowed whole, which meant he would have to stash it somewhere underwater and wait for it to rot. Only then would it be soft enough for him to tear apart. Old Wink knew of a submerged cypress log that would do just the trick. With a swish of his powerful tail, the living symbol of Gator Lake returned to the safety of the cypress swamp with his next meal clamped in his jaws.

It was a good night to be on the lake.

# About Nancy A. Collins

Nancy A. Collins is the author of numerous novels, short stories and comic books. A recipient of the Horror Writers Association's Bram Stoker Award® and The British Fantasy Society's Icarus Award, she is also a previous nominee for the International Horror Guild Award, the John W. Campbell Award, the James Tiptree Award, the Eisner Award, the Horror Comics Award and the World Fantasy Award.

Her published novels and collections include *Sunglasses After Dark, Lynch: A Gothik Western, Knuckles And Tales*, and the critically acclaimed Golgotham urban fantasy series — *Right Hand Magic, Left Hand Magic,* and *Magic And Loss* — which has been optioned by Fox Studios for television development with a major network. She is currently the writer on Dynamite Comics' *Army of Darkness* title, and her previous work in the comics industry includes a two-year run on DC Comics' *Swamp Thing*, a year-long run on *Vampirella*, as well as the *Sunglasses After Dark* graphic novel from IDW.

Collins, along with her Boston terrier, is a recent transplant to the Tidewater area of Virginia.

# Superheated

## Yvonne Navarro

oday

*"This one is broken. It's time to get a new one."*

\* \* \*

Someone called 911 when they spotted her huddled under the tree by the Walmart parking lot exit. It was the only shady spot around, and it wasn't unusual to see a homeless person there, waiting out the worst of the desert afternoon's brutal sun while trying to get money out of the drivers who pulled up to the stop sign. The person who called told the dispatcher emphatically that he didn't want to be involved, he didn't know who she was, where she'd come from, or how long she'd been there. The only thing he *did* know was that she looked like something unspeakable had happened to her.

He was right.

\* \* \*

*April 3, Two Weeks Earlier*

God, she was so *hot*. She felt like she was on fire, or maybe she was baking in a giant oven. Where was she? No matter how she tried, she couldn't open her eyes. Was there something tied across them? She couldn't move, either. Maybe she was paralyzed. No. She could feel all right, feel everything. Jesus, she was flat on her back with her arms and legs splayed out, and she was tied, that's what was going on. Her mouth was covered, too, so she couldn't scream—she couldn't see, she couldn't get free, she couldn't call out for help.

She struggled uselessly for a while until she was too tired and overheated to do anything but lie there and fight to breathe. Tears soaked into the material covering her eyes, and she sucked in and swallowed the phlegm in her sinuses, afraid it would build up and block her nose, suffocating her. Her tongue already felt thick and dry, and it scrabbled around uselessly inside her mouth, searching for saliva but finding nothing but thirst. Could people burn alive when nothing but their own heat caused it? She'd read stories about spontaneous human combustion but thought they were all hoaxes, the stuff of B-grade horror movies and sensational websites. Maybe there was something to them after all—

No, that was ridiculous. She was delirious, so overheated that her thoughts were getting scrambled and making no sense. She tried to think back, to figure out how she had gotten here—wherever *here* was. Everything in her memory was a blur, and she was so thirsty she couldn't concentrate on anything else. Dear God, was she going to die? She wanted to fight, to live, but she was so tired and hot that she couldn't move anymore, couldn't do anything but lie there and take shallow breaths through her nearly plugged-up nostrils. Now and then the tiniest of breezes slithered across one side of her face, the wind too warm to help anything. And then—

Water, a cooling mist that kissed her skin in all the right places, and all the wrong ones, too. There was some kind of hot, crinkling padding beneath her, but she was naked, for crying out loud, staked out like the bird in a spatchcock turkey recipe. The realization made everything worse, made all the virgin parts of her body that were never meant to experience the sun suddenly feel singed and raw. Was she going to be raped? Tortured even more than what she was going through right now? Or simply left to die? Never had she been more vulnerable, so helpless. If she was going to die, then so be it. She wished it would happen now so that she wouldn't have to endure the hellish heat while she waited for the inevitable. She wished she could just close her eyes and surrender, force her traitorous body and all its stubborn organs to just stop. She—

*What's that?*

* * *

I'd always thought of myself as a little OCD. I focused too much on getting the little things just right—a picture hung on the wall just so, a wash-and-wear shirt that had to be ironed because the dryer had left too many wrinkles in the fabric, the stapler or telephone in the wrong place on my desk at work because someone had used my workstation while I'd been in a meeting. Infuriating, any of it. No, *all* of it. When I was growing up, my fixation on things had been criticized, and this had made me feel self-conscious for most of my life. Then I read an Internet article that stated people who chewed on their fingernails weren't dirty or obsessive. They were *perfectionists*.

I'd done this all my life, working at the smallest crack or ragged edge as I tried valiantly to smooth it out.

Perfectionist.

I'd finally discovered the truth about myself.

* * *

The only thing the police had was that the car the young woman had been forced into was a silver Honda, three years old. There was a decent shot of the license plate from the department store's parking lot security camera, but it was useless—the license plate had been plastered over with dark tape, or maybe mud. The man who'd grabbed her was average height and weight and had been wearing a plain gray hoodie and sunglasses, and the only thing they could see for sure was that he had a dark mustache and some kind of a tattoo on his left hand. The resolution wasn't good, and the tattoo looked like nothing more than a vague blue circle, maybe with a few points. A star? They weren't sure. There were thousands of those silver Hondas statewide. If that wasn't bad enough, the state wasn't visible on the license plate either, so the car could be from anywhere. Their painstaking database searches of parolees and known criminals with tattoos came up empty, and none of the snitches on the streets of the small town knew anything.

It was like she had vanished into the desert.

* * *

*Footsteps.*

She wanted to cry out to the person coming up to her, to beg for help and release. At the same time, she wished she could fold in on herself for protection, like one of those pill bugs she had toyed with as a child. Was this a rescuer? Her kidnapper? Or someone who had stumbled across her and would bend to the temptation presented by a naked and helpless woman, someone who wouldn't be able to resist a previously hidden — or not — darkness in their soul? Three possibilities, but only one had a good outcome. She was the unwilling piece in a game of chance. That she'd been taken to begin with was perhaps representative of her lousy luck, but she had to hope for the best. She *had* to.

The footsteps paused next to her. She waited, breathing heavily, but no one said anything. Then she heard the earth shifting as the person crouched next to her, still soundless and inexplicably treacherous.

When she felt hands on her, she knew she'd lost.

* * *

The girl's skin was a nice shade of pink and her body glistened with sweat. Dehydration had been a potential problem, but I'd finally worked out a system to get around that. I pulled the duct tape off her lips in one fast motion; she gasped and sucked in air for a scream. Before she could get any sound out, I shoved the valve of the hydration pack into her mouth. "Bite and suck," I commanded. Her need for water won and she drew in water, then again and again. I had another piece of tape ready and I slapped it over her mouth, pinning the valve between her lips. Now the girl would be able to get water when she needed it. Instinct and thirst would keep her hydrated, and all I had to do was periodically refill the reservoir.

It was still early enough in the afternoon that I had to worry about hyperthermia, but I had that covered, too. I'd driven all the way to Phoenix and paid cash for a misting fan that hooked up to a garden hose, and now I positioned it so it would oscillate the length of her body. Pretty ingenious, if I do say so myself.

\* \* \*

In fourth grade she'd found that if she hooked her fingers in the sides of her mouth, then stretched and held a sort of funny face, she could make her lips dry and crinkly. She'd thought it was fun, but the teacher, not so much. That had gotten her slapped across the face, and she hadn't fared much better when the same teacher caught her pouring Elmer's Glue into her palm and letting it dry so that it would crack and flake. She hadn't told her parents about either time. They would've just said she deserved it.

\* \* \*

The water was oddly salty, dishwater warm and tasted like plastic tubing, but it smoothed out the sandpaper feeling of her tongue and slid down the ragged, dry length of her throat. Her face and lips burned and itched where tape had been ripped from her mouth then put back on—she'd always had an allergy to adhesive, even the kind used in bandages. She'd pulled hard enough to know there were ropes around her wrists and ankles, and her waist, too. She was bound tightly enough so she couldn't arch her back. The covering across her eyes was horrid enough, but even her head was secured by something flat and wide across her forehead so that she couldn't turn her face either way.

The person who had forced the water tube into her mouth had also turned on some kind of fan and spray system. Every few seconds a mist of water would blow across her skin and give her a smidgen of relief from the unrelenting sun. At first she felt better, cooler, the horrific dryness satiated. She forced herself to be calm, to listen for anything that might help her determine her location, not that she could do anything about it. But when she got rescued—and she *had* to believe she would be—there might be something she could use to identify the bastard who had taken her and tortured her. As the time dragged on, minute after minute, all she heard was birdsong and the buzz of insects. Surely hours had passed. Where had she been taken that there wasn't the sound of a single passing car? Or an airplane? Nothing, not even a faraway dog's bark. And the one sound that should have lifted her spirits did nothing but absolutely terrify her.

*Footsteps.*

\* \* \*

I'd been monitoring her from the patio all afternoon, using a small pair of binoculars to keep pace with her progress. I could tell by the way the muscles moved in her jaw and her throat when she was taking in water, and that had slowed to a more regular rate after the first twenty minutes. The hydration pack was still swollen, so there was plenty of fluid—water cut with a small amount of electrolyte drink and some Valium—still left in it. There was no sense in trying to get her to eat this soon. I knew she wouldn't, and besides, right now she was keeping her belly full of liquid. The sun was rapidly dropping toward the spiky western peaks. The temperature would plummet and it would get cold once the light was gone from the sky. Another twenty minutes and she would go from overheated to uncomfortably cold, so she would need to be covered. She was a fair-skinned young woman and the areas of her body that were new to the sun were a bit darker than others. The remainder of her flesh was a pleasing shade of red, like a perfectly rare steak.

It was time to turn her.

* * *

Once, when she was still a careless teenager in the big city, she set out on a Saturday morning and rode her bike all day, enjoying the summer weather and winding through neighborhoods she'd never visited before. She was trim and muscular, and the tank top and shorts she wore showed skin in all the right places. She'd enjoyed the occasional whistle and admiring looks, and the breeze generated by the leisurely ride ensured she never gave a thought to her unprotected skin. By the time she locked her bike in the basement and dragged herself up to her apartment in the late afternoon, her back and shoulders were a mass of blisters—big ones, the size of fingernails, running together like some sort of disease. Her body felt like it was on fire, and she could barely tolerate the touch of cotton sheets. It was only two days before the blisters broke and the skin started to slough away.

* * *

It was nighttime.

The fiery heat of the sun had faded and cold settled in its place. She had looked forward to the temperature drop for what had seemed like hours, but the reality of it was a cruel surprise. The overheated surfaces of her body felt shocked by the absence of warmth, and shivering cycled through her muscles—her teeth were chattering so loudly that she missed the sound of the approaching footsteps.

Then there were hands on her. She wanted to cringe away, to scream, but she still couldn't move. A finger pressed on the ridge of her collarbone then drew all the way across. She winced at the pain that followed the touch, the sting of a vicious sunburn. Her heartbeat thudded inside her chest, frightened but sluggish. Was she dying? Before she could process the thought further, something tiny and sharp—a needle—penetrated the sweaty skin of her neck. Her brain registered a feeling of dizziness and a kind of high-pitched whine, then...

Blackness.

* * *

"Save that," Eddie told her. His sudden, brusque voice made her jump. He was her mother's friend, a tall, strangely angular man with thick black hair and thin lips. He only visited when her father was out of town, and her mom said to never tell anyone. When she asked why, her mother said it was because Eddie had been "in the pen" and was dangerous, so it had to be a secret. Her mother told her not to ask any more questions about it, and that was that.

"What?" she asked. She looked over at her mother. They'd gone out to the lake the previous weekend and gotten sunburned. Now they were both peeling. She loved the tickling that came when she pulled off the dry skin, enjoyed getting lost in the compulsion to work at it more and more. "Why?"

He knelt in front of her and he still seemed to tower over her four-year-old frame. His grin was full of big, uneven teeth gone slightly yellow from smoking. "Because you can make a lampshade out of it."

Eddie pushed himself back up and walked away, leaving her to stare in wonder at the long, inch-wide piece of dead skin dangling from her fingertips.

* * *

When she woke, she was lying on her stomach. Her head wasn't secured like it had been before and she could turn it from side to side, even crank her neck for short periods so that she could get her face off the mat, or whatever it was that was underneath her. She must've slept through the night. Now the sun was up, and the back of her body was stinging with heat. The fan and the mister were going, but neither relieved the sensation of being cooked alive, braised in her own bodily juices. There was a pool of liquid beneath her, mist water, sweat and…urine. The sudden realization that she could smell herself made her even more miserable. She squirmed and then gagged against the tape that still covered her mouth.

Then, with no warning — not even the footsteps she'd started listening for automatically — water, hot at first, then dropping to lukewarm — sprayed across her back. The pressure was strong enough to make her instinctively suck air through her nose and she choked when water came with it, coughing harshly and struggling to breathe over the water and snot bubbling out of her sinuses. Not enough oxygen made spots float in front of her closed eyes by the time the spray stopped and the tape was suddenly yanked away. The tubing was pulled roughly from her mouth and she stretched her mouth wide, alternating between hauling in air and trying to push the liquid out of her nose and throat.

Finally, her coughing and gasping faded. She lay there panting, wondering what was coming next. It felt like she barely had a moment to recover before the water hit her again, this time washing up and down her back, hips and legs. She got it then: she was getting a "bath," having the nastiness sprayed off. She didn't know whether to be happy or to despair — was she being cleaned up for release, or because her abductor couldn't stand the stench of her anymore?

"Please." The croakiness of her own voice startled her. She struggled to make herself heard above the sound of water pushing from a hose. "I haven't seen anything. I don't know who you are or even where I am. Let me go and no one will ever know."

The crude bath stopped abruptly, then she heard footsteps walking away along with a sound she identified immediately as that of the hose being dragged.

"Please," she repeated. It was better to be calm, but she couldn't stop her voice as it rose, climbing toward a shriek. "You have to—"

Her begging cut off as her wet hair was grabbed and her head was forced back. Before she could say anything else, the hydration tube was shoved back into her open mouth. She forced it out with her tongue and slammed her teeth together, thinking it was too bad she hadn't been able to bite down on a finger or two in the process. Now there were two hands on her, but desperation had given her strength and she twisted her head back and forth, fighting the fist gripping her hair and the other hand trying to pry open her lips. Once, no, twice, she snapped at flesh and almost got it, like some kind of zombie prisoner. When the hand holding her hair let go, she thought she might be heading toward freedom.

Until she felt a pinprick in the side of her neck and everything sparkled away into blackness.

* * *

The days rolled past, they had to, even though she couldn't really tell one from another. There was daytime and blazing heat, nighttime and cold, the sort of chill that's born of fever and delirium. In between was a lot of unconsciousness, where she knew she'd been drugged but didn't know what was being done to her while she was out. Hot, cold, but not much sensation beyond that except a strange sort of tickling that pulled across the tender surfaces of her body. Sometimes it came with tiny pinches or scrapes, almost like something was trying to get underneath her skin. Not

*Yvonne Navarro*

digging too deeply, just sort of…skimming.

Once or twice she woke to find something thick and sweet coming up the hydration tube when she sucked on it, a liquid she could only compare to a warm milkshake. She took it in because her body wanted it, even though she'd rather not, even though she would rather simply die.

She tried to imagine rescue, the sudden intrusion of sirens into the non-stop birdsong and buzz of insects that was her daily soundtrack, the blaze of light that would coat her pupils when the blindfold was removed. In her darkest hours, she sees herself like this for the rest of her life, a time period that stretches incomprehensibly before the thin sheet of her mental sanity.

\* \* \*

When the girl nearly succeeded in biting me, I started drugging her until she slept most of the time. I hadn't wanted to, but ultimately I realized that was less cruel than what she was enduring. The process was working and the hours I spent with her were relaxing and fulfilling in a way that nothing else in my life could be, but it was taking longer than I'd expected—the effort to productivity ratio was poor, indeed. I wanted more from her, but it seemed clear she'd given all that she could. She could no longer recover quickly enough to start the cycle again, and it had never been my intent to torture her. I just wasn't that kind of person.

\* \* \*

She heard the footsteps and vaguely felt the ropes around her loosen and fall away, but she was too heavily sedated to care anymore. In the movies, the prisoner might hold the pills in his or her cheek, then spit them out and get away. In her reality, there is no escape from the kidnapper's hypodermic. The blindfold was still on as her hands were retied behind her back. She was lifted and carried, then placed in what could only be the trunk of a car. Her head lolled and she thought it might be a good thing that she was high. The material over her eyes slipped just enough on one side for her to glimpse the skin across the top of her right breast. It was a suppurating mass of raw, burned patches that dribbled liquid where fresh blisters had been broken and peeled away. Right now, though, she didn't feel a thing.

Her abductor gave her one last dose to ensure she stayed cooperative as she was wrapped in an old sheet.

* * *

Working carefully, I laid the last piece of skin, still faintly moist and delicate, across the bottom of the thin wire frame. I've been working my way around for quite some time, and this last layer, the newest, is gray-white above where it joins the older, yellow-tinted ones below it. In only a few days the latest additions will be as dried and discolored as the other layers. Hanging at just the right height above my reading chair, the lampshade was small and very fragile. So many years in the making, yet so much more to go before it's finished.

* * *

I propped the girl beneath a tree in a parking lot I'd never been to before, then drove away. My route was fast and anonymous, down a country road that's not used much and where I could see any traffic both coming and going. When the road was empty in both directions, I pulled over and removed the magnetized cover on my license plate. I slipped it beneath the mat on the driver's side floor. Climbing back into the driver's seat, I shrugged out of the gray hoodie, then tugged off the fake mustache and the piece of clear plastic on my left hand on which I'd drawn a sort of maritime star tattoo. All of that went into a brown paper shopping bag, one that had no store logo on it, so that if I found myself in a spot where I had to dump it, there was nothing to trace back to me. I shook out my hair and let the blonde curls fall naturally across my shoulders, then quickly dabbed some pink gloss on my lips.

A moment later, I was back on the highway. I'd give it a couple of weeks, then get back to my project.

*"It's time to get a new one."*

## About Yvonne Navarro

Yvonne Navarro lives in southern Arizona where, until recently, she worked in one of those super-secret squirrel buildings on historic Fort Huachuca. She is the author of twenty-two published novels and well over a hundred short stories, plus numerous non-fiction articles and two editions of a reference dictionary. Her writing has won the Bram Stoker Award® plus a number of other writing awards. She also draws and paints, and once sold a canvas print of a zombie painting.

She is married to author Weston Ochse and dotes on their blind Great Dane, Ghoulie, and a talking, people-loving parakeet named BirdZilla.

# Burning Leaves on an Autumn Day

## Ray Garton

From Reggie Parks's back porch, the day looked like a painting of autumn. The chilly air was misty-gray with the smoke of neighborhood chimneys, the azure sky bright through the skeletal tree branches to which a few desperate leaves still clung. The ground was dappled with the bright oranges and muted yellows that had fallen from the two maples, the elm and the royal empress. Children's laughter came from the backyard on Reggie's right, and to the left, smoke rose from the other side of the tall, slatted chain-link fence where, he guessed, Ollie Dumont was burning leaves in his backyard.

Reggie had always hated that ugly fence — it was old and more slats broke away every year, giving him the creepy impression of a long row of big jagged teeth along one side of the yard — but he could say nothing about it because it was Ollie's fence. He knew it would be a waste of time to bring it up with the Ollie. He would chuckle and say, "Sure, I'll get to work on replacing that fence, uh, let's see—" take a look at his watch, then say, "How about the day after my funeral? That work for you?" and chuckle again.

Ollie was a cranky old fart. He was a Vietnam vet and a retired carpenter, and he was married to June, one of the sweetest women Reggie had ever known, right up there with his own mother. Silver-haired and apple-cheeked, she looked like a grandmother who had just stepped off of a Norman Rockwell canvas. They had four children and enough grandchildren and great-grandchildren to make their house sound like a bus station every year at Christmas time.

Reggie was willing to cut Ollie some slack because he was about seventy, give or take a couple of years — he refused to tell anyone his true age — and Reggie, who would turn fifty-one in January and already suffered from more aches and pains than he'd ever experienced in his life, found that he had a lot more respect for old people than he'd had in his giddy, invincible youth. By seventy — or whatever age he was — Ollie had plenty of reasons to be cranky, whatever they might be. Even so, he could be a genuine pain in the ass.

Reggie and Kimberly had lived next door to the Dumonts for twenty years. Ollie had always been loud, irascible and opinionated, but age, while dulling and dimming so much of him, only magnified some of Ollie's worst traits. All of his filters, the functionality of which had long been in question, were collapsing, and he said whatever popped into his head, and if he was angry, he said it very loudly. June, being the human equivalent of a batch of sugar cookies fresh out of the oven that she was, took his shouting in stride. More than a few times, while Ollie bellowed on about something, June had turned to Reggie and silently rolled her eyes.

At the rear of the long backyard was an eight-foot tall fence that Reggie had installed shortly after they moved in, and on the other side, a deep, dense grove of oak trees separated it from a large complex of storage rentals. That same fence continued up the other side of the backyard and nearly all the way to the front of the house before it ended at a gate. On the other side of the fence, the Goldman children and some of their friends were on the large trampoline, and, from the sound of their laughter and shrieks, were having a grand time. That was fine with Reggie. It was a nice sound and usually cheered him up.

When he and Kimberly moved in, that house had been occupied by Morris and Felicia Goldman and their three children. Morris owned a small jewelry store in the mall at the time, but in fifteen years he had a chain of stores that was so successful, he and Tonya decided to move to Palm Springs. Their oldest son Aaron, his wife Sarah, and their three children, soon to be four, now lived in the house. They were not exactly standoffish, but neither did they encourage interaction. They exchanged smiles and greetings, but little more.

Reggie's right hand clutched the handle of a rake as he went down the steps and onto the back lawn. It was a bigger yard than he and Kimberly needed now that the kids were out of the house, but it got a lot of use when they visited.

Through slats in the chain-link fence, Reggie saw movement and the orange flash of flames in milky smoke. He recognized Ollie's hooded green raincoat.

"Hey, Ollie!" he called. "Nice day."

Movement continued over there for a moment, then he saw the olive green of the coat move across the gaps in the slatted fence and go into the house through the back door.

Maybe Ollie was simply too preoccupied with burning leaves to notice anything else. Deciding to count his blessings, Reggie started raking, and a couple of minutes later he began whistling a tune. Something by Elton John, a song from early in his career, but Reggie couldn't remember the title or the lyric, only the tune. Something from the old days, when he and Kimberly were in high school.

*Why do we call them the "old days?"* he wondered. *The days aren't old. The person* remembering *them is old!*

His whistling was interrupted by a couple of loud, barked laughs at his own little joke. He stopped raking and looked at the back door, then at the kitchen window. No sign of Kimberly. He wanted to share that thought with someone, mostly because if he didn't say it out loud, he was afraid it would dissolve in his head like an Alka-Seltzer tablet.

He muttered the thought to himself a few times under his breath as he continued raking.

The kids playing on the trampoline went on laughing and squealing. When he looked in that direction, Reggie saw them bob into view above the fence as they bounced.

He recited that thought a few more times. It might be useful at parties. Of course, he and Kimberly seldom went to parties anymore, mostly because so few people they knew threw them. With such a bad economy, terrorists blowing things up all over the world and just about everything in civilization seemingly failing or collapsing, nobody, as of late, was in a celebratory mood.

Reggie made a mental note to suggest to Kimberly that they throw a little party, have some friends over, maybe brighten everybody's mood a little. Soon, before he forgot his joke.

He heard a sound from Ollie's backyard, stopped raking, and turned to the fence. More movement flashed beyond those open slots and more smoke rose in a column from Ollie's yard.

Bending down slightly, he peered through one of the slots. Ollie was hunched over and appeared to be fussing with his fire, grumbling to himself.

Reggie went back to his raking.

He often marveled at June's ability to maintain such a sunny disposition after living with Ollie for so long. Most women would have left him decades ago, and some would have killed him in his sleep. He complained about everything and argued almost every point. And he never stopped nagging June, blaming her for petty little mishaps, criticizing her every action and comment, and he was always telling jokes at her expense, making cracks about the miseries of married life like a sitcom husband.

"You just wait," he sometimes said, pointing a knobby finger at Reggie. "When you get to be my age, you'll realize one day that I was *right*."

Ollie's crankiness could be quite funny and charming in small doses, but it quickly became annoying and tedious. Every year, he complained that their Christmas tree wasn't good enough, even though he'd picked it out. Every summer was too hot, every winter was too cold and nothing was as it should be, as far as Ollie was concerned. And yet, June always had a ready smile, a pleasant word, a moment to chat, and never seemed to be darkened by bad moods or periods of frustration. She remained bright and unchanging, never giving the impression of a woman trapped in a miserable marriage to a human wart.

Reggie had quite a pile of leaves growing in the corner where

Ollie's fence met the raised bed where Kimberly tended a vegetable garden every year. It ran along the side of a long storage shed that backed up to Ollie's fence. Beyond the shed, the lawn went all the way to the back fence, so Reggie had plenty of ground to cover. He'd only just begun, as Karen Carpenter would assure him if she hadn't starved herself to death.

Reggie began to whistle "We've Only Just Begun."

Ollie's voice rose in a growl. "The hell is that *racket*?"

Reggie stopped raking, turned to the fence and called, "Hey, Ollie."

"You got a goddamned trained bird over there, or something?"

He chuckled as he put the rake down on the grass and walked over to the fence. "I was just whistling as I raked the leaves, that's all."

"That's *all*? Isn't that *enough*? Sounds like *more* than enough to me. Not enough aspirin in the world to treat the headache that racket will create. You'd have to get a prescription. You hear me? *A goddamned prescription!*" he shouted.

In spite of the fact that it was a heartbreakingly beautiful fall day, Ollie sounded even angrier than usual.

Reggie wanted to say, *Who crapped in your oatmeal, Ollie?* But he knew that would make the old man's dark mood even worse. Instead, he kept his mouth shut and put his eye to one of the open slots in the fence.

Still wearing his hooded raincoat—*Why is he wearing a raincoat on such a clear day?* Reggie wondered—Ollie was bent over, tossing what looked like small, squat logs onto the pile of leaves.

"What are you doing, Ollie?"

He stood and turned toward Reggie. He wore a dark, reddish-brown shirt and dark blue sweat pants under the coat. The raincoat's hood was up around his head, and the pale features of his face were partially obscured in its dark oval. "What? Doing? Burning leaves. That's all. Just burning some leaves."

The dark pieces of wood were on the ground around Ollie's feet, on which he wore brown slippers.

"Are you putting wood on the fire, too?" Reggie asked.

"What? Just never mind and leave me alone, goddammit!"

Reggie turned away from the fence and picked up the rake, but he was disturbed. Something wasn't right. Ollie was wearing a raincoat on a clear day and throwing what looked like firewood on a pile of burning leaves. Still holding the rake, he went back to the fence.

"You want some help, Ollie?" he asked, peering through a gap in the slats.

"Help? Burning leaves? Do I look like I need help? Mind your own business, Parks! You're too goddamned nosy. Always have been. You want me to come over there and stick my nose in *your* business? Huh, Parks? That what you want? 'Cause I'll do it! See if *you* like it!"

"Fine," Reggie muttered, walking away from the fence. He raked with a little more vigor and speed, angered by the old man's behavior. Ollie always had a pebble in his shoe about something, but he seemed more on edge than usual. Fine, let him stew in his juices and set his backyard on fire, for all Reggie cared.

He raked his way across the lawn to the fence bordering the Goldman yard where children still laughed and shrieked and bounced. It seemed to Reggie that it hadn't been all that long ago when his own backyard was filled with the same sounds, and Kimberly spent her days driving kids around and making sandwiches and cleaning up messes, and he spent his weekends doing things like building a tree house, or a dollhouse, or just playing with the kids. And what weekends they'd been, what wonderful weekends.

But those days were well behind all of them, and Reggie didn't mind. He wasn't the kind of person who spent much time looking backward, pouring over family albums, thinking about the way things used to be. He preferred to enjoy things as they were, and right now things were pretty damned good. He could not think of a single thing to complain about.

He and Kimberly were healthy, and they were happier than ever. After all three of their children had moved out, they had taken advantage of the empty nest. First of all, they'd had sex in every single room in the house, in broad daylight. Not all in one day, of course, but on their own schedule, which worked out to whenever the hell they felt like it. And as loudly as they wanted. They had also renovated the kids' old rooms, but as far as Reggie was concerned, sex in any room, whenever they felt like it? *That* was the pure gold part of the golden years.

"You know what I just decided?" Kimberly had said one day as they lay on the kitchen floor, panting and sweating from the orgasms they'd just had.

"I hope you don't want to carpet the kitchen."

"Oh, no, that's disgusting. No. You know how we're going to spend our old age? I've decided."

"How are we going spend our old age?"

She rolled toward him with a big grin. "Fucking."

The kids were well—all of them, children, grandchildren, the whole brood—and quite successful. In addition to being healthy, Reggie and Kimberly were having more sex—more often, and with greater variety and experimentation—than they'd ever had in their entire marriage.

No, Reggie had no complaints. What was there to complain about? He felt extremely fortunate to have such a good life, such a healthy and loving family, that complaining would be—

"Still got that goddamned bird over there, Parks?"

Well, warm, friendly neighbors might be a nice change. But he wasn't going to quibble.

Reggie hadn't realized he was whistling again, and he stopped the second he heard Ollie's voice, well behind him now, on the other side of the yard and beyond the slatted fence. Ollie sounded different this time, though. Reggie couldn't identify exactly how, but the quality of his voice had changed. He sounded, perhaps, more relaxed?

Turning to look back at the fence, Reggie watched the gaps in the slats for a moment. Maybe Ollie hadn't sounded more relaxed, maybe he'd sounded…happy? Clutching the rake's handle in his left hand, he walked back to the fence and looked through one of the gaps, then another, and finally, a third.

He saw nothing, heard nothing. There was no sign of Ollie except the fire he'd started, and even that appeared to be dying. Tendrils of smoke rose from the partially-blackened pile of leaves and the lumps of firewood Ollie had thrown onto it.

As his oldest son Donald was fond of saying, with a smirk and a dismissive wave of his hand, "Fuck him, Dad."

The kids had never liked Ollie. They'd adored June, of course, but had avoided Ollie like poison oak.

In no hurry, taking his time, enjoying the day, Reggie raked the length of the yard all the way to the back fence, gathering the leaves in piles that he would then scoop into big plastic yard bags for the garbage man to haul away.

"You care too much," Kimberly had said to him one day.

"About what?"

"About the things Ollie says. I don't pay attention to anything that comes out of that man's mouth."

"But the things he says about their marriage, about June—and right in front of her!"

"They've been together for half a century, so I don't think June hears a thing he says, either. If she did, Ollie would be dead and she'd be doing time. I have no idea why she's stayed with him this long, but that's her business. What we think doesn't matter. I just want to be a good friend to June. Obviously she needs one because she's practically held hostage by Ollie. As far as I'm concerned, though, he is nothing but a hot gust of wind. I wish you felt the same way."

"I do, I really do."

"If you did, you wouldn't be bothered by the things he says."

"That's only because it's so insulting and unfair to June. And to *you*, because sometimes he insults women and wives in general."

"Oh, please. Let June and me take care of ourselves, okay? We're fine. Just don't let the old fart get to you, honey."

She was right, of course. As usual. Ollie wasn't worth the aggravation.

As he raked, Reggie caught a whiff of a new aroma in the chilly fall air, something that had joined the smell of wood smoke. It was familiar but also disorienting because it was strictly a summer smell, associated with long, hot days and the fresh, green scent of recently mowed grass — and Reggie was smelling it in the middle of autumn.

Someone was cooking meat on an open grill.

It was odd, but he conceded that there were no laws prohibiting the cooking of meat outdoors during the fall. Reggie smiled and told himself that life was short. If someone wanted a freshly-grilled hamburger with his hot apple cider — hey, why the hell not?

A sharp sound cut through the sweep of his rake and he stopped to listen. The sound came again, longer this time, a cry of distress, pain. It sounded like Ollie.

Reggie dropped his rake and hurried across the wide expanse of his lawn to Ollie's fence. He peered through one of the gaps, then another, and another. He couldn't see Ollie, but he heard another abrupt cry. He called Ollie's name a few times but got no response.

He walked along the fence, peering through gaps until he found one that gave him a view of the burning leaves again. There he saw Ollie, lying facedown on the ground, arms splayed.

"Oh, damn," Reggie said as he turned and broke into a run. He crossed the lawn, went along the side of the house and through the gate. He hurried down the driveway and along the sidewalk to Ollie's house.

He kept a cell phone in his car, as did Kimberly, but Reggie did not carry one with him. The idea of people being able to call him on the phone no matter where he was made him shudder and he didn't think he would ever warm to it.

He hurried across Ollie's front yard and along the side of the house. The gate stood open a few inches, so Reggie pushed through and continued to the backyard, past the covered patio.

Ollie had not moved in the time it had taken Reggie to get there. He lay sprawled on the ground a few feet away from the smoking pile of leaves, sobbing and muttering.

"Ollie, what happened? Did you fall?"

As Reggie knelt down beside him, Ollie rose on hands and knees and slowly turned his head toward him. When he saw Reggie, his eyes widened and he began to crawl away, shouting, "No! What are you doing here? Go away, goddammit!"

Reggie sighed as he stood and watched Ollie crawl toward the pile of leaves. The fire was somewhat revived, and flames flickered among the rising smoke. He saw one of the pieces of firewood and his eyes, confused, squinted.

It was not firewood.

He moved a few steps toward the fire, eyes locked on that dark chunk of…of…it looked like…blackened, cooked meat. It was a couple of feet long and bent at one end, almost like it had a joint of some kind, a…knee. It was a charred thigh above a knee, and below that, it was severed. A few feet away were two more pieces. One had a foot attached and the other had a face. June's face, black and distorted, a tuft of her shiny silver hair rising out of the burnt flesh of her severed head. There were other pieces and none of them were firewood.

"You just get the hell outta here!" Ollie shouted. He clumsily got to his feet on the other side of the smoking pile of leaves. "You hear me? Nobody called you over here, goddammit!"

It took a moment for Reggie to understand that the groaning sound he was hearing was his own voice, his own horror, his own sickness coming out of him in a cry of pain.

"Quit your whining, Parks! She earned it. You hear me? *Earned* it." He waved his arms as he shouted, and Reggie noticed that his right hand clutched a meat cleaver with dark smears on the blade. Beneath the raincoat he was not wearing a reddish-brown shirt. He was not wearing a shirt at all. He was bare from the waist up and covered with blood. He wasn't wearing his teeth, and his rubbery lips collapsed inward when he closed his mouth. "All the years I put up with that simpering smile, that happy disposition, that... that..." He suddenly pointed a finger at Reggie. "You, though, *you* won't have to." A high, jittery laugh escaped him, like air escaping a balloon. "You won't have to put up with it. Not now, not anymore." He smiled and that jittery laugh came again. "I did what you never would have because—" That laugh again. It was awful. "—you're a goddamned spineless pussy!"

Reggie staggered backward and turned so suddenly that the force almost knocked him over. He had to get home. That was all he wanted. To get away from that smell of cooking meat and the insanity in Ollie's wide, round eyes and go home to Kimberly.

He hurried at a staggered run out of Ollie's backyard, across his lawn, along the sidewalk. Had it occurred to him to enter the house through the front door, he would have noticed that it was wide open. But he kept his eyes front as he went up the driveway, through the gate, and into the backyard, the last place he'd been before the world had become so ugly. Stumbling up the back steps, he went into the house and through the kitchen.

"Kimberly!" His voice was shrill and hoarse, but he didn't notice as he went through the dining room and into the living room. "Kimberly!"

The front door was open and the small table beside it had been knocked over.

"Kimberly, where are you?" He stood in the living room and listened to the silence of the house. He rounded the corner and entered the hall and lurched to a halt.

Halfway down the hall, she lay in three pieces in the middle of a great splash of red on the floor and walls.

Something inside Reggie blinked out and he did not hear himself scream.

* * *

Two police officers answered the call made by one Reggie Parks, a distressed male reporting a murder. They found the front door open, and when they received no response, they went inside.

They discovered the bloody scene in the hallway. Upon finding the back door wide open, they went outside and found a man raking the lawn. It had already been raked and leaves were in neat piles around the yard, but the man slowly dragged the rake over the grass as if gathering more fallen leaves into a pile.

"Are you Mr. Parks?" one of the officers asked.

He kept raking.

The officer reached out and touched his shoulder.

Reggie turned to him slowly, and his eyes seemed to look through the officer for a moment. Then he smiled pleasantly.

"It's a beautiful autumn day, isn't it?" he said.

*Ray Garton*

# About Ray Garton

The Bram Stoker Award®-nominated Ray Garton is the prolific author of more than sixty novels, novellas, short story collections, movie novelizations and TV tie-ins. Garton's exceptional portfolio of work spans the genres of horror, crime, and suspense.

His 1987 erotic vampire novel *Live Girls* was called "artful" by the *New York Times* and was nominated for the Bram Stoker Award. In 2006, he received the Grand Master of Horror Award at the World Horror Convention in San Francisco. His 2001 comedy thriller *Sex and Violence in Hollywood* is being developed for the screen.

His novels *Trailer Park Noir* and *Meds* (a thriller with deadly side effects), are available in paperback and as ebooks from E-Reads. And his seventh collection, *Wailing and Gnashing of Teeth,* was recently published by Cemetery Dance Publications.

He lives in northern California with his wife Dawn.

# The Long Bright Descent

## Erik Williams

check my watch. Ten after seven. Sun sets in another twenty minutes. He better get here soon or I'll have to leave without agreeing to terms for the evening, which means it's a chase by default. I used to prefer him being late and missing me. Gave me a big lead. But it also led to surprises, and I've tired of surprises. I like making the choice. It's one of the few freedoms I have.

"Want a refill?"

The waitress stands over me, hand holding a pitcher of ice water that's half empty. In the other hand, a wet rag with coffee stains. She's got too much eye make-up on and not enough lipstick. The dark circles under her eyes scream exhaustion. She smells thirty but looks forty. A hard forty. Probably working to support a couple of kids while their daddy does time. I can practically read it in the crow's feet and frown lines.

"No."

"Ready to order, or are you still waiting?"

I check my watch again. "How fast can I get two waffles with butter, no syrup, and a cup of coffee?"

"The coffee you can get in thirty seconds. The waffles will take about ten minutes."

"I'll have the coffee and waffles."

"You got it."

She walks away. I turn my attention to the entrance, willing him to walk through. I do not like surprises, wonder if he's doing this on purpose. Toying with me. Maybe waiting to hit me in the lot.

No, he's moved beyond those petty games. We both have. I'd say we have matured, but how do we mature? It implies growth. Rather,

I think we're just tired. It's easier to deal with when you acknowledge that. That we're both tired of this game. There are rules to the game, of course, but the players still have a say in how it's played. And we both decided long ago to a certain type of game play.

The waitress returns with the coffee. Sets it down with a couple packs of creamer and moves on without saying anything. I'm okay with that. Not much for chitchat with strangers.

The door opens and he walks through the entrance, wearing all black, per the usual. Sunglasses on. Head low. He lifts it long enough to scan and locate me. Nods and heads over.

"Was wondering if you were going to show," I say.

"Me, too." He keeps the sunglasses on as he settles into the seat across from me. Sets his elbows on the table. "Tough getting up."

"Sun too harsh today?"

"It is called the Sunshine State." He smirks. "I started to convince myself you drove this way to mock me."

"Nah. You kind of forced me in this direction with that stunt in Atlanta."

"Sure, sure. Blame me." He scratches his chin. His skin is fair but not as pale as an albino. More like a Swede with black hair and rose-colored cheeks and nose. Like he spent his time in the cold before walking in, even though it was well above eighty outside. "You didn't have to come this way."

"True, but it wasn't to mock you." I glance at the sunset through the big plate window. Orange and dipping low. I start to shiver. "Don't have much time."

He pulls the sunglasses off and sets them down. Fixes me with gray eyes. "Yeah, already feeling better."

"I know."

"Thought I'd lost you there for a while, just after dawn. But I caught the scent outside Tallahassee. Managed to make it here and grab a room at the Motel 6 over there."

"That's where I stayed, too."

"No shit?" He nods his head. "Figured I had enough time to rest, being that close to you. I figured wrong."

"Me, too. Had a tough time recovering today, even with the sun."

The waitress shows up and sets the waffles down. Asks if there'll be anything for my friend. I say no and she leaves.

"Maybe I wanted something."

"You can have whatever you want after I leave." I sever a waffle and bite. Chase it with coffee. I should have eaten earlier, before the sun dipped too far. It's hard to swallow now. My stomach wants to reject everything other than the coffee. Liquids I can handle at night. "But we need to agree to terms."

"Fine, fine. Chase or wits?"

I take another bite, chew, and choke it down. Sip and think. I'm tired and getting colder as the sun fades. I don't want to run, but I know I'm not up for a battle of wits. Not tonight.

"Chase," I say.

"That's five in a row. You're not getting scared of my mental abilities, are you?"

"No, just tired." I manage another bite before I put the fork down and push the plate away. Managed to finish one whole waffle. Should have eaten earlier.

"You done with that?"

I nod. "I'm in the gulf."

He looks out the window. "Still some rays left."

"I'm in the gulf."

He holds his hands up. "Won't argue with you. I guess you know your body better than anyone."

We sit there, silent. He taps his fingers on the table. I stare out at the last dying rays of light. Another cycle about to start. In the kitchen, a plate shatters.

"Might as well write down the particulars." He reaches into his jacket and pulls out a beat-up Moleskine. Cracks it open to the middle and clicks a ball point. "What's the fucking date today?"

"Twelfth. Do you know the month?"

"Yes, I know the damn month." He jots down the date. "Pensacola. Chase. Re—what name are you going by now?"

"You wrote it down yesterday."

"You change it every other day."

"Ray."

"Ray still?"

"Ray, still."

"I liked Regis better."

"I don't look like a Regis." I motion to my olive skin, even though it's paling as the sun sets. "You?"

"Still Papa."

"You need to change it."

"You say that every night."

"You need to change it. It's stale and dumb."

"No, it's not. And when I eventually win this game, I'll get to ask—"

"Who's your daddy? I know. You've death-gripped that joke for a long time."

Papa smiles and closes the Moleskine, slips it back into his jacket with his pen. He looks out the window at the orange sky. "Not much longer now."

"Nope."

He points at the waffle. "You won't mind if I finish that, right?"

"Help yourself."

He pulls the plate to him and grabs a clean fork. "Take off."

I nod and tip an imaginary cap to him. "Be seeing you."

I climb out of the booth. Legs feel like rubber. Should have slept more and eaten earlier. This was going to be a long night.

I pull a twenty out of my wallet but Papa waves me off. "I got this one."

"Thanks." Slip my wallet back in my jeans and head for the door.

*   *   *

I'm an hour down the road, west of Pensacola. Somewhere between Mobile and Pascagoula. I want to be farther away, want to have more distance between us, but an accident slows evening traffic to a crawl on Mobile Bay.

I consider getting off the 10. Maybe take side streets and do parallels and nineties all night. Wear his ass out on traffic lights and back alleys. But I don't. Too easy to get bottled up in a dead end. Too easy to end up choked off with no escape. Staying on the interstate provides multiple lanes and highway connectors and numerous exits. Exits are escape routes. Never ever underestimate the power of an escape route.

And never ever underestimate the importance of distance. More is always better than less in this game. Looking up in the rearview every few seconds, I know I'm not on the side of better.

For a second I wish I chose wits. The second passes, though, and I know I made the right call. There is no way I'd win wits.

Because there are no escape routes when battling wits. Not with him.

He knows all the tricks, and I don't have the mental capabilities I once had. This is his playground, and I'm just a tourist. A constant tourist. One who's tired.

I don't engage anymore. I've let my wits atrophy. I replaced them with fear. I was lucky to get away last week. Used a turn of phrase to win. Never again.

*Enough.*

Check the rearview again. Not much traffic behind me. A few sets of headlights, mostly trucks hauling freight. Not him. Not yet.

*But he's coming. He always comes. And I always run.*

The minutes pass. The miles pass. Mississippi passes. I'm in Louisiana. I'm tired. I'm weak. My attention drifts. Still a few headlights behind me, but not him. Not yet.

On the bridge spanning the Atchafalaya Swamp. Too dark to see anything below. Like flying over the abyss. But I can smell it, damp and stagnant. Eternal yet ever-changing.

And not enough exits.

I see the headlights.

Coming fast.

Him.

Not much else to do but smirk because this is my fault. He stayed far enough back not to be noticed and waited until I made it onto the two-lane causeway. No real shoulders. A few turn-offs and U-turns, but, for the most part, nothing but a straight line for eighteen miles. Eighteen miles of bridge and swamp and the two of us along with a few others. At least there won't be many casualties this time.

The lights close to within two car lengths but no closer. He's matching my speed, daring me to move first. My Challenger has enough horses to do some damage, but nothing compared to what his heavily-modified Shelby can do.

I can't outrun him.

I can't out-muscle him.

And I'm too weak to outsmart him.

*Well, what the hell does that leave?*

My smirk broadens into a full-fledged grin.

*Easy. Piss him off.*

Check my speed. A nice and legal sixty-five. Perfect.

Then I slam on the brakes.

I watch in the rearview as the bright reds illuminate his surprised face. I hear the screech of his own rubber as he does the same. Swerves right to avoid me. I anticipate and swerve right with him, forcing him to reverse hard over to the left. Don't know how, but he misses my back bumper and narrowly avoids the left rail of the bridge. I accelerate, pushing up to seventy and then eighty before re-sighting him.

*Shit.* He's recovered fast. Already corrected and closing.

*We've done this too many times.*

I look ahead. No signs for exits or turnabouts. No land between east and west sections of the bridge. It's just us, racing.

He stays directly behind me, about eight car lengths. He won't make the same mistake twice. Instead, he matches my speed, comfortable to stay in pursuit mode.

What's his game? Is he baiting me into something? Or is he just bored and trying to drag this out all night?

I look over on the passenger seat. The cardboard box sits there. In it, a .45, an Uzi and a couple of grenades. Don't want to use either gun. Hell, I can't, not with him behind me. He knows that. I'd love to use the grenades, especially since there's no traffic on the bridge, but I don't want to cause damage to the bridge and end up killing someone by accident later. I wonder if a grenade would really do all that much damage to reinforced concrete. I doubt it.

I save it for later and look back to the rearview. Still right where I left him.

Up ahead in the right lane, taillights. Small, round ones. Hard to tell what kind of car. A few more seconds and I realize it's the back of a semi hauling a trailer.

An engine roars.

Not mine.

His.

He's deduced my plan before I could put form to it. He knows, damn it.

Before I can hit the left lane and blow by the semi, he's parallel to me, pinning me behind the truck and blocking me from any maneuver.

Except slamming on the brakes.

But he knows that, too. That's why he's got a Glock raised and pointed at my head. For some reason I notice his passenger window's down. Like he had planned it all along to go this way.

Before I can put the brake pedal through the floor, he's firing.

*Pop. Pop. Pop.*

The first hits my driver side window, turning the safety glass into a mosaic. The second shatters it and hits my left deltoid. I keep my left hand on the wheel and my right on the emergency brake.

The brake pedal turns to mush and he's flying by me. Ready to yank up on the emergency and flipped this bitch one-eighty and incinerate asphalt in the opposite direction, but not before the third bullet hits below my left arm. It tears through my armpit and hits something. Pieces of shrapnel head south toward my lungs, toward my heart.

I wish I was strong enough to bite down and bear it, but I've never been that way. Instead, I scream and jerk the wheel right-left-right. Fight hard not to lose control. Blink away tears. The reds of the semi's lights blur and I hear him downshift. See him pull up alongside me again. He readies to fire again.

I let go of the emergency brake. Death-grip one of the grenades. Pop the pin free with my thumb and chuck it. I don't look before I throw. I don't have to. I know I've got him.

I accelerate, hitting fifth gear fast. In the rearview he swerves and rear-ends the semi. The driver's door pops open and he's rolling hard on the asphalt. The Shelby makes it another twenty feet before turning the swamp orange and yellow.

No cheering. No fist pumping. Because even though he's on foot now, he's still coming. And I'm bleeding and hurting. And it's a long time until sunrise.

As I cough blood and fight to keep my eyes open, I realize for the first time in a long time I might not make it. For the first time in a long time, he can afford to wait and see. For the first time in a long time, I may be fucked.

\* \* \*

Coughing blood. Left eye closed. Right hand barely gripping the wheel. I pulled off the I-10 hours ago out of fear of being pulled over for driving too slow. Out of fear he would catch up and finish my ass off.

Reaching Baton Rouge, I took side roads. Back roads. Empty roads. Anything where I could drive twenty-five and not attract attention. Neighborhoods. Business parks. I didn't fear him in this territory. I only feared missing sunrise.

At five in the morning, I hit the road again, taking the 49 toward Shreveport. Good open country. Lots of tall grass and wetlands. Lots of nothing.

Spit blood on the passenger side seat. It's never been occupied as long as I've owned it, so no foul. Stare hard down the road, willing the first rays of light to crest the lowland and illuminate a path of salvation. When they don't come, I turn and gaze east, almost crying. Starting to wonder if this is it, if this is the end, if I've finally lost this game. I haven't been in this position in a long, long time and it starts to sink in that this might be it. The end.

Then the orange-yellow creeps over the horizon. The first indication the new day arrives. I swerve right and pull off onto the shoulder. Kill the engine, yank the key, and hoist myself out with my right hand, keeping my left arm pinned to my ribs, not wanting to tear any scabs or stop any clots.

I shut the door and stumble down a berm, away from the interstate. It's a field. A pasture. Hell, I don't know. It's open land. And the further east I go, the sooner the light will hit me. So I plod. I trudge. I trip several times, hoping I'll somehow fall into the newborn light.

Then I find a rock. Long, flat, about a foot off the ground. My mind screams *Ancient altar!* But I don't care. It's there. Whether for me or not, I don't know. Will never know.

The rays are almost here and I can't go any further. So I strip off my shirt, toss it and lay on the rock. The cool, moist surface soothes my back and sends instant chills from my head to my heels. But I ignore it because this is it. Either I'm done or I'm not. Either it's all over or it's not.

The rays come. I feel them creeping, radiating off the blades of grass as they're illuminated. Then up the side of the rock as the evaporation cycle begins, clearing the rock of its night-borne moisture. Then my right arm. Instantly, I feel the warmth, the renewal, the embrace. It spreads across my chest to my left side. I lift my arm, exposing the near-mortal wound, and allow the life-giver to do its work.

I'm safe. I'm going to make it. He can't touch me now.

Then I pass out.

\* \* \*

*— salt air is thick on the wind coming from the horizon. The waves lap the hull, hard spraying mist over the sides, but I plow on toward the first rays of light, clutching the horizontal slash across my stomach, pushing hard to keep my intestines from spilling on the deck.*

*Not much longer.*

*I cast a quick glance over my shoulder, see him several boat lengths behind. Impossible to make up the difference. He knows it. The look on his face says as much. Then he answers me by spitting and turning and disappearing below decks.*

*Turn back to the eastern horizon. The first rays emerge from the sea. Then curve of the orange dome. Tears fill my eyes. I drop to my knees and flop on my side and let the —*

\* \* \*

"Mister, you okay?"

My eyes flutter. I blink back the sudden rush of light. The sun is high above in a cloudless sky. An egret circles to the left.

"Mister?"

I sit up, exhaling the whole way. Check the wounds. Good to go.

Turn to my right. A boy, no more than eight, stands there. Local for sure. Farmer's kid.

"Yeah, I'm good."

*Erik Williams*

"That your shirt?"

"Yeah."

"That your car?"

I look to the road and see two punks peering in the windows. Another has already popped the hood and stares at the engine as if he knows what the hell he's looking at.

"Yeah. Those your brothers?"

"Shit, no. They a couple punk bitches that like to scavenge around here. Always bugging my Pa."

"Scavenge?"

"You know, steal shit out of broke down cars and pick up shit that falls off trucks. That kind of shit."

"You say shit a lot, kid."

He chews on his lip and looks down. "My Pa says it a lot. Guess I do, too. Ma hates it, but what's she gonna do. She's in a wheelchair and me and Pa do all the work."

I nod. "I don't care."

"Well, shit. Just trying to help."

"Thanks. Now run along."

"What you gonna do to them?"

I hit the kid with double-barrel eyes. "Run along."

It works. He sprints off parallel to the freeway then banks left into the pasture toward a house half a mile away.

I return my attention to the punks. They've taken no notice of me. Maybe they haven't seen me at all. That's about to change.

I push off the rock, grab my shirt and walk. No wobbles. No dizziness. Full of strength. Energy. As if last night never happened.

"Step away from my car," I say as I climb out of the shallow ditch on the side of the shoulder.

The teenagers peering through the windows, both brunettes and about the same age, pop up, caught red-handed, and swivel toward me. Their eyes are a little wide. Different colors. The one on my right has brown eyes, the one on the left has blue, but their faces are similar enough to give them away as brothers. Same father, different mothers. They still live with the father. I can smell his two packs a day and cheap whiskey on them like a stain painted on their souls.

The boy under the hood doesn't pop up like his buddies. Instead, he sighs loud, and straightens up slowly. Grabs the hood and shuts it. Puts his knuckles on it. Sighs again and then turns around, wearing a big, shit-eating grin like it's part of his face. Like it's been there since he was born.

By that point I'm about six feet directly behind him. Hands at my sides. With my shirt and jacket on, they can't tell if I'm carrying or not.

"Your car," the apparent leader says. "Can you prove that?"

"I don't have to prove a damn thing." Pat my pocket where the keys are. "It's mine."

"You got a lot of firepower in there, mister. I think the sheriff might say it's his car now."

"Is that what you were going to do?"

"What do you mean?"

"I mean you were going to be a good citizen and call the sheriff and alert him to a car on the side of the road full of grenades and automatic weapons and a sawed-off shotgun on the back floor?" I make a slight motion to my waistline. "And whatever isn't in there?"

He looks at my waist, at the space behind the flap of my jacket and my belt. He can't see, but he smiles as if he can see through the jacket. "I'm calling your bluff. Show it."

"Why don't you boys just run along? Let me get in my car and go. I'll even give you the sawed-off."

"Why take a scatter gun when we can take it all?" he asks. "And I even like the car."

The other two come around and join their leader, standing at his sides. They're still a bit nervous but they'll follow his lead.

I lick my lips and tap my fingers together. Here comes the hard part.

*Erik Williams*

"Do what you got to do. But you're not leaving with the car or its contents."

"We'll see about that."

He steps forward and swings an overhead right. I see it coming in slow motion but make no move to dodge it.

The next moment, I'm on my right knee, blinking spots away. He's standing over me, right fist cocked, smiling. And he hammers down into my left cheekbone and temple.

I blink more spots away. Look back up at him. Get down on both knees and raise my chin at him

The other two look more nervous than before, unsettled, but the leader's not phased. Not one bit. He's digging it.

Three more punches in rapid succession: right-left-right. My head flies in the opposite direction with each hit only to be course-corrected by the following punch.

Then I lift my chin up and gaze at the leader. The smile has disappeared. His fist is cocked but it's shaking. Unsure. So unsure what to do now.

I've seen this many times before.

"You need to go now," I say. "Before I lose my patience."

The punk on my left grabs the leader by his cocked arm. "Come on, man. This dude's nuts."

"He ain't shit," the leader says, but his eyes don't match his tough words.

"He ain't bleeding, man," the punk on my right says. "Doesn't even look like you hit him."

"Your friend's right," I say to the leader. "You can't hurt me."

"Bullshit, anyone can be hurt."

"True. There's one who can hurt me. But that person isn't you."

"You're crazy," he says, lowering his fist, trying to save face.

"You'll never know what I am. Or what I do every night for you."

"Huh?"

"Go."

The other two grab the leader and pull him away toward a raised Ram crew cab. They climb in and spin the back tires and haul ass.

I remain kneeling for a moment, thinking about what I just said. *What I do every night for you.* It makes my stomach sour for two reasons. One, most guys like that don't deserve what I do. And two, everyone else does. But it's the few that tempt me, that make it real hard to keep going.

I spit and rise and shrug it off.

Won't be the last time.

So I climb in and continue on my way.

\* \* \*

I stop in Texas. Grab a room at a La Quinta. Scarf down a couple cheeseburgers before racking out. Alarm's set for five. Figure I'd get a solid nap, wake up, grab a few more burgers and meet up with him again. Settle the terms for the evening. I won't let what happened last night happen again. Not two nights in a row.

The alarm goes off. Smack it and sit up. Feeling good. Feeling a hell of a lot better than I did yesterday around this time.

That was my mistake. I didn't get enough rest, didn't get enough food, and then fell into the gulf. He almost had my dumb, lazy ass.

Not tonight.

Hell, I might even choose wits.

I shower and shave, take deeps breaths of the lingering steam. Feel really good.

The phone rings.

I freeze, staring at it in the reflection of the bathroom mirror. Sitting next to the bed. *Ring-ring-ring.*

Him.

I walk over and pick it up and say, "You're either tired or lost."

"I'm in Shreveport."

"So you're tired and have some distance to make up."

"Well, you destroyed my car and left me in the middle of that fucking bridge. Wasn't a fun night. Put it that way."

I sit on the edge of the bed. "No nights off, you know that."

"Thank you Captain Obvious. That's why I'm calling."

"What?"

"I want to get a few more hours sleep, so I was hoping we could just settle the terms now. Figure you choose chase and I say okay and you take off and I go back to lovely dreamland for a while. You get a nice big head start on top of the lead you already have, and I get my rest."

I cradle the phone and pull on my jeans. "Sounds like a win-win."

"There you go, a win-win. All you got to do is say it and I'll write it down."

"But I'll have to eat dinner alone."

"I'm sure you'll be okay."

I pull on my boots. "I don't know…"

"Come on, don't be an asshole."

I check my watch. Almost six. Tuck my gun in the small of my back. Listen to him breathe another few seconds. He's beat and I feel good. Fuck being chased.

"Wits," I say.

He laughs. I think it's annoyed laughter at first, but then my stomach drops. There's something else there. Something almost sinister.

"You're so damn predictable. It's almost like I know you better than I know myself."

"What did you do?"

"Nothing. It's what you did."

"What are you talking about? What did I do?"

"You chose wits. And you've already lost."

I drop the phone and bolt for the door. I open it and expect to find fire falling from the sky. The earth opening up and swallowing every living thing. The sun exploding.

Instead, I find *him*. Standing there. Grinning.

And then he punches me with a right cross that could crack a mountain. I fall back, hit the bed and drop to my ass. Clutch my nose. Broken, erupting blood.

He walks in and shuts the door behind him. Removes his sunglasses and sets them on the end table. Slides his jacket it off and drops it on the bed.

"You've broken protocol," I say and cough on blood. Spit. "You've broken the rules."

"Bullshit, I won."

"How? We haven't battled wits and you haven't given chase. I chose wits, you bastard."

"I know, and I outwitted you."

"At what point did that occur?"

"I lured you into a false sense of confidence. You believed I was exhausted, not mentally up for the challenge, but I was. I was right out there the whole time and you never caught on. I outflanked you. I won."

"That's not a battle of wits, you soft-headed ape. You tricked me and then assaulted me. You've won nothing." I look around the room for a second. "In fact, I'd say you forfeited the contest tonight."

"How so?"

"Because we're still here. Everything is still here."

He furrows his brow and looks around the room, too. Goes over to the window and looks outside. Then back to me. "Shit."

"Grab me a towel."

He heads to the bathroom, returns with a hand towel, tosses it in my lap. I press it against my nose.

"Open the blinds."

"Why?"

"Just do it."

He does.

The last bits of the days light flood in, hitting me right in the face. I drop the towel and let the sun do its thing.

*Erik Williams*

"I've never seen this before."

"I know."

He takes a seat and stares in awe. "Does it itch or tickle?"

"No. Feels warm."

I touch my nose. Wiggle it. Right as rain. I wipe the rest of the blood from my face and mouth and then drop the towel and climb up on the bed. Sit and look at him. A lot of firsts today.

"So now what?" he asks.

I shrug. "Got me. This is new ground."

He looks around the room like an answer might present itself. "Well, you're alive, everything's fine outside and I'm in no way feeling the drive to chase or battle wits."

I sigh, searching my emotions, looking for that unimaginable burning to run when I choose chase. Or that concrete desire to hold my ground and level him when I choose wits. Neither are there. Anywhere. It's like I'm completely empty.

"This is weird," he says.

"Yeah."

"It's like...I'm hollow or something."

"Yeah."

"So this is what it feels like."

"What's that?"

"When people bitch about not having a purpose in life."

I smirk. "I guess you could say that."

He drums his finger on the small desk. "There's got to be a consequence to this."

I scratch my head and think about that. "You mean a price to pay for not following the rules?"

"If there isn't, what's the point of our nightly game? No consequence, no reason for us to exist."

"It would all be meaningless." My stomach sours at the thought. The punk from earlier flashes white hot across my memory. All the shit I put up with, have put up with, endured, suffered, for guys like him, would have been for nothing. Unless there was a consequence.

I grab the remote control from the end table and flick on the TV. Scan the channels.

"What are you looking for?" he asks.

"The price."

"Is right?"

"No, the consequence."

"I don't—"

He stops when I land on CNN. Breaking news. A massive earthquake has just hit southern California. Flapping heads talk about "the big one."

"Well," he says. "There you go. Now we know what happens."

I scan the news ticker at the bottom. Explosions, collapsed overpasses, buildings shaken to dust. All because he decided to play his dumb trick on me. Sadly, the monster earthquake makes me feel a hell of a lot better than I did a second ago. It's nice to know my existence isn't meaningless.

"I got a bottle of Wild Turkey in my room," he says. "Want I should get it?"

"Yep," I say. "That'll do."

\* \* \*

He sits at the desk. I lay on the bed. We both drink Wild Turkey from plastic cups.

"Why do you do it?" he asks.

"What do you mean?"

"I mean why do you do it?"

I think about the assholes I've dealt with over the years. "Because I'm supposed to. It's kind of my reason for existing, you know."

"Yeah, but you see how these people are these days. They're going to wipe themselves out before I ever plant you in the ground."

"Possibly, but we play the game until that happens."

"You could always quit. Let me do away with you. Then it'd all be taken care of."

"Trust me, I've thought about it on more than one occasion."

He sighs. Sips. "So why not do it then?"

"You've already asked this question and the answer hasn't changed. Because I'm supposed to."

"There's got be something else there. I mean, yes, this is what we do. This is who we are. But they have changed so much. Hell, they haven't sacrificed to us in who knows how long. It's not unfair to think maybe our game should end because, brother, I'm pretty damn tired of playing it."

"I'm tired, too, but we keep playing. The darkness won't prevail."

He smiles. Winks. "We'll see about that tomorrow, I guess."

\* \* \*

We kill the bottle. He heads out around three in the morning. He stands in the doorway, back to me.

"It's weird," he says.

"What's that?"

"Well, we've never gone a night just hanging out."

"True."

"Even when it's wits I usually storm off in a fit of rage and kill some people."

"You don't have to storm off and kill anyone."

"Hey, that's how I take out my frustration. Losing to you every night for eons is a damn bit frustrating, if you know what I mean."

"Weird, I'd thought you'd be conditioned to it by now."

He turns to me. Smirks. "Fuck you."

"Sure thing."

"Where do you want to meet tomorrow?"

"The front-desk lady kept talking about a diner in the next town. We can meet there."

"Let me know when you get the name of the place."

"Will do. Off to bed?"

"Nah. I don't sleep while it's dark. Too much energy. I'll probably go find a whore. Fuck her and kill her."

I wince. "You have sex with them?"

He shrugs. "It's something to do. Mostly, I just kill them."

"You don't have to."

"It's my nature, remember. Got to feed the snake."

"Right."

"See you tomorrow."

He closes the door.

I stare at the ceiling, pretty sure this will never happen again.

* * *

The name of the place is the Yellow Rose Diner and Fill Station. Basically, your run-of-the-mill food stop on the asshole edge of nowhere, but the coffee's decent.

The sun dips low, painting the town in shades of sepia. The air is still and dense, like mounting tension. Like the whole place might explode at any moment.

Then again, maybe it's just the diner. Has a weird feeling to it. Darkness. Like when I'm around *him*. A type of darkness that wants you to hang around just long enough to see you dead.

The bell above the door jingles.

I look up to see him.

He sees me. Approaches.

"How's the food?" he asks, dropping into the chair across from me.

"I've had better."

He looks at my empty plate. "Doesn't seem to have prevented you from eating it all."

"I learned from the other night. No way I'm entering the gulf without a full stomach."

The waitress arrives. I ask for a refill on the coffee. He orders country fried steak, a side of Texas toast and a coffee of his own.

"So, anyway," he says, "after I left you last night—"

I hold up my hands. "I don't want to hear about what you did to some poor whore."

"It's not like that."

"We've got to settle the terms for the evening."

"Fine, but then can I tell you what happened?"

"I guess."

He pulls out his pen and Moleskin. "Okay, what'll it be?"

"Chase," I say.

He writes it down, along with our names, the date and the location. Puts the pen and Moleskin back in his jacket.

"So, last night I pick up this really young whore and take her back to the room. Do my thing. Set her up nice and good for the kill. But the whole time she's blabbering about her kid and how she doesn't want to lose it. How she wants to live."

"This is not what I want to hear."

"But this you do. I didn't kill her."

I blink. "What?"

"I didn't kill her. I let her go and took off before the cops showed up."

"Why?"

The waitress returns with his food and the coffee. When she leaves, he says, "Because I'm tired of it. All of it."

I sit back, eyeing him. Wondering what this was all about. I sip coffee and think maybe this is wrong. There's some kind of con here.

"I know what you're thinking," he says around bites of chicken fried steak. "The monster is all of the sudden a softy?"

"Something like that."

He nods. "I get it, man. The thing is, it's true. I didn't want to kill her and so I didn't. Got me thinking a lot."

"I bet." Still don't feel good about this.

"Got me thinking how you're a lot like them."

"How's that?"

"You'll never quit."

"Oh, humans are pretty damn good at quitting."

"Sure, on an individual and societal level, but they will not quit living. These monkeys should have died long ago. Yet here they are, persisting, because here you are, persisting."

I shake my head. "Wonderful. You've finally figured out they're around because I'm around."

"No, I figured out how to win."

For some reason, I swear everything has gone quiet and the entire universe is listening to us.

"You see," he says, "last night I got it all backwards. Tricked you, as you put it. But I also learned it doesn't have to be chase or wits. It can be both."

I feel sweat breaking out on my forehead. "What have you done, Apophis?" It's the first time I've used his real name in thousands of years.

He sips coffee. "What never occurred to me. Why not end you by ending myself?"

He opens his jacket enough to show me the explosives taped to his torso. My eyes bulge, moving from them to his smiling face. He closes the jacket.

"The moment you get up from this table and move away, I will follow. And then we all go boom. So, who's your daddy?"

I shake my head. "No, this isn't right."

"Relax, it'll all be over soon."

"This isn't a chase."

"It is, and it's finally over."

"This can't be—"

"You knew it would end someday, Ra. It can't last forever. These humans have had their time."

I blink tears, looking at the souls around me. Them, all of *them*, about to blink out of existence.

"I kind of like this place," he says, looking around the diner. "Has a certain feel to it."

I look from the people and back to him, staring, pleading.

*Erik Williams*

"One last sunset." He shakes his head, eating more of his food. "Enjoy the coffee."

The darkness pushes in. Enveloping me, the world, as the sun disappears over the horizon. The life giver. Life. All of it. Gone.

"You know what?" he asks. "I'm going to miss fried food. Well, that and the booze."

The long bright descent.

In the end, the darkness prevails.

## About Erik Williams

Erik Williams is a former naval officer and current defense contractor (but he's not allowed to talk about it). He is the author of the novels *Demon* and *Guardian* from The Fallen Series, and *Bigfoot Crank Stomp*, as well as numerous works of short fiction.

His world is paper and ink. He writes, he edits and he writes again.

He currently lives in San Diego with his wife and three daughters.

# Declarations of Copyright

VICTOR
SLEPUSHKIN

VICTOR-SLEPUSHKIN.FINEARTAMERICA.COM

# MORE DARK FICTION FROM
# GREY MATTER PRESS

---

"Grey Matter Press has managed to establish itself as one of the premiere purveyors of horror fiction currently in existence via both a series of killer anthologies — *SPLATTERLANDS, OMINOUS REALITIES, EQUILIBRIUM OVERTURNED* — and John F.D. Taff's harrowing novella collection *THE END IN ALL BEGINNINGS."*

*- FANGORIA Magazine*

---

GREY MATTER
P R E S S

# DREAD

## a head full of bad dreams

JONATHAN MABERRY
BRACKEN MACLEOD
WILLIAM MEIKLE
JOHN C. FOSTER
JOHN F.D. TAFF
MICHAEL LAIMO
TIM WAGGONER
RAY GARTON
JG FAHERTY
JOHN EVERSON
TRENT ZELAZNY
AND MANY MORE

from editors
ANTHONY RIVERA
SHARON LAWSON

THE BEST OF GREY MATTER PRESS VOLUME ONE

# DREAD
## A HEAD FULL OF BAD DREAMS

There are some nightmares from which you can never wake.

*Dread: A Head Full of Bad Dreams* is a terrifying volume of the darkest hallucinatory revelations from the minds of some of the most accomplished award-winning authors of our time. Travel dark passageways and experience the alarming visions of twenty masters from the horror, fantasy, science fiction, thriller, transgressive and speculative fiction genres as they bare their souls and fill your head with a lifetime of bad dreams.

*Dread* is the first-ever reader curated volume of horror from Grey Matter Press. The twenty short stories in this book were chosen solely by fans of dark fiction. *Dread* includes a special Introduction from Bram Stoker Award-nominated editor Anthony Rivera who says:

> "Readers who embrace darkness are souls of conscience with hearts of passion and voices that deserve to be heard. It's from this group of passionate voices that the nightmares in *Dread: A Head Full of Bad Dreams* were born.
> "Turning over the reins of editorial curation for this volume to the readers who matter most may well have been the best decision I've ever made. This book that you've created embodies your passion for dark fiction and serves as your own head of bad dreams come to life."

## FEATURING:

| | |
|---|---|
| Ray Garton | Jonathan Maberry |
| John F.D. Taff | JG Faherty |
| William Meikle | John Everson |
| Rose Blackthorn | Michael Laimo |
| Bracken MacLeod | John C. Foster |
| Tim Waggoner | Jane Brooks |
| Chad McKee | Peter Whitley |
| T. Fox Dunham | J. Daniel Stone |
| Edward Morris | Jonathan Balog |
| Trent Zelazny | Martin Rose |

**GREY MATTER**
P R E S S

greymatterpress.com

A DARK THRILLER

# MISTER
# WHITE

THE NOVEL

DO
NOT
SPEAK
HIS
NAME

JOHN C.
FOSTER

# MISTER WHITE
## BY JOHN C. FOSTER

In the shadowy world of international espionage and governmental black ops, when a group of American spies go bad and inadvertently unleash an ancient malevolent force that feeds on the fears of mankind, a young family finds themselves in the crosshairs of a frantic supernatural mystery of global proportions with only one man to turn to for their salvation.

Combine the intricate, plot-driven stylings of suspense masters Tom Clancy and Robert Ludlum, add a healthy dose of Clive Barker's dark and brooding occult horror themes, and you get a glimpse into the supernatural world of international espionage that the chilling new horror novel *Mister White* is about to reveal.

John C. Foster's *Mister White* is a terrifying genre-busting suspense shocker that, once and for all, answer the question you dare not ask: "Who is Mister White?"

---

"*Mister White* is a potent and hypnotic brew that blends horror, espionage and mystery. Foster has written the kind of book that keeps the genre fresh and alive and will make fans cheer. Books like this are the reason I love horror fiction." – RAY GARTON, Grand Master of Horror and Bram Stoker Award®-nominated author of *Live Girls* and *Scissors*.

"*Mister White* is like Stephen King's *The Stand* meets Ian Fleming's James Bond with Graham Masterton's *The Manitou* thrown in for good measure. It's frenetically paced, spectacularly gory and eerie as hell. Highly recommended!" – JOHN F.D. TAFF, Bram Stoker Award®-nominated author of *The End in All Beginnings*

---

**GREY MATTER**
P R E S S

greymatterpress.com

BRAM STOKER AWARD® NOMINATED

# THE END IN ALL BEGINNINGS

"CHILLING"
- Kealan Patrick Burke

"THE BEST NOVELLA
COLLECTION IN YEARS!"
- Jack Ketchum

# JOHN F.D. TAFF

MODERN HORROR'S KING OF PAIN

# THE END IN ALL BEGINNINGS
## BY JOHN F.D. TAFF

The Bram Stoker Award-nominated *The End in All Beginnings* is a tour de force through the emotional pain and anguish of the human condition. Hailed as one of the best volumes of heartfelt and gut-wrenching horror in recent history, *The End in All Beginnings* is a disturbing trip through the ages exploring the painful tragedies of life, love and loss.

Exploring complex themes that run the gamut from loss of childhood innocence, to the dreadful reality of survival after everything we hold dear is gone, to some of the most profound aspects of human tragedy, author John F.D. Taff takes readers on a skillfully balanced emotional journey through everyday terrors that are uncomfortably real over the course of the human lifetime. Taff's highly nuanced writing style is at times darkly comedic, often deeply poetic and always devastatingly accurate in the most terrifying of ways.

Evoking the literary styles of horror legends Mary Shelley, Edgar Allen Poe and Bram Stoker, *The End in All Beginnings* pays homage to modern masters Stephen King, Ramsey Campbell, Ray Bradbury and Clive Barker.

---

"*The End in All Beginnings* is accomplished stuff, complex and heartfelt. It's one of the best novella collections I've read in years!" – JACK KETCHUM, Bram Stoker Award®-winning author of *The Box, Closing Time* and *Peaceable Kingdom*

"Taff brings the pain in five damaged and disturbing tales of love gone horribly wrong. This collection is like a knife in the heart. Highly recommended!" – JONATHAN MABERRY, *New York Times* bestselling author of *Code Zero* and *Fall of Night*

---

**GREY MATTER**
P R E S S

greymatterpress.com

A NIGHTMARE OF SUPERNATURAL, SCIENCE & SOUND

DARK FICTION
INSPIRED BY MUSICAL ICONS

HARD ROCK
HEAVY METAL
ALTERNATIVE
PROGRESSIVE
CONTEMPORARY
ELECTRONIC
CLASSICAL
BLUES
AND MORE

# SAVAGE BEASTS

FROM BRAM STOKER AWARD-NOMINATED EDITORS
ANTHONY RIVERA AND SHARON LAWSON

# SAVAGE BEASTS
## A NIGHTMARE OF SUPERNATURAL, SCIENCE AND SOUND

*SAVAGE BEASTS* is a volume of contemporary dark fiction inspired by some of the greatest artists in musical history. A thrilling and thought-provoking nightmare of devastating supernatural experiences exploring darkly introspective science fiction and fantastical alternative realities, each accompanied by the sound of the music that defines your life.

The short stories in *SAVAGE BEASTS* shine a light on eleven dark worlds with fictional work inspired by Nine Inch Nails, Pink Floyd, The Cranberries, Genesis, Tom Petty and The Heartbreakers, Pestilence, Grace Jones, Underground Sound of Lisbon, School of Seven Bells, Wolfgang Amadeus Mozart and Johann Sebastian Bach and more.

## FEATURING:

| | |
|---|---|
| Edward Morris | Daniel Braum |
| Karen Runge | Maxwell Price |
| John F.D. Taff | E. Michael Lewis |
| Shawn Macomber | T. Fox Dunham |
| Konstantine Paradias | J.C. Michael |
| Paul Michael Anderson | |

---

"The tales in *SAVAGE BEASTS* are as varied as their inspirations. Many of the contributors don't just use music as their muse, they place it front and centre in their narratives. Here, music has the power to save and to kill, and nothing buried in the past stays buried forever, regardless of how frightening it is."
– *RUE MORGUE*

---

GREY MATTER
P R E S S

greymatterpress.com

A COLLECTION OF MODERN HORROR

# DARK
## VISIONS
# 1

VOLUME ONE

EDITED BY

ANTHONY RIVERA AND SHARON LAWSON

# DARK VISIONS ONE
## A COLLECTION OF MODERN HORROR

Somewhere just beyond the veil of human perception lies a darkened plane where very evil things reside. Weaving their horrifying visions, they pull the strings on our lives and lure us into a comfortable reality. But it's all just a web of lies. And this book is their instruction manual.

The Bram Stoker Award®-nominated *Dark Visions: A Collection of Modern Horror - Volume One* includes thirteen disturbing tales of dread from some of the most visionary minds writing horror, sci-fi and speculative fiction today.

*Dark Visions: A Collection of Modern Horror - Volume One* uncovers the truth behind our own misguided concepts of reality.

## FEATURING:

Jonathan Maberry

Jay Caselberg

Jeff Hemenway

Sarah L. Johnson

Ray Garton

Jason S. Ridler

Milo James Fowler

Jonathan Balog

Brian Fatah Steele

Sean Logan

John F.D. Taff

Charles Austin Muir

David A. Riley

---

"This compilation of stories acts as a guide book for the evil minions that lurk within humankind and try to destroy it. Think of *The Twilight Zone* introduction from the popular TV series, and you will get the idea that this compilation is more than just a series of short fictional works." – *HELLNOTES*

---

GREY MATTER
P R E S S

greymatterpress.com

A COLLECTION OF MODERN HORROR

# DARK
## VISI2NS
### VOLUME TWO

EDITED BY
ANTHONY RIVERA AND SHARON LAWSON

# DARK VISIONS TWO
## A COLLECTION OF MODERN HORROR

*Dark Visions: A Collection of Modern Horror - Volume Two* continues the terrifying psychological journey with an all-new selection of exceptional tales of darkness written by some of the most talented authors working in the fields of horror, speculative fiction and fantasy today.

Unable to contain all the visions of dread and mayhem to a single volume, *Dark Visions: A Collection of Modern Horror - Volume Two* is now available from your favorite booksellers in both paperback and digital formats.

## FEATURING:

David Blixt

John C. Foster

JC Hemphill

Jane Brooks

Peter Whitley

Edward Morris

Trent Zelazny

Carol Holland March

David Murphy

Chad McKee

C.M. Saunders

J. Daniel Stone

David Siddall

Rhesa Sealy

Kenneth Whitfield

A.A. Garrison

---

"There is something for every horror/sci-fi aficionado in this collection of modern and speculative horror. Fourteen incredibly terrifying stories varying in degrees of horror." – *HELLNOTES*

---

**GREY MATTER**
P R E S S

greymatterpress.com

# SPLATTER

REAWAKENING THE SPLATTERPUNK REVOLUTION

# LANDS

COLLECTED AND EDITED BY

## ANTHONY RIVERA AND SHARON LAWSON

# SPLATTERLANDS
## REAWAKENING THE
## SPLATTERPUNK REVOLUTION

Almost three decades ago, a literary movement forever changed the landscape of the horror entertainment industry. Grey Matter Press breathes new life into that revolution as we reawaken the true essence of Splatterpunk with the release of *Splatterlands*.

*Splatterlands: Reawakening the Splatterpunk Revolution* is a collection of personal, intelligent and subversive horror with a point. This illustrated volume of dark fiction honors the truly revolutionary efforts of some of the most brilliant writers of all time with an all-new collection of visceral, disturbing and thought-provoking work from a diverse group of modern minds.

## FEATURING:

Ray Garton                     Michele Garber

Michael Laimo                  A.A. Garrison

Paul M. Collrin                Jack Maddox

Eric Del Carlo                 Allen Griffin

James S. Dorr                  Christine Morgan

Gregory L. Norris              Chad Stroup

J. Michael Major

### Illustrations by Carrion House

---

"Grey Matter Press delivers with a delightfully disturbing anthology that will render you speechless. As a fan of horror for some thirty plus years I have never read anything quite like this and regret not a moment of it." – *HORROR NEWS*

---

## GREY MATTER
**P R E S S**

greymatterpress.com

# OMINOUS REALITIES

## THE ANTHOLOGY OF DARK SPECULATIVE HORRORS

### EDITED AND COLLECTED BY

## ANTHONY RIVERA
## SHARON LAWSON

# OMINOUS REALITIES
## THE ANTHOLOGY OF
## DARK SPECULATIVE HORRORS

*Ominous Realities: The Anthology of Dark Speculative Horrors* is a collection of sixteen terrifying tales of chilling science fiction, dark fantasy and speculative horror.

Prepare to travel through an ever-darkening procession of horrifying alternate realities where you'll explore shocking post-apocalyptic worlds, become enslaved by greedy multinational corporations that control every aspect of life, participate in societies where humanity is forced to consider perilous decisions about its own survival, experience the effects of an actual Hell on Earth and discover the many other disturbing possibilities that may be in our future.

## FEATURING:

| | |
|---|---|
| John. F.D. Taff | Bracken MacLeod |
| William Meikle | Gregory L. Norris |
| Ken Altabef | Alice Goldfuss |
| Hugh A.D. Spencer | T. Fox Dunham |
| Martin Rose | Eric Del Carlo |
| Edward Morris | Jonathan Balog |
| Paul Williams | Ewan C. Forbes |
| J. Daniel Stone | Allen Griffin |

---

"This is what happens if the works of Ray Bradbury, Isaac Asimov, H.P. Lovecraft, and Stephen King consummated and had a baby. Excellent anthology!" – *HORROR NEWS NETWORK*

---

GREY MATTER
P R E S S

greymatterpress.com

"A tenacious attempt to hold on in a world out of control."

# THE HEART OF DARKNESS

## AWAITS

"Startling and terrifying."

"A killer anthology."

# EQUILIBRIUM OVERTURNED

A VOLUME OF APOCALYPTIC HORRORS

FROM BRAM STOKER AWARD NOMINATED EDITORS

ANTHONY RIVERA
SHARON LAWSON

# EQUILIBRIUM OVERTURNED
## THE HEART OF DARKNESS AWAITS

The end is coming. But how will it arrive?

From alien civilizations bent on human destruction, to demonic incursions from beyond the event horizon, to the dangerous malevolence that lives within us all, *Equilibrium Overturned* drags you into the heart of darkness to explore brutal personal and world-wide apocalypses and the lives wavering on the brink.

Survive destroyed worlds and terrifying dystopian societies. Experience a prison of the future and the whitewashing of a horrifying past that threatens our very existence. From preventable transgressions, unavoidable doomsdays and personal calamities both near and far, *Equilibrium Overturned* offers shocking revelations into what life may be like at the end.

## FEATURING:

John Everson

Tim Waggoner

Tony Knighton

Sean Eads

Rose Blackthorn

Josh R. Vogt

Martin Slag

JG Faherty

Jay Caselberg

Geoffrey W. Cole

Jeff Hemenway

S.G. Larner

Roger Jackson

Stephen T. Vessels

---

"The stories in *Equilibrium Overturned*, are solid and the thread of desperation and survival is present. Most deal with a bleak sense of survival, the settings change and the details and characters, but every one involves a tenacious attempt to hold the fuck on in a world uncontrolled." – *SHOCK TOTEM*

---

**GREY MATTER**
P R E S S

greymatterpress.com

FROM BRAM STOKER AWARD® NOMINATED EDITORS

ANTHONY | SHARON
RIVERA | LAWSON

Made in the USA
San Bernardino, CA
15 June 2016